Praise for the Novels of Eric Pete

Don't Get It Twisted

"An engaging novel full of vibrant characters, a compelling story line, and lots of emotional impact."
—*New York Times* bestselling author Zane

"Eric Pete has done it again! An exciting page-turner that you'll find impossible to put down."   —Bestselling author Karen E. Quinones Miller

"An entertaining story that rings with mature truisms about the relationship phenomenon and the blessing of friendship."
—The RAWSISTAZ Reviewers

"Deserves applause for its fabulous writing and refreshing originality."
—Romance Reader at Heart

Gets No Love

"*Gets No Love* will make people think, it will make people realize that you cannot escape the past, and it will have people remembering the characters and the story line long after the last page."
—*New York Times* bestselling author Zane

"Intrigue, scandal, and true-to-life characters . . . a wonderful read."
—Kimberla Lawson Roby, bestselling author of *The Best-Kept Secret*

"*Gets No Love* demands your attention and refuses to let you put it down until the last page. Passion, friendship, heartbreak, and secrets that will shock you: Eric does it again as he mixes all of these together to form one intense concoction."   —Dwayne S. Joseph, author of *The Womanizers*

"One of the best reads for me in a long time. *Gets No Love* provides intrigue, sensuality, love, fear, hesitation, and joy all rolled into one."
—Rochelle Ragas, The Sistah Circle Book Club Inc., Dallas, Texas

ERIC PETE

Lady Sings the Cruels

NAL | NEW AMERICAN LIBRARY

New American Library
Published by New American Library,
a division of Penguin Group (USA) Inc., 375 Hudson Street,
New York, New York 10014, USA
Penguin Group (Canada), 90 Eglinton Avenue East, Suite 700, Toronto,
Ontario M4P 2Y3, Canada (a division of Pearson Penguin Canada Inc.)
Penguin Books Ltd., 80 Strand, London WC2R 0RL, England
Penguin Ireland, 25 St. Stephen's Green, Dublin 2, Ireland
(a division of Penguin Books Ltd.)
Penguin Group (Australia), 250 Camberwell Road, Camberwell,
Victoria 3124, Australia (a division of Pearson Australia Group Pty. Ltd.)
Penguin Books India Pvt. Ltd., 11 Community Centre,
Panchsheel Park, New Delhi - 110 017, India
Penguin Group (NZ), cnr Airborne and Rosedale Roads, Albany,
Auckland 1310, New Zealand (a division of Pearson New Zealand Ltd.)
Penguin Books (South Africa) (Pty.) Ltd., 24 Sturdee Avenue,
Rosebank, Johannesburg 2196, South Africa

Penguin Books Ltd., Registered Offices:
80 Strand, London WC2R 0RL, England

First published by New American Library,
a division of Penguin Group (USA) Inc.

First Printing, November 2006
10 9 8 7 6 5 4 3 2 1

REGISTERED TRADEMARK—MARCA REGISTRADA

LIBRARY OF CONGRESS CATALOGING-IN-PUBLICATION DATA

Pete, Eric.
    Lady sings the cruels/Eric Pete.
        p. cm.
    ISBN 0-451-21954-6 (trade pbk.)
    1. Sings—Fiction. 2. African-Americans—Fiction. 3. Houston (Tex.)—Fiction. I. Title.
PS3616.E83L33 2006
813'.6—dc22   2006011447

Set in Palatino   •   Designed by Elke Sigal

Printed in the United States of America

PUBLISHER'S NOTE
This is a work of fiction. Names, characters, places, and incidents either are the product
of the author's imagination or are used fictitiously, and any resemblance to actual per-
sons, living or dead, business establishments, events, or locales is entirely coincidental.
    The publisher does not have any control over and does not assume any responsibil-
ity for author or third-party Web sites or their content.

WILDERMUTH

To the survivors of tempests—
be they of the literal, emotional, or spiritual kind.
And to the people that have shown them love and compassion.

Thank you.

ACKNOWLEDGMENTS

I thank God for allowing me and my family to see this day. Five novels, several long nights at the computer, a natural disaster or two, and only a few gray hairs later we're here. And where is "here"?

Here is another place, not just the new environment I find myself calling home, but a different way of looking at things so many of us take for granted. Things that can disappear in the blink of an eye. Don't blink, people. Don't blink. Keep those eyes open a few seconds longer each day.

Here is also this book you've decided to pick up and crack the spine of, another insane story cooked up for you to judge. Careful. You hold hazardous materials in your hands. It's raw . . . wild . . . *caliente,* but most important, I hope "true" to you. So without further ado . . . *DeeJay, hit my music. Bartender, bring me a Crown and Coke.* Yep. I still like it smooth. *And you?* Get whatever you want. It's an open bar tonight, kid.

A special thanks to Traci Pullum and Tommy Johnson. Without you two, this story might not have been. Ki, a real songbird, thank you mainly for your friendship, but also for the conversation that cold, dreary day downtown. Tommy, thank you for answering the gazillion questions I e-mailed you night after night. I appreciate both of you.

Marsha and Chelsea, thank you for staying by my side through all the chaos and uncertainty of the past year. You make me want more, to do better . . . to see you do better. I love you guys.

Mom, keep cheering. It's fourth and long with one minute to go. I can hear you in the stands. You'll get the game ball when I've silenced the crowd. (*My mom doesn't watch much football. She might not get this. When you see her on the street, explain it to her.*)

To the rest of my family, friends, and new faces in my life—thank you for the support you offered Swiss Family Pete. I can't name you all, but you're in my heart and your prayers were felt. To the people of Houston, our new home—your kind smiles and open arms meant more than you ever could know. Joseph and Demetrius, I know you're tired of me thanking you, but I can't stop . . . won't stop. *smile* Never have I known a more selfless couple.

My fabulous ghost readers—Shontea, Jamie, Carmel, Jacqueline (Waiting on your novels, Mrs. Scott), and Shelia. Thank you for your time and your constructive criticism.

To my agent, Elaine Koster, and the folks at New American Library: Kara Cesare, Lindsay Nouis, Paola Soto, Kara Welsh, and everybody behind the scenes who makes this tick—thank you. Rose Hilliard, even though you've moved on, can't forget ya. Thanks to Cross the Network for keeping my Web site tight.

To all the booksellers and my fellow authors—keep striving and providing for us readers. We may have different appetites and diets, but we are all hungry. There's room at the buffet for all.

Special shouts to: Michele Lewis of the Afro-American Bookstop, Vera Warren-Williams of Community Book Center, Adekunle Odusanwo of Nu-World of Books, B'Randi and Trenton Marshall of B's Books 'n More, Danielle and Holly of Waldenbooks–Prien Lake Mall, Monica and Travis of Barnes & Noble–Harvey, and Emma Rodgers of Black Images Book Bazaar.

I have to acknowledge the bookclubs and reviewers, some of which I've listed: Sistah's on the Reading Edge, Jackson Mississippi Readers Club, GAAL, Delta Rho Sorority Inc, Delta Sigma Theta, Central Arkansas Alumnae Chapter Red Hot Readers, Voices Beyond the Pages, Circle of Friends, Brothas Well Read, Barnes & Noble African-American Book Club–Harvey, Sisters with Books, Sister Friends, Cover 2 Cover, Essence of Sistahood, Nubian Sistas, Sirens, Hee Say Shee Say, the Good Book Club, Divas Read 2, Fusion, Black Women with Book, the Sistah Circle Book Club Inc., RAW Sistaz, Souls of Sisterhood, Sister-Friends, the G.R.I.T.S., APOOO, Readin-color, and Sisters Sippin' Tea.

Special shoutout to those in the media who took the time out of their busy schedules to hear me: Tessa and Baby J. of Da Breakfuss Club, Adai Lamar, Erik Johnson, Gina Cook, Monica Pierre, Hal Clark, Kelder Summers, Kandi Eastman, Jackie Simien, Nancy Parker, Michelle McCalope, Cynthia Arceneaux, the Madd Hatter Morning Show, Janine Haydel, Glenn Townes, Joyce Davis, Damien Lemon, Patricia DeLuca, Michael Baisden, Angela Jenkins, Gail Norris, Michael Addison, Misherald Brown, Tonyasue Carther, Heather Covington, Chezon Jackson, Wali Muhammad, Don Lee, Jason McDonald, Don Tracy, Pamela Yvette Exum, and Nathasha Brooks-Harris.

If I've left anybody off, it wasn't intentional. Give yourself a pat on the back for taking it in stride.

In closing, I have to thank you who still hold this book in your hand after this long-ass acknowledgments. Thanks for entering my world and for allowing me to be a part of yours. Hope you come back again and again.

Now . . . more than ever . . . say it like you mean it and know that it's true.

Can't stop. Won't stop. Believe that.

—Eric

PROLOGUE

DO YOU KNOW WHAT TIME IT IS?
CHECK THE CLOCK.

"Your girl gonna win, Bodie?" Ro asked in his laid-back drawl, thick like molasses from a can.

"You know what time it is. Think somebody out here got a better voice?" I answered over the screwed and chopped verses of Prince's "The Beautiful Ones." The trunk of the old Cadillac convertible rattled violently with each lazy note as if about to fly off its hinges. My niggas, the Fontenot brothers, rode up front, tossed back on that syrup. When they were mixing the codeine 'n' shit, I passed. *Need my head on straight for my boo, Amelia,* I proudly thought. She was downtown at the Four Seasons tryin' to change things in her life, so why shouldn't I?

"That show's full o' shit, if you ask me," Aaron volunteered as he wheeled the big orange slab down North Main, his normally blue eyes dyed bloodshot red from all the drank he'd been hittin'. Both the Fontenot brothers looked like white boys if a nigga didn't know better. I guess that's why they were always overcompensatin' 'n' shit— permanent scowls and always ready to break a nigga down if they got outta hand.

"That's just it. Nobody asked you," I snapped back. Ro laughed but you could barely hear him. He'd plopped a couple Xanax in his drank back at the crib. Even with all that, only half his edge had been taken off. Of the two, he was the scary one. If Aaron was the sound, Ro was most definitely the fury.

Aaron continued in spite of me. "Them stupid TV shows all outta a nigga's control 'n' shit. Dressin' folk up like some dolls and makin' 'em sang that gay shit. Who wanna hear some Barry fuckin' Manilow? Ya know? Shit ain't real like it is out here. What we do is real. If one of them judges came up in my face, tellin' me how bad I handle my business, I'd show him he's a wrong motherfucker. One time." He looked around for his Glock .40 to wave for emphasis, but couldn't find it. I just shook my head.

"Just drive, man. I wanna pick this up before she finishes. I wanna see her face when she walks out from her audition and I plant that boulder on her finger. Ya know?"

At the EZ Pawn, Aaron and Ro let me out the car so I could handle my business. Abdel, the Arab cat I'd been dealing with, recognized me and buzzed me in when I rapped on the door. I'd been to his store three times this month, putting some ends down on my shit. Well . . . Amelia's shit.

I was a Northside nigga and Amelia was a Southside girl from Missouri City, or Mo City as we called it here in Houston. She was my ride-or-die chick and had put up with much noise from me since we'd met. We'd almost broke up again last week when I realized she was out for good if I didn't quit my ways. Sometimes a nigga gotta burn shit out his system, y'know? I ain't gonna front. What I was gonna do today was big. Life changin', y'know? Yeah, I was scared.

I was giving Abdel a pound when Ro and Aaron caught the closing door. He stared at them, thinking they were white boys at first . . . and in the wrong neighborhood, until I spoke.

"They with me, bruh," I vouched, exchanging a look that told him not to sound an alarm or reach for whatever he kept behind the glass case. They were supposed to stay in the car, but true to their nature they did whatever the fuck they wanted.

"Oh," he replied. As he watched their demeanor, he smiled, realizing he'd been fooled by their features.

"Yeah, they's niggas too. Got that Louisiana shit in 'em." I laughed, just low enough for them not to hear. They were prowling around the other cases, eyeing all the good shit people had pawned. Abdel had clued me in on my last visit. High-end niggas losing their jobs at Enron had allowed gutter niggas like us to get high quality for cheap.

I reached in my pocket, pulling out the fat roll of bills to seal the deal. Abdel's eyes lit up at the sight. He still had some reservations about my boys fawning over the items behind the glass, but went in back to get the ring for me.

"Damn, look at that one," Aaron said to Ro, bringing his attention to a bunch of new jewelry on display. The glow reflected in his hazed eyes.

Ro shuffled over in his white tee and baggy jeans and scratched the brownish-blond fuzz on his chin. He nodded as if responding to voices unheard by the rest of us. His gaze was clear and focused when he twisted slowly in my direction. "Bodie, why you didn't tell us 'bout this here?" he asked.

" 'Cause I know how you crazy motherfuckers be actin'," I replied. In fact, the only reason I was catching a ride with them today was because 1) they were my boys and 2) my Lac was off Westheimer getting dipped in some fresh candy paint. A lapse in judgment was nothin' new on my part. I'd have Amelia's ring soon, so it didn't matter.

"How much you payin' for her shit?" Ro asked.

I held up the fingers, each one indicating a grand.

"Daaamn," Aaron gushed. Ro said nothing.

Abdel came back with my ring in a jewelry box. "She's going to love this," he said. He opened it, allowing me to inspect. I didn't trust anyone when it came to matters of money. I held the solitaire up to the light and my world changed.

As slow as the Fontenot brothers had been previously, it was like someone lit a fire under them. I'd seen that fire in action before. And it was nothin' nice. Abdel's eyes spoke to me as I paused from admiring the ring I was to propose with. His gaze met mine, wondering how I could betray him. I was shaking my head in denial when

Ro's 9 mil swung across his head, leveling him. Dumbstruck, I just stood there.

"Don't even think about an alarm, boy." Ro slid around me like I was a store fixture and hopped the counter in one smooth move. He leveled his 9 on Abdel, on whom he'd opened a nice cut. Aaron followed his brother's lead. After checking the front door, he pulled out his gun. I guess he'd found his Glock after all. They were wildin'.

"You gettin' that ring for free, bruh," Aaron gleefully proclaimed. "And then some."

Abdel began pleading for his life, to which Ro shouted, "Shut the fuck up!"

"Get the tape, bruh! Get that shit!" Aaron yelled at me. I didn't come here for this, but the time for talk was done. Without hesitating, I was back in that fucked up mode too. Abdel wouldn't be telling anyone anyway. Not if he didn't want us coming back to pay him a visit. I stowed Amelia's ring in my pocket and ran to the video recorder in the back office. Coming from the front of the pawn shop, I could hear cases being shattered and glass shards tumbling to the floor. The store tape was in my hand when I looked at my watch. I was gonna have Aaron drop me off at the Four Seasons when we got outta here. It was a "when." An "if" never crossed my mind. It should've.

"Check for the money while you're back there!" one of them urged as I left the office. My stupid ass listened, stopping to look around. On Abdel's junky desk, I saw a framed photo of his family. I didn't get a chance to find anything else.

A raucous scream I recognized as Ro's rang out. I heard Aaron curse before the alarm went off and shots rang out. I dropped the tape and ran back to investigate. On the floor behind the counter lay Abdel's twitching body, a piece of his head having been blown off. In his dying grip, he held one of those taser guns. Aaron was helping a limping Ro out the front door and didn't even bother looking back for me. Torn between wanting to help the dying man and get the fuck away, I went on instinct and ran like O.J. It would've been all good except my foot caught the blood gushing from his wound. Slipping, I took an express trip to the concrete floor where my head hit with a hollow thud.

It took a second for me to get back up and shake it off, but by then I could hear the loud exhaust on the orange Lac as it sped out the parking lot. Fuck this. I wasn't getting tagged for something that wasn't my idea. Alarm still blaring, I burst out the front door and ran for daylight.

Just make it home was what my racing mind repeated again and again.

I

BODIE

"On five!" he hollered.

The corrections officer, or CO, at the end of the row repeated him. The second time in two weeks my cell had been through shakedown. I came closer to check things out.

"Don't know why you're diggin' around my mattress," I said, looking over his shoulder. I maintained a safe distance while, on his knees, he checked the mattress frame for a shank. "You won't find nothin'."

He didn't answer but, finishing his inspection, moved to my pictures pinned on the cell wall. Winters, a CO about the same age as me, was better than most motherfuckers. Some of them liked makin' your life a living hell. He made sure you knew he was just doing his job. That earned him a nigga's respect on most days.

Winters lifted the pictures, making sure no contraband was hidden behind them. We weren't supposed to put shit on our walls. He could've been a dick and yanked them down. When he lowered them back in place, he stared at my girl's for a sec. Next to a wrinkled picture of my custom Lac was a picture of Amelia taken a year before I went away. She was just a young'un then, posin' all seductive in this camisole I'd gotten her.

"Nice, bruh."

"Ain't she though."

8 ERIC PETE

"Waiting for you when you get out?"

I laughed. Ten years is a long time. "I dunno. Ain't seen her in a minute. She special though."

"Sure seems like it," he muttered before moving on.

Winters thumbed through the pages of my book, *The Autobiography of Malcolm X*, leaving the page I'd marked undisturbed. Rather than tossing it on the floor, he handed it to me. "Great book," he said. "Sure made me get my act together. Maybe if you'd read it sooner, you wouldn't be in here."

I wanted to punch him for trying to talk down to me, but it wouldn't have done any good in the long run. Each day on the inside was helping me understand how I should handle things on the outside.

After sentencing, I'd done my first two years in Huntsville before being transferred to this new facility by the airport. Every day, I'd hear the planes flying overhead, imagining I was on one of them in a first-class seat to Mexico or maybe Rio for Carnival, where bronze, boomin' asses would shake in my face all night long. Yeah. Prisons are a booming crop in Texas and folks like me are the seeds they water to make them grow.

"Close five!" Winters hollered, his search completed. My cell door clanked shut. Before he left, he lingered by the bars. "Don't mean to preach, Bodie."

"S'all right. I know. Instead of 'hangin' with you, I should be with my girl on the outside. She could sing her ass off, y'know? Without even tryin'."

His face grimaced. "She doesn't sing anymore?"

I paused. "No."

He didn't say anything else. Just moved on to the next cell on his list.

I set the book down to fix my mattress. As I bent over, I heard a tapping sound behind me. I thought Winters had returned and expected to hear his voice.

"Nice ass, Antoine."

No one but my grams called me by my birth name. And this bitch wasn't my grandmomma. I ignored her and kept putting things back in place.

"Ain't gonna talk to me, Antoine?" I heard her say something in the radio on her shoulder. My cell door started opening. I counted to ten before acknowledging her.

"Cell check," CO Arnold proclaimed as she stood there, ready to mace me if I got out of hand. The HNIC on this block, she was one of the worse ones. Don't get me wrong. Arnold was fine as fuck. She was around five-six, the color of a good cigar, and thick in the hips, and her hair was always done up. Today, she rocked one of them bought ponytails. I would've tapped that country ass on the outside. But because she was an evil ho who liked making life miserable for niggas on the inside, she was never getting it from me. That seemed to make her angrier.

"Winters just came through," I snapped, knowing she really didn't care.

"And it looks like he missed something."

I looked around the tiny space, imagining some crevice he hadn't touched.

"There," she said, pointing at the wall near the head of my bunk. My pictures.

She kept her hand on her radio, daring me to make a sudden move to stop her. I wasn't getting my head caved in today. She smiled as her leg brushed against mine. I wanted to trip her.

"You know you're not supposed to hang anything on the wall."

I raised an eyebrow, keeping my hands on the bunk and my mouth shut.

She snatched down the pictures of my Cadillac and Amelia and looked on the back of each.

"This your car?"

"Yeah."

"This your girl?"

I nodded my head, not really knowing anymore if Amelia was

"my girl." Her last visit had ended with us screaming at each other across the table.

"Which one of your boys you think is fucking her now?" I bit my lip. She saw my eye twitch and laughed. *"Manslaughter?* You're gonna be here a while, Antoine. You might as well get used to things."

The picture of my Lac, she balled up and dropped on the floor. Amelia's picture, she slowly ripped in half before letting the pieces fall as well.

"Oops," she said with a shrug. "You better pick that trash up. You know we don't allow littering."

I was putting the pieces of Amelia together when I heard, "Close five!"

2

AMELIA

"9 7.9 The Box. Can't stop, won't stop. You're on the air."

"*Yeah. I wanna hear that new song from Natalia.*"

"*Well, we're giving it to ya! That new joint from Houston's oooooooown Nataliu!*"

I was trying to get to my waitress job at Mirage, but when I heard it, I focused on nothing else. The cars honking on the 610 Loop went silent. The construction crews hammering away on the latest expansion project disappeared. All that was there was me and the voice, the voice of my best friend.

"Yeah!" she screamed frantically as she emerged from the ballroom that day. It was as if the Holy Ghost had jumped inside her and wouldn't let up. She was crying uncontrollably and the cameras were eating it up. I was so happy for her; I ignored the number pinned to the front of my blouse and began jumping too.

"You did it! You did it!" I screamed as I ran, embracing Natalia hard enough to crush her.

"I'm going to Hollywood, Amelia! I'm going to Hollywood!" She then went into another fit, which made the other *U.S. Icon* contestants either nervous or happy, depending on their mental state. It didn't matter to her because she'd made it past the preliminaries. Hollywood and all that TV exposure awaited. It didn't matter to me because she was my best friend . . . and my time to shine was coming up. At her mom's house the night before, we'd discussed how we would handle it when we were the final two contestants on *U.S. Icon*. We were going to handle it with dignity and class. No cat fighting or backstabbing. Yep. Represent for H-town. Beyoncé had already gotten hers. Both me and Natalia remembered running into her and the rest of them girls at talent shows around town. She had the looks and her momma 'n' 'em behind her, but we had the voices. We were on the come-up now.

Natalia wiped her eyes as she came down to Earth. She'd quit hyperventilating. A lady behind us who'd been rejected was pitching a fit and now stealing the show. The cameras rushed with great zeal to cover every single curse word. Natalia rolled her eyes. "Girl," she said as she tried to put her matted hair in place, "they're going to be calling you in there soon."

"How were they? How did they act? What did they say?"

She laughed at my bombardment. "Well, that one guy, the asshole from Europe. He kept a straight face the whole time. I know I blew him away, but he tried to play it off."

"Wow."

"Yeah, girl. We're going to Hollywood!"

I felt uneasy when she included me. I hadn't gone before them yet. They might have reached their quota of fine young sistahs from the South. Well, they were just gonna have to make room for one more.

One of the production people called out my number to let me know I'd be going before the judges soon. Natalia had been holding her pee all morning and ran off before she burst. I felt a case of nerves coming on and tried to breathe.

Bodie promised he'd be there, but he wasn't. Just like him. *Either high or sleeping off a high*, I thought. He'd let me down so much, but I was stupid enough to get involved with him. One of them Northside knuckleheads he was—dangerous and with plenty money I never asked about. He treated me like a princess whenever he was trying to make up. I was finished with making up. He wasn't here when I needed him most. It was time to move on.

The contestant just ahead of me was called into the ballroom. I watched her give her parents a final hug. On the wall above her, the Four Seasons hotel had a TV monitor affixed to keep us hostages entertained and off the show's back. I noticed KPRC interrupting for late-breaking news.

The scene switched from *The Golden Girls* to a shot from their news helicopter as police cars chased a black man on foot. Other than a white T-shirt, I couldn't make out a thing about him other than his quickness. He did *something* stupid, I thought. It would've been easier on him if he just quit running. The scene was a replay from earlier and was just being re-aired. Losing interest, I looked around for Natalia again. She was still in the bathroom or maybe on the phone with her boyfriend.

When I looked back, the details were scrolling across the bottom of the screen. Someone had tried to rob a pawn shop. Somebody had been shot. The production assistant signaled me that it was time to go to staging. I lingered a second longer to see the suspect. His arrest photo flashed, filling the entire screen. *Antoine "Bodie" Campbell* was the name displayed beside his image.

"*Ma'am*, you're up next," the production assistant repeated with emphasis.

Natalia's new song ended, bringing me back in the now. She'd called me from Miami last week wondering what I thought of her new CD. I lied to her and said I thought it was the bomb. I hadn't bought it. I was gonna have to get it soon, but couldn't bring myself to just yet. Besides, I was late for work . . . again. I sped up, but knew I could never outrun the thoughts running through my head.

3

IKE

"Ike, you going out for drinks with us, right?" my sergeant asked as she stowed her gear in her locker.

"Gotta take a rain check," I answered.

"C'mon now, Winters. Why you're always passing on hanging with us? I don't bite. *That much.*"

The other COs in the locker room laughed. Since transferring to this facility, I'd quickly learned Serena Arnold was persistent in getting what she wanted out of inmates and COs alike. It's not that she wasn't at all attractive. It was her stank attitude that was the big turnoff.

"Cut Winters some slack, Serena," one of the other sergeants, a graying Hispanic man named Tomas, said as he joined the conversation. He added, "Isn't it obvious? He's got someone to go home to unlike you."

Only half the locker room laughed this time, some afraid of being put on shit detail by Serena. She rolled her eyes at Tomas.

"And who says I don't have anyone to go home to?"

Tomas shook his head. "I meant on a steady basis," he shot back. I tried holding back my laughter, but couldn't.

"Is that true, Winters? You got somebody?" Her attention was back on me.

"Yeah. You could say that," I answered while tying my shoe.

"Oh?" she said, taking a seat beside me on the bench. "What's his name?" she asked in typical locker room humor, which got the laughs and snickers she wanted. I looked at Serena like she was crazy. "Hey, a sistah never knows these days."

"Her name's Deryn."

She chuckled. "She got your nose all open, huh, Ike? Probably got her on your mind the whole time you're in here."

"Nah. I do my job," I said confidently. I stood up to leave.

"I'll bet you do, baby. I'll bet you do." She licked her full lips and blew me a kiss.

As I left, I meant to ask her about Bodie, the inmate whose cell I'd shaken down earlier. I saw Serena enter after I'd finished and wondered if I'd missed something. She hadn't said anything, so I decided to let it go and escape while I could.

Knowing I was out of beer, I stopped at the Shell on FM1960 on the way home. I was only a few blocks from our house, so I popped the cap on a Miller Light and took a swig before I got there. I'd barely turned onto North Bambridge, but I could see Deryn's car wasn't home. Parking my old truck on the side, *where the neighbors couldn't see it*, I came in the front door and threw my bag down. *Another late night*, I thought as I punched the keys on the alarm to our new home and looked around. I really couldn't say much as Deryn had paid for most of what we had. Even the house was solely in her name although I scraped up enough every month for the taxes. Thank God for love, because my bad credit would've had us back in Third Ward renting from my momma.

An hour later, Deryn came through the front door. I was starving, but had waited for her before eating. I was feeling Pappadeaux's, but was on a Jack in the Crack budget till payday. Ending her conversation, she closed her cell phone shut with a snap. *Just like her abrupt personality*, I thought. She set her briefcase down by the front door and stepped out of her Jimmy Choos.

I'd gone to work while she slept and was seeing her in her gray pin-striped suit for the first time. I was admiring how she rocked it when she removed her jacket. She came to the couch where I was resting and bent over. She planted a long, sensuous kiss on me; her soft hands caressed my face and traced the outline of my beard. With that one taste, I forgot all about my stomach's hunger and greedily reached for one of her breasts visible through her white blouse. She swatted my hand and stood back up, putting one of her brown curls back in its place.

"Not now, Isaac," she said, calling me by my birth name. "I'm starving." She threw her jacket onto the sofa beside me and was off to the kitchen.

"His Honor the Mayor still piling on the work?" I asked.

My girlfriend cut me a look, then smirked, her hazel brown eyes twinkling at the notion. She answered, "Yes, but he's not the mayor . . . yet."

"And he won't be if I have to vote for him," I said with a defiant wave of my hand.

After we graduated from Prairie View A&M, Deryn got on with the city of Houston and was now assistant to Marshall Patterson, its chief administrative officer. Marshall was a bougie, pretender who irked the fuck out of me. While I used my National Guard experience and became a corrections officer, she moved up to the big leagues, leaving me choking in the dust. One day I was afraid she wouldn't bother looking back. Of course, I wouldn't tell her about my fears. Men don't talk about shit like that.

In the kitchen, Deryn fetched a bowl and filled it with pretzels, one of which she plopped in her mouth. She rejoined me on the couch, where she continued our exchange.

"Isaac, instead of hating on Marshall, maybe you should let him get you a real job. With your experience, he can probably place you with a security firm or something. Anything's better than watching those killers and rapists."

"My job's not that bad," I answered as I took a few pretzels from her bowl.

She laughed. "Whatever. I just thought you might like something more—"

"Safe?" I said, cutting her off.

"Actually I was going to say 'profitable.' "

It always came back to the money, or my lack of it. I wanted to check her on the putdowns, but bit my tongue. I turned on the TV and began flicking through the channels with the remote.

"Isaac?"

"Yeah."

"Speaking of the mayor, I need you to go to a party with me."

"Damn, girl. You know I'm uncomfortable around those people."

"And?"

"And I don't want to go."

Deryn's eyes locked on me. I tried ignoring them, pretending I was more interested in *Fear Factor* at the moment. "It's for my job," she said in my ear as her hand came to rest on my leg.

You mean for your future job, I thought without saying.

She blew softly, almost cooing, letting the warmth of her sweet breath caress my ear. I closed my eyes. Her legs resting under her, she inched closer to me. Her hand playfully slid off my thigh and moved to something a little more firm under my shorts. I came to life and grew at her expert command.

"You like that, don't you?" she whispered. Her teeth bit into the fleshy part of my ear.

"Mmm-hmm," I mumbled.

She applied more pressure to my swollen dick, coaxing the inches forth and working my head to a steady throb. I let go of the remote and began cupping her ass. She tugged on my drawstring and released it. My dick was free and eager to taste what it had been missing for over two weeks. I was going to hit it and hit it right. My mind was already racing to the positions I was going to have her in.

Suddenly she stopped.

"Well, Isaac, if you want that and more, then I guess you're going to that party with me after all."

Disappointed and aroused to no end, I opened my eyes. Deryn had got up and was walking off. She unbuttoned her blouse as she took to the stairs.

"Where the fuck are you going?"

"Shower," she casually snapped.

4

BODIE

"Why did you do this to me?" he asked, his heavy Middle Eastern accent stressing each word.

"Man, I didn't do a fuckin' thing."

"I had a wife and three children. Remember? We talked about them when you first came by my shop. I showed you their pictures. Remember?"

"Yeah. I remember," I answered calmly, hiding the panic clawing beneath my skin. Everything in the pawn shop was the same as that day. "But I didn't kill you. I already told you that shit."

"Sure, you did," he said as he rose from the floor soaked in crimson. Chunks of Abdel's brains spilled onto his shirt as he came closer. He turned his head sideways, giving me a better view. "See."

In the middle of the brains, blood and squirming worms sat Amelia's ring.

Wanting to scream, but unable to, I woke up in a cold sweat, banging my head on the bunk above me. My heart was still jumping like a jackhammer as I swallowed deep breaths of cool air.

"You all right, celly?" asked the head peering at me upside down from the bunk above. It startled the fuck out of me, as my nerves were still on edge. I jumped away, pressing against the cell wall as if to go through it before catching myself and manning up.

"Damn it, nigga! I almost fucked you up. Don't jump out at me like that," I snarled in the darkness.

The upside-down face of my cellmate, Rewind, laughed. "You the one jumpin', celly. You were knocked the fuck out when they released me."

"Damn. I must've been," I said, realizing I'd slept through someone entering my cell. That shit wasn't cool on my part. "How you healin'?" I asked.

"I'm straight," the skinny brother with gold teeth replied. I didn't know what Rewind was in here for, but that's the way it is. No one asked those kinds of things unless you wanted to get fucked up. Besides, it was a two-day sentence for all of us—the day you came in and the day you walked the fuck out.

Rewind worked detail in the prison metal shop. Word got out that he was goofing off and backed into a grinding wheel. There was also another word that said different. Don't let his size fool ya; Rewind was quick to air a motherfucker out. My guess is that's what got him here and probably what led to his "accident" in the metal shop.

"Sorry 'bout wakin' you up."

"S'okay," Rewind replied from up top. "Wasn't sleepin' no way. Side's killin' me. I'll be glad when these stitches come out."

"Why you didn't stay in the infirmary? You had a better bed and that thick nurse to look at."

Rewind laughed. " 'Cause them fuckers wouldn't give me no more pain pills. S'okay. Imma have my own tomorrow."

I joined in his laughter, finding anything to latch on to in this place. From the other cells, I could hear someone telling us to shut the fuck up and go to sleep while others wanted to know what the deal, desperate to latch on to something too.

The light from the windows across the way cast a glow through the bars and onto the wall. I'd put Amelia's fractured picture back up after that bitch Arnold ripped it. One half of her torn face was visible to me. Rather than head back to my unsettling dreams, I stared at it. My hand reached down into my shorts, thinking about better times and Amelia letting me know her shit was mine without a doubt.

"Bodie?"

I wanted to ignore Rewind and get back to things. Instead I slid my hand back out. "What?"

"Who was spookin' you like that?"

"Nobody," I said at first, trying to keep my mind on more pleasant things like the night I was going to have with Amelia. "Just some dude."

When morning came, I was gonna check on things. I needed to make sure my lawyer was still sending those anonymous payments to Abdel's wife and kids. Unlike the funds I had set up for Amelia, theirs never came back.

5

AMELIA

I stowed my purse and tried to act like I'd been at work all along. I was hustling toward my assigned tables for the night, but my manager, Tookie, had already covered them. As she brought the food orders to the back, I watched her confident stride, her thick legs carrying her as if she hadn't a care in the world. Before she got to the kitchen doors, she saw me lurking. She looked at me, then to her watch.

"Sorry I'm late," I said, sincerely meaning it. I nervously adjusted my skirt. Tookie did my cousin Me-Me a favor when she gave me this job. Both of them had come up waiting tables here at Mirage before Me-Me moved on with the cook who started his own place, Lullaby's, over in Third Ward. Tookie had followed them, but came back when Mirage offered more money.

"Child, you're just like your cousin. I guess that's why I like you," she chuckled. "Here. Take these orders to the kitchen. And try not to get your salads mixed up. It looks like a good night for tips."

"Thank God," I huffed, not meaning to sound so desperate.

"Broke?"

"Am I?" I said with a laugh. Just yesterday, I'd marked the newest envelope from Bodie's lawyer *return to sender* and delivered it to his Sharpstown office. When I felt the thickness of the dollar bills inside, it took all my might not to just sneak a peek. *I'm not going back to that life,* I told myself before I shoved the envelope through the anonymous mail slot I knew to be his.

I brought the orders to our cook, hoping he was sticking around longer than the others. Tookie told me about the heyday of Mirage before the cook Neal left for Lullaby's. Seems like all the cooks since were just passing through or simply sucked.

The owners of the place were putting a lot of pressure on Tookie to keep things going, but it wasn't all her fault. She hustled more than anyone else to keep things afloat. This made me feel even guiltier for my tardiness. In the mirrored reflection of the kitchen counter, I checked out the curly, short mess atop my head, then hurriedly grabbed several plates of salads.

Bringing out the salads to my tables, I hadn't the benefit of seeing the people who gave the orders. I could hear Tookie's voice warning me, but I hadn't paid attention. Loaded with plates, I gambled.

"Miss?" *And lost.*

"Yes?" At the table I'd just left sat a balding tourist and his tanned wife. I knew he was a tourist from the *Don't Mess with Texas* T-shirt and fanny pack he wore. She was a little better, just a *Texas: It's a Whole Other Country* sun visor obscuring her weathered face.

"I ordered my salad with ranch dressing," he replied.

Seeing what appeared to be his salad in front of his wife, I swapped their salads and apologized.

"Miss?" he asked again while I emptied my hands.

I looked back as cheery as possible. "Something wrong, sir?"

"This isn't mine either. I explicitly asked for no cucumber and wanted bacon bits."

The customer was right. I ran back to the kitchen, where I found his salad waiting where I'd hurriedly left it. Apologizing profusely, I hoped my tip wouldn't be reduced too much.

As he dug into his salad, chomping loudly with his mouth open, his wife eyed me curiously. She then broke into a big smile.

"You know who you look like?" she squealed.

I shook my head, hoping she didn't embarrass herself.

"That singer," she said as she wagged her finger. "The one that won that competition. The black one." I closed my eyes and prayed I didn't hear about Natalia again today. People always said we had similar facial features. I watched her mouth begin to pronounce the name.

"Fantasia!" she barked. Huh? "You look like Fantasia!"

Her husband finished chomping his first shovelful and egged her on. "Dorothy. You're right!" he said as if some incredible revelation had come over him.

If not for being associated with a winner, I would've slapped the caps off her teeth. Why, Lord, did all black people look alike to white folk? I blinked and went to fill drink orders, knowing today was a classic.

When it was closing time, I stayed late, working past my shift so Tookie wouldn't be the last one in the place.

"Don't get me wrong. I appreciate it," she said as she took one last look over the restaurant, "but you didn't have to do this." She slid her blouse out of her skirt, shaking it vigorously to cool off her ample bosom.

"Hey, I don't have anywhere to be."

"You? As pretty as you is?" she responded in her country drawl. "Where's your man?"

I fought back the urge to say, "In prison." Clearing my head, I answered. "I don't have one." Not anymore.

Tookie paused to analyze what I'd said. "Uh-huh. You got a story."

"Why do you say that?" I asked, pushing a chair back into place at the table I'd cleaned.

"Because we all got one."

A loud tapping on the restaurant door interrupted us, saving me from a walk down memory lane.

"Tookie, you in there?" ushered forth in deep tones through the thick tinted door glass.

She broke her concentration and ran toward the voice. "Hold up," she said, darting away.

The lock clicked as Tookie let the person in. A tall, fine black man placed his hands around her waist as he mumbled something in her ear. When he began nibbling on her earlobe, she giggled, pulling away.

"Ahem. Montez, this is my friend Amelia."

Montez, upon realizing they weren't alone, straightened up. His dark dreads whipped back atop his head as he flashed a smile in my direction. He looked younger than Tookie, probably younger than me, I thought.

"Hey," I said, waving and feeling like a fifth wheel.

"What it do," he answered. Yes. He was definitely younger. He had an athletic build that showed through the white button-down and jeans he sported. Probably played football for U of H or TSU, I surmised. I was coming to learn my full-figured manager had a way with men.

"Tookie, if we're done, I can leave," I offered, figuring on giving her and her ride some time alone.

"Yeah, we're done, child. Where you off to?"

I chuckled. "Home," I answered.

"That's all you do, huh?"

"Pretty much," I sighed as I took my purse to leave. "Gotta make sure the bills get paid."

Tookie and Montez traded looks. He nodded.

"Where you live?" Montez asked.

"Stafford."

He looked at his girlfriend and shrugged his shoulders. "Fine with me," he said. I wondered what was going on.

"Child, we're gonna follow you home so you can change."

"Change?"

"Yeah," Tookie answered. "Unless you're going out with us in your uniform. Montez got his grant check today and it's his birthday."

6

IKE

Serena had me on shit detail, sending me to check the same damn cells over and over again. All it could do is piss the inmates off at me. That's probably what Serena wanted. She had remarked about my not drawing the line like I should and trying to be a counselor when it was my job to break heads instead. I paced down the line until I stood before the familiar cell.

"Step away from the cell door."

"Sure thing, *boss*," Rewind replied, using the backward term for what they really called us—Sorry Son of a Bitch. The skinny inmate, barely filling out his white prison-issueds, Rewind earned his time and nickname by being a repeat offender with a violent temper.

"On five!"

As the cell door clanked open, I stood at the ready. I'd already searched Bodie's bunk, but Rewind had just returned from his latest "accident." I didn't need any surprises lurking for use in his retaliation. I had him turn around and initiated a search of his person before ordering him to step back as I went through his stuff. As I undid the sheets on his mattress, I sensed he was a little too close.

"Back up," I commanded Rewind, not feeling comfortable with my back to him. Another corrections officer stood outside the cell, just in case. He'd just been hired and was barely out of training. I hadn't bothered to learn his name although he'd given it to me along with how much he bench-pressed more than once. Although bigger than both me and Rewind combined, he was scared shitless. It showed all over his fresh face. I ain't gonna front; I was the same my first week on the job. Rewind winked at him as he watched my back.

"Big man will be gone in a week," he chuckled loud enough for both of us to hear.

I cast a scathing glance at Rewind, then went back to inspecting his mattress frame for any loose pieces. On the cell wall below was the picture of Bodie's girl. It had been ripped in half, then put back together. Even with her face split in half, she was hauntingly beautiful. I'd thought that when I first saw it, but this was my first time dwelling on it. How had Bodie wound up with her?

There were always the pretty ones that went for the dope men and that fast, easy life. In the end, they usually learned nothing was easy. Was she one of those? I didn't want to think that of her.

"Ya ain't gonna find nuthin' there, so don't think about plantin' sumthin'," Rewind grunted, uneasy at my taking so long around his bunk.

I stopped daydreaming and turned my focus back to the search. "Plant something? You know me better than that," I answered as I passed my hand one last time.

"I don't know you at all, boss."

"Where's your cellmate?"

"Bodie? He usin' his phone privileges. Why you interested?"

"No reason. Just making small talk."

"Uh-huh," he said with a laugh. He'd moved back into my space, oversized clothes and all. "You miss him or sumthin'? CO Arnold told me about you. Said you like men. That true?"

He smiled gleefully. Something about the way he stepped to me. Like a challenge, but more like a proposition, got under my skin. I wanted to knock the gold caps off his teeth. "Stay the fuck back and shut the fuck up before I—"

"Before you rough me up, boss? You wanna hit me? Knock me around?"

I wanted to all right, just not in the way he was suggesting. Rewind was a troublemaker, but I was more angered at the notion of my sergeant starting this. Inmates with time on their hands liked to spread rumors, but a backhanded joke by Serena at my expense wouldn't surprise me.

I pointed at Rewind, choosing my words carefully before I spoke. "I guess that big, dumb mouth on you is why you have so many shop accidents."

"Your momma didn't complain when I used this big, dumb mouth on her last time I was on the outside."

"Bruh, that was my grandma and she said you didn't know what you were doing. Said she had to coach you because you kept drooling all over her Depends."

He flinched as to make a move on me. I didn't blink.

"Everything okay in there?" my forgotten backup asked as he'd worked up the courage to move closer to the cell.

"Yeah. It's fine, man," I replied, still not recalling the name. "No problems," I stressed with a fake smile and even faker Jamaican accent for Rewind's benefit.

I brushed him off as I shoved my way past him.

"Just watch your back," he whispered without looking at me.

I cocked my head, getting in his face. *"Are you threatening me?"*

"Nope, boss," he replied with a sigh, moving his face away like my breath stunk. "Just expressin' concern. From one black man to another and all that shit."

I stole a final glance at the torn photo, its now uneven eyes peering from a different time, a different place. I was way too fixated about why it was now ripped and the circumstances of how it happened. "Watch *your* back," I said, clearing his cell. "Close five!" I yelled.

When my shift ended, I was glad to be out of there. I knew it was going to be another day of Deryn coming home late, so I drove into town, to my old neighborhood in Third Ward, to relieve some stress.

My old gym welcomed me with open arms as I donned the boxing gloves again and did a little sparring with some of the young dudes coming up. I also emphasized that they stay in school and keep their heads on straight so I didn't see them on the inside. My old trainer made sure to embarrass me, joking about how good I was in my amateur days before I turned traitor and chose Prairie View A&M over the neighborhood school, Texas Southern. To top that off, I then moved out to the North Side. Funny. When I was boxing, all I can remember is him telling me I wasn't shit. In all honesty, I wanted to attend TSU, but instead followed Deryn to Prairie View. In those days, she had my nose open. *Still does,* I thought, not too enthusiastic at admitting it.

As I left the gym feeling sore, yet invigorated, I decided to call Deryn since she was on my mind.

"Whatcha doin'?" I asked, when my lady answered.

"Working," she replied after pausing.

"Still?"

"Yes. Somebody has to pay the bills." She just wouldn't let up. "Where are you? You're off your shift?"

"Yeah. Went by my old gym. Did a little sparring too," I proudly announced while playing with the radio stations. I stopped when I heard some old UGK and began nodding to the groove. I continued. "Gonna check in on my momma while I'm out here."

"You're down in Third Ward?"

I smiled, recognizing an old building on Nagle I used to hang out in front of before things went down. More fond memories. "Yep," I answered.

A long sigh escaped her lips. "I hate going back there. Tell your mother I said hi."

"Aight. When will you be home?"

"Soon. I'm helping Marshall prepare some reports for the city's budget meeting."

"Oh." My attitude changed at the mere mention of his name.

Ignoring my mood shift, she pressed on. "Thought some more about the party we talked about?"

"You mean the one *you* talked about."

"Whatever."

"Yeah. A little. I'll discuss it with you when you come home."

I ended the call to let her get back to work, then finished my drive to my momma's home on Rosalie Street. My family had been a part of this community since the 1930s, when my grandfather, an educator, moved here with his family from tiny Nacogdoches, Texas. My momma, a retired teacher herself, had served as a writer for some of the city's black newspapers and still lived modestly despite the property she owned around town.

I eased alongside the ditch that lined the street in front of the yard, careful to leave enough room for passing cars. Even though it was bricked years ago, my momma's house still held its charm. As I hopped onto the front porch, I lamented over how much the neighborhood had gone down. Two houses over, all that remained was the burned shell of a home with a sign THIRD WARD NOT FOR SALE in the front. A few old tires had been thrown in the ditch too. When I was ready to leave, I was taking them with me to dispose of.

"Boy, you stink," my momma said as she hugged me. A lock of brown hair mixed with gray dangled from beneath the blue scarf she wore when turning in for the night. Her reading glasses dangled from the cord around her neck. In her hand, she held a copy of Victoria Christopher Murray's *Grown Folks Business. Probably for her book club,* I thought. If I'd asked her what it was about, she would only tell me to read it myself. She claimed I didn't read enough as it is.

"Hello to you too," I said with a laugh. "Just finished sparring. Don't worry. I'm going straight home when I leave."

"Hmph. You better. I know I raised you better than that." It was dusk, but she took the time to survey me before letting me pass. "And that hair. That beard. Boy, why can't you be clean cut?"

I just laughed. "Now that you finished your inspection, can I come in?"

"I guess," she said facetiously, rolling her eyes for added effect. "Come on in, baby."

She poured a glass of her fresh lemonade, then brought it to me on the couch, where I sat. She lowered the volume on her O'Jays album, then joined me.

"What's new?"

"Just people getting on my last nerve, Isaac," she said, referring to me by my birth name. "That juke joint, Lullaby's, over on Elgin has people parking in front of my house at all times of night. Between them and those developers always calling me wanting to know if I'm selling my house, I'm going to lose the last bit of brown hair I got."

"You could always dye."

"Die?" she replied, clearing some distance between us as if to slap me.

"Yeah. Dye. Your hair," I answered, pointing for emphasis.

"Oh." She laughed to herself at the misunderstanding.

"Need any work done around the house?"

"Nah, baby. Mr. Vernon comes around and checks on things. He's been fixing the rent houses too." Mr. Vernon was my momma's boyfriend, but she'd never admit it. She was always private about her personal life after lung cancer claimed my pops. "How's Deryn?" she asked, wanting to change the subject.

"Workin'."

"You say it like it's a bad thing."

I drank more of my lemonade. "She spends too much time wrapped up in it. She's never home."

"And what about you? You work odd hours at the prison, right?"

"That's different, Momma."

"Why? Because you're a man?"

"Nah. Nothing like that. You raised me better than that. It's just that she's always pushing and riding me about what I'm doing. Now she wants me to go to this party the mayor's having."

She chuckled. "I'd like to go to that, baby boy. Tell him what I think of his funding for projects around here."

I gave her a look.

"Baby, you know how that girl came up. Deryn had it hard. With all them kids her momma had, she's the only one that did something with her life."

"I know, but what about that?"

"Y'all have been together since high school."

"Yeah. And?"

"And you need to be a little more understanding and supportive. Try giving more of yourself, baby. It may be hard, but try understanding her."

I took my momma's words to heart as I picked up a bottle of Deryn's favorite wine and a tray of cheeses on the way home.

After showering and setting everything out to surprise Deryn, I dimmed the lights, lit some candles and waited. *Be more understanding*, I said to myself as I waited some more. As the hours went by, I opened the bottle of wine and began drinking it myself.

7

BODIE

No one accepted the charges. I removed the receiver from my ear, tapping it on the table while I thought out things. Amelia wasn't home, otherwise she would've answered, I reassured myself. I didn't want to consider she was too busy to pick up. Or what would have her that busy.

"One call, Campbell," the CO who was monitoring my call uttered.

"I know, man. It didn't go through. I think I messed up."

"Uh-huh," the CO answered skeptically. I didn't mess up because he'd placed the call for me from my visitation list. Those were the only calls I could make . . . usually. "You're lucky I'm in a good mood today. Hurry up."

Amelia was on my mind. I began thinking about other people I could call. I wasn't waiting another thirty days for my normal phone privileges to roll around.

"I need to call a different number."

The CO was looking over his uniform like he had a date or something. He pulled a loose thread from his gray shirt before acknowledging me. "Excuse you?" he said, irritated.

I played with my ear and repeated it, softly this time. "I need to call another number."

The other CO nearby, the one I had been bribing since my transfer, caught the signal. On cue, he walked over and whispered something in my babysitter's ear. Feeling relieved of watching me, he gladly left to groom himself some more. Bitch.

Number two sat down in his place. He looked at my visitors list as if dialing from it, but actually dialed the number I motioned with finger signs. I would've smiled, but I had nothing to be happy about. I'd paid more for this call than I had for a good lap dance at Harlem Knights or Ice Cream Castles when I was on the outside. That's just it. To this day, I still had trouble accepting that I could no longer do what I wanted when I wanted. Like a soldier, I put on my game face every fuckin' day and did what I had to do to get by. It's just that it wasn't living. That said, it was more than what Abdel was doing these days.

"Hello?" the groggy voice belonging to Aaron said after accepting charges.

"Hey."

"What it do, man?" he greeted as he perked up.

"Can't tell."

I didn't much talk to Aaron or his brother, Ro, since things went down. We never discussed that day when we did talk. Aaron knew what this call was about. It was usually the only thing on my mind.

I motioned for the CO to stop monitoring the call and give me a little privacy. "Make it quick," he muttered.

"You aight, bruh?"

"Yeah. I'm straight. We can talk now. What's your boy doin'?"

Aaron laughed. "Man. Ro doin' contractor work now. Thinks he's a handy man or sumthin'. Y'know, all them houses comin' up west o' here?"

"No. I wouldn't know."

"Oh. Yeah," he stated, his voice trailing off as he suddenly felt foolish. "Well, he's doin' that. Got him a house out by Katy 'n' shit."

"What she's doin'?"

"Straight to it, huh?"

"Yeah. It's like that."

Aaron cleared his throat. "I ain't seen her in a while," he answered.

"What?"

"Calm down, bruh. I've been goin' through some thangs—car trouble 'n' shit. I'm doin' what I said I'd do though."

"So what *do* you know?"

"She mainly go to work, then come home. She waitin' tables now. She don't go out much. She rents a lot of movies. That's about it."

"What about that dude?"

"Man, that was last year. Me and Ro paid him a visit. He ain't come around since."

"You sure?"

"Oh, yeah. I'm sure." I knew better than to ask what that meant.

"She know?"

"Nah. He understand the reality of the situation."

"Where she singin'?"

"She ain't."

"Damn. Still?"

"Fo sho."

The CO motioned to me that time was up.

"How's my Lac?" I asked, signaling to Aaron that I was about to be monitored again.

"It's shined up and waitin' on you, little daddy."

"Good. Keep it that way. Don't forget to check under the hood."

"I won't. I'll drive by and check thangs out soon. Just to make sure it's runnin' like it should."

"Do that."

"Consider it done."

"Look, I gotta go. Boss starin' a nigga down 'n' shit."

"All right then. Bruh, keep yo head up and I'll see you tomorrow," he said, meaning he'd be there on release day. Too far away for me to stress over.

I hung up and watched the CO as he watched me.

"Everything okay?"

I chuckled. "Like you care. Man, take me back to my cell."

8

AMELIA

Montez and Tookie followed me home, where I hurriedly showered, teased my hair and changed into something more appropriate—a Nicole Miller top, a pair of designer jeans, and my favorite boots. As I applied my makeup in the mirror, I struggled to remember the last time I'd had fun of any sort.

I thought I'd had some chemistry with this guy I met last year, but he freaked on me and quit returning my calls. I never understood that because we really seemed to hit it off. Other than that one rare occasion, there had always been Bodie. With the history we shared, it was hard cutting him loose. I wasn't naive about his lifestyle, but I still didn't want to believe he'd murdered someone. In spite of my desires, I had nothing else to go on. All I had was what the local news said every night—that and the tortured images of him running from the police, the murdered man's blood staining his clothes. Bodie refused to talk about it, barely cooperating with his attorney during the trial. In spite of what he'd cost me, I stuck around as long as I could. One day, I realized that, for my sanity, I had to free myself and quit holding out that if he ever lived through his sentence he would emerge from prison a changed man. I still took calls from him, but my last visit to the prison was almost the hardest thing I'd done.

Almost.

I blinked to prevent from tearing up and finished applying my

eyeliner, telling myself that I deserved the occasional bit of happiness
in spite of my secret sin.

"How do I look?" I said to Tookie and Montez, exiting my bedroom with a false smile to mask my dismal thoughts.

After leaving in my car, I followed them to Tookie's house for her
to change as well. Of course, she wouldn't let us leave without a few
shots of cognac to get things crunk. Montez decided to be the night's
driver, so I left my car at her place. Our before-the-club dinner con-
sisted of Timmy Chan's off I-610, where we laughed at Montez as he
did his Ricky Smiley impersonations. Tookie's boyfriend left my
stomach in knots to where I couldn't finish my delicious wings, rice,
and gravy.

Montez didn't have a preference on where to celebrate his birthday, so while searching on the radio, we heard Mega 101 hyping reg-
gaeton at one of the Latin clubs, Babilonia.

"Why not?" we all agreed. I loved me some Daddy Yankee, even if I
couldn't understand what he was saying. For the night, Tookie and me
were Dominican. Montez, just to be different, decided he was Cuban.

At the club, it didn't take long for the pounding rhythms to drive
Tookie and Montez to the dance floor. They tried to get me to join
them, but I decided to ease into things. Tonight, I was only dipping
my toe in the pool, I told myself. I nursed an apple martini while
watching them heat up.

Tookie was like a thick Lisa Nicole Carson grinding on the floor,
fiery and fully confident in the power of her sexuality. Watching her
plump ass pressing against Montez' pelvis caused a stir in me.
Maybe it was my martini, but I felt flush as a wave of heat dissected
me from my chest down to the damp treasure between my legs. I
could feel my clit swelling inside my jeans. Gawd, it had been way
too long since someone had torn this up. Not tonight though. I shook
my head and looked at my drink before pushing it away from me.

"*Muy fuerte?*"

It took me a second to realize the bronze-ish gentleman was talking to me. "Excuse me?" I replied.

He seemed puzzled at first, then let out a hearty laugh. I thought he was crazy or drunk. That didn't stop me from noticing how attractive or well-dressed he was. *"No Español?"*

I was embarrassed to admit it, but did so. "No," I answered, like he'd been let in on a big secret. Hell, I could count the amount of definite black folk in the place on my hand. "Shhhh," I whispered, more tipsy than seductive, "I'm pretending I'm Dominican tonight. Don't tell anyone."

He smiled as if he wanted to laugh at me, but held it together. "I was asking if your drink was too strong. If it is, I can get another one for you."

"Aren't you a sweetheart?" I was flirting. No more drinks for me. "But I'm fine."

"Can I at least have a dance with you? Such a *mujer bonita* shouldn't let her friends have all the fun."

I agreed, learning his name was Filiberto. We danced, wild and free, and had a good time in each other's company. I remember chanting along with Nina Skyy to the song *"Oye Mi Canto"*, *"Boricua! Morena! Dominicano! Colombiano! Cubano!"* And finally *"Mexicano,"* to which the whole club erupted on cue.

"You wanted to go home with him, huh?" Tookie teased me later on. We were finally leaving the club. I was still buzzing in the backseat, where she and Montez had safely placed me.

"Nope. I just met him. I got his number though," I admitted, before giggling like a small child. I didn't mention how close we'd danced or how aroused it had left me.

"How long has it been?"

"Tookie!"

"Girl, it's just me, you and Montez up in here. And he ain't gonna put your business on blast. You already told me at work you ain't got a man, so I hope someone or *something's* been servicing your kitty. At least a Silver Bullet."

"You are a trip" was my only response.

"Ain't I though? Child, the way you were dancing out there

looked like you were about ready to gush in yo pants. I thought I was bad. Just promise me you'll give that Mexican dude a few days before you have him over," she said with an evil laugh before turning around and resuming her proper position in her seat.

Once Tookie had her fun, the drive was mostly quiet, so I took the time to cool off. My shirt had faint traces of perspiration visible between my breasts. I blew down my shirt to cool them off. Tookie and her man continued carrying on once they thought I'd fallen asleep. I was just resting my eyes, but they held my curiosity. He'd whisper something to her, laugh and she'd do likewise. We were stopped at a red light before jumping on the freeway when I noticed Tookie was no longer visible. Rather than saying something, I continued pretending I was asleep. Barely over the music, low bass-filled moans could be heard escaping Montez' lips. As the top of her head came into view between his legs only to disappear again, I imagined the voracious slurping sounds she must've been making as she enveloped his dick in her mouth . . . and jealously wished I had a man of my own to please like that. I decided to take a nap the rest of the way rather than bother my drunk, tired mind with such stuff.

I awoke back at Tookie's, and was in no shape to drive, so they insisted I stay the night. As I had an off day tomorrow, I didn't make a big stink about it. Besides, Tookie and Montez were too distracted to notice me at the moment. As she placed the key in her front door, Montez' dark, muscular arms enveloped her. He worked to undo the buttons on her blouse, eager to get a handful.

"Down, boy," she teased, swatting his large hands away.

"But it's my birthday."

"Was. Was your birthday. Boy, it's after midnight."

I was silently following Montez in the door when he suddenly stopped. I clumsily walked right into him. "So I'm not getting any?" he asked.

Twirling her keys on her finger, Tookie turned around and smirked. "I didn't say all that. Now get your ass in here. You're blocking Amelia."

Tookie put on some music, Heather Headley's new album I be-

lieve, then served us some Arbor Mist from the fridge. I found myself humming along to the music, careful not to break out in song,
even though my soul cried out. We sat around conversing until
Tookie abruptly jumped up off the couch as if jarred by a memory.

"Y'all want some weed?" she asked, attempting to be a good hostess in her own special way. From working with her, I knew she was
a wild one, but this night was definitely revealing.

I shook my head. The glass in my hand was all I needed to end my
night.

"Nah," Montez answered. "They test me at school."

She stood there, frowning at the two of us, hands on her hips.
"Fuck y'all," she commented. "I'm gettin' lifted."

Tookie went to her bedroom, then came out with a Ziploc bag of
weed and papers, which she promptly began to roll. Before she could
fire it up, I asked to use the shower and for something to sleep in if I
was going to be spending the night. She led me to the bathroom and
gave me one of her bathrobes.

"Child, you look like you wanna pass out. If you want to, you can
use my bed. Me and Montez gonna be up a while."

I thanked Tookie for breaking me out of my routine, then left her
to her man and her weed, in no particular order. I found a spare
shower cap, then took a warm, steamy shower. I exited the shower,
reaching for the towel and saw myself in the fogged mirror. I took the
time to seriously assess myself, turning slowly as the fog and steam
subsided. Sure I'd put on a few pounds, added a little curve to my
swerve, but minus the long hair I no longer wore, I was still the slender showstopper from my young, dumb and fun days. The changes
life had brought me had me feeling ugly despite what my eyes com-
municated.

After toweling off and putting on the oversized robe, I was
greeted by the distinctive aroma of marijuana and the sounds of giggling and thuds beyond the bedroom door. I chose to go to bed and
leave them alone, but I had to be nosy.

As I approached the partially open door, I heard another thud. I began to simply push it shut, but was drawn like a moth to the flame. I peered around the corner of the door.

On the throw rug in the middle of the living room floor, Montez lay writhing on his back. His shirt lay open, jeans and boxers down to his ankles. Tookie was nude from the waist down, her blouse undone and hanging past her shoulders. She was straddling him backward, allowing him to watch her full hips as she slapped them up and down on his pelvis. She swallowed him inside her with every drop she took. Harder and harder she smacked, riding him as if caught on a train she couldn't . . . didn't want to get off. As if in a trance, she hummed, eyes closed, as she clenched her bottom lip in her teeth. I recoiled away from the door, afraid of being seen, but took one final look.

"Damn," I said, feeling hot myself. I then crawled into Tookie's bed and forced myself asleep. My dreams were a swirling, intoxicated mix of our night out and surprisingly the last time I'd made love to Bodie. It was the last time I'd shared myself with anyone.

I couldn't have slept more than an hour or two before Tookie and Montez stumbled in, high and drunk. I thought it might have been part of my dream, until their intertwined bodies tumbled beside me on the bed, jarring me from my slumber. The smell of sweet sex mixed with marijuana covered their bodies, further awakening me. I wanted to get up, to move. As drained as I was, I decided to stay. *If I lie very still, they'll eventually stop,* I thought.

Planting his hand to brace himself, Montez caused part of my robe to pull open, exposing my thigh. I said nothing. He hadn't noticed and probably didn't see me. All he saw was Tookie's inviting pussy before him, singing its enticing song. To them, I didn't exist.

"Fuck me some more, big man," Tookie demanded, panting with each breath. She lay right beside me in the dark. As he obeyed, I found myself getting aroused. They wouldn't notice. I slowly, delicately, arched my exposed leg and slid my fingers inside of me. I was already so wet. With my index finger probing in and out, I took my thumb and began playing with my clit. They were so loud anyway that they wouldn't hear my moans. Before long, I began to orgasm. By this time, Montez was rocking her bottom, her legs held open to take it all in.

I was cumming all over when I opened my eyes and saw Montez looking dead at me. I flinched upon being found out and suddenly stopped. Rather than stopping, he just smiled before turning his attention back to fucking the shit out of Tookie. I glanced her way. I was no longer invisible. My scent now mingled with theirs and hung heavy in the air.

She yanked on the robe's sash, fully exposing my nude body. Montez' eyes lit up lustfully. Instead of running out of the room or tying the robe back, I did nothing. Tookie turned on her side and whispered in my ear.

"Want some?" she asked, barely audible. The room was suddenly very still.

I didn't speak, just nodded. Yes.

Montez had stopped doing the do, not sure of what he heard. He looked to Tookie, wanting to be certain before . . .

"It's your birthday," she said. "Go, Montez. It's your birthday," she sang like that Luke song, but in a sexy, playful way that was quite different.

He flipped his head back, sending his dreads flying, then resumed his long strokes, sweat now covering his massive muscular chest. While he fucked her, his hand ran up my thigh, stopping at my percolating pussy. My breathing became shallow. I spread my legs ever so much, as two of his fingers slid right in. My eyes rolled back as rivers flowed once again. What was I doing? Didn't matter.

With his firm hand still lodged between my legs, I felt another, softer hand on my breast, then a pair of full sensual lips. Tookie startled me. I blinked, having to do a double take, but allowed myself to be taken somewhere I'd never been. With my hard nipple in her willing mouth and Montez fingering me to no end, I let loose with a loud scream. I came uncontrollably.

I eventually lost it, sitting up to actively join in. I kissed Montez all over his beautiful self and he kissed me back, cupping my ass in his hand.

"You wanna fuck her, baby?" Tookie asked him.

He paused from kissing me and nodded.

Tookie eyed him for a second, then chuckled. "Go get a condom."

I was fully awake and energized now, eagerly awaiting the gift I was about to receive. As I waited, Tookie started things back up. She pulled me atop her. With me straddling her full figure, the heat between our bodies was intoxicating. Our breasts brushed against each other. Her nipples were large and inviting. I paused.

"Oh, just let it go," she said with a smile. I brought my lips to hers and plunged my tongue into her mouth. Our hands explored everywhere as we pressed against each other, causing a rush of sensations I'd never felt. Goose bumps popped up all over me. I rose onto my elbows, allowing her to cup both my breasts in her hands, kneading them skillfully like baker's dough. She knew just how to touch them. Tookie moaned as I kissed up and down her neck before trailing down her body with my tongue.

"Mmmm. Damn, girl," she moaned.

I'd momentarily forgotten all about Montez, but quickly remembered. As I pleasured Tookie, I felt his hands on my raised ass, then their sure grip, steadying me. I gasped and let out a yell of sheer pleasure as I felt his swollen head enter, parting my yearning walls from behind. Tookie cradled me to her bosom, allowing me to eagerly suck on them while he pounded me doggy style, wearing me out to no end.

"Is it good? Is it good?" she asked.

"Uuuu . . . uh-huh," I mindlessly replied, cumming harder and harder.

"Damn right it is," she affirmed as her man's pelvis smacked against my ass cheeks. Even as I backed against him, I begged for mercy, lost in contradiction and wave after wave of orgasms.

9

IKE

I waited for Deryn, buzzing off the wine I'd been drinking. The candles I'd lit flickered, some near the end of their wicks. Another episode of *Busted*, the TV show where people in Houston caught their lovers cheating, had just gone off. I'd flipped the TV off, leaving the house bathed in only the candles' glow.

She'd said she was working late, but this was past late. I had her cell number, could've called her, but I wasn't the chasing type. I didn't know about the world she worked in. I worked my shifts and tried to separate myself from the job whenever I could. Deryn, on the other hand, wrapped herself in hers. Maybe that was it. It was a career to her and I was one of those pieces that didn't fit.

The lights from a car turning into our driveway temporarily illuminated the living room. I put my goblet of wine down on the coffee table and went to the window. Inside the black Acura, I could make out her silhouette. Deryn was talking on her cell phone. Again. I was relieved to see her, but the longer I waited for her to get out the car, the more my anger returned.

It was all about understanding tonight, just like I told my momma. The candles were still lit, so I returned to the couch, determined to be patient.

"It's open!" I yelled as she fumbled for her keys.

Most of the wine gone, I tried appearing sober as she came inside.

Deryn wore a white blazer and matching skirt with a pink top underneath. She looked more as if she'd been out than spending a hard day (and night) at work. She stepped out of her designer shoes at the door, just as she always did, before noticing the flower petals covering the wood floor before her feet. Then she saw the candles and me waiting on the couch. She was stunned.

"Is . . . is that a Verité?" she asked.

I was confused until I remembered that was the brand of wine I'd bought. "Yeah. It was. Good stuff," I said. I fumbled for her goblet, filling it with the remainder of the bottle. "I got tired of waiting. You hungry? I have some cheese too."

"No. I already ate." She closed the door, then sauntered over to take the glass from my hand.

I kissed her hand before releasing the glass. "Where you been?"

She swirled the wine around in her glass, admiring its color. Again, I was tuned out. "Work."

"Uh-uh. Not this late," I reminded her. "Where were you?"

Deryn was surprised by my demeanor. She quit playing with her wine. Rather than being pissed or trying to put me in my place, she smiled. "I had some dinner afterwards. I thought you'd eaten, so I stopped on the way home. Are you mad at me, Isaac?"

"What the fuck do you think?"

She took a sip of her wine, then embraced me with her free arm. I didn't return the hug. "Well, I'm here now. Seriously though. It's lovely. You haven't done something like this in a while. Thank you, Daddy," she purred. As my reward, she kissed me, her tender lips tasting like the Verité I'd been drinking too much of. Nonetheless, her mouth tasted good. I kissed her back, our lips meshing. My pulse raced as our tongues intertwined. Deryn's nails dug into my neck. I felt the electricity as she dragged them up into my scalp, where she grasped the back of my head. I laced powerful kisses across her neck, then moved her jacket aside so I could savor her smooth golden shoulders. She moaned, almost falling back, but I caught her.

"Still love me?"

"Mmm-hmm," I answered, looking into the dazzling eyes of the woman I'd loved most of my time on this Earth. "And I want to understand you . . . like I used to. Be there for you."

She swallowed the last of her wine, then threw her goblet over her shoulder. It shattered in the corner. It felt like old times. She removed her blazer. Her top underneath barely contained the perfect Cs, courtesy of the implants she'd treated herself to last year. They always looked a little off on her slender frame, but tonight they were perfect. She saw me eyeing them. "You want me, don't you?"

My dick answered, filling out the front of my pants, even though I wasn't trying to have one of those nights. She reached down to feel it, but I backed off. "Yeah. I want you, but I have something to show you first." I walked over and reached on the side of the sofa. I pulled out a box I'd stowed early.

Deryn recognized the label. "You bought me shoes?"

"Just a little sumthin'," I answered. I'd maxed out my credit card on them at Nordstrom in the Galleria. I'd seen enough of her brands in the bedroom closet to know what she liked.

"What's the occasion?"

"Just thought you might need them when we go to the mayor's party."

Her mouth hung open. She eyed the black sandals, then locked in on me again. She was impressed. "I . . . I didn't think you'd go. Marshall said you'd change your mind, but I—" she cut her comment short, but it was too late.

"Marshall? What are you doing talking about me to Marshall?"

Her eyes blinked rapidly, like a hummingbird's wings. "It was nothing. I was just saying that you didn't want to go and—"

"Wait. Wait." I closed my eyes, regaining my mind back from the wine and the emotions I'd felt less than a minute ago. "Where did you eat?"

"Excuse me?"

"Where were you tonight? You said you had dinner."

"Look, I'm not going to get into this with you. I—"

"Deryn. Just telling me where you fuckin' were."

"La Colombe d'Or."

"Never heard of it."

"Inside your little prison world, you never would," she snapped in as nasty a tone as she could summon. "It's a French restaurant. Somewhere you'd never take me."

"And you went there tonight? After work?"

"Yes. I said I was hungry."

I laughed, not because it was funny, but because it was better than the alternative. "Ate there alone?"

"No. How would I look eating there by myself?" She picked her jacket from off the floor. Some of the flower petals stuck to it, and she quickly picked them off. "Marshall offered when we finished work."

"You kept me waiting at home while you went out with your fuckin' boss?" I clenched my fist, something I'd just used earlier in the gym.

"I didn't go out with him. It was just dinner. Don't try turning it into something it isn't, Isaac." She noticed my clenching and unclenching my fist. "What? You want to hit me now?"

"No. It's not worth the effort."

"You weren't saying stuff like that a minute ago when you wanted to fuck me."

"Look, Deryn. This isn't what I had in mind for tonight," I said, waving my hand at her. "I'm gonna cool off before I do or say something both of us will regret."

"You want to get rough, Daddy?" she said in a seductive baby voice. Deryn was a closet freak and I knew where she was headed.

"Look, don't start that." I put my arms up to keep her at bay.

"Why not, Daddy?" she said as she grasped my arms. She pulled them down to my sides, allowing her to press her breasts against me. "You know I like to get you worked up."

"C'mon now. You need to back up. I'm not up for the games tonight."

"But you know that's how I like it. *You don't want to play?*"

"Naw. Go on now."

"I made you mad, Daddy, didn't I?"

"Stop this shit, Deryn."

"You don't want me to stop," she laughed. "If you do," she said as she whispered in my ear, "then make me stop. I've been bad tonight. Why don't you punish me?"

The faint glow from the candles reflected in her hazel eyes. I said nothing, but she knew she had me back where she wanted. Her jacket fell to the floor again, this time followed by the rest of her clothes as she slowly stripped for me. When she was finished, she stood there revealed. Her beautiful sultry body desiring my touch, my taste.

"You did all this for me and I made you mad. Now I have to pay. Are you going to make me pay with that, Daddy?"

When I looked down at the bulge she was referring to, I knew my resolve was gone. My anger and passion had fused. She was going to be the object of my wrath . . . just as she wanted. I began taking my pants off. She helped me with my shirt, popping the buttons as she pulled to get it off me. She jumped into my arms, wrapping her toned thighs around me like a constrictor. She feverishly worked on my neck, biting mixed with licks from her tongue. As I gave in to Deryn's passion, my head instinctively went in search of her tight, sweet home. She slinked farther up my body as I carried her, making it easier for me to penetrate.

"I want it on the stairs, Daddy," Deryn instructed.

She rode my dick, sliding up and down, as I carried her to the staircase. Still inside of her, I sat down, and she grabbed the rail with one hand, bracing the other on the wall.

"Mmm. That's it. That's it," she mumbled as she bounced up and down on me. Each time, she rammed harder and harder, her sweet honey clinging to me. I wanted to explode in her so bad, but fought it.

"You want to cum, Daddy? Huh?" She smiled sadistically.

"Y-yes, yes," I cried out. Her pussy felt so good.

"Are you still mad at me?"

I could barely get the answer out, but she knew what I meant. As she came down, she began winding her ass on me like a top. My hands grasped her, but they were merely along for the ride. Her juices flowed all over my lap. When she came down again, I gripped one of her cheeks, allowing my finger to enter her ass. As soon as she felt it, Deryn cackled as if insane. Her pace quickened.

"Oh yeah! Oh yeah! Oh yeah! That's it," she chanted. "Keep it in there, Daddy."

My breathing became labored. I buried my face into her sweaty body, tasting her salt and perfume. I slid forward on the step, giving me a better angle. As she leaned back, she maintained her grip in every way. Her motions became more and more violent as she thrashed about on every inch of me.

"Oh Gawd. I'm gonna cum," I said.

"That's it, Daddy. Cum with me. Cum with me," she panted.

With that, I exploded inside her, releasing every ill feeling, suspicious thought and bit of bitterness I'd had pent up inside. Her body trembled and quivered as she rode down on me one last time. She gasped for air through the matted hair that covered her eyes. For minutes, we didn't move, collapsed onto each other in a heap.

Deryn suddenly got up, jarring me from semiconsciousness. "Don't get up," she said, patting me on the shoulder as I started to move. "I'm going to clean up. I have a long day ahead of me tomorrow," she snapped, as if she'd had a personality transplant. It wasn't what she'd said as much as the dismissive tone that had returned. It said she was through, as if what we'd just had was simply a distraction for her. I looked at all the broken glass on the floor from the goblet and wondered if my resolve hadn't been just as easily shattered by her tonight.

"Oh and, Isaac?" she said from the top of the staircase, having forgotten something.

"Yeah?" I answered, buck naked and drained.

"You need to get a haircut. Your shit's looking rough."

10

BODIE

I lay on my bunk listening to the chopped and screwed version of the rapper AK's last album. My hand rested across my head while, eyes closed, I mouthed the lyrics along with his grimy, slow delivery. To be back on the streets and runnin' thangs.

Something tapped against my foot. I removed the earpieces.

"Antoine?" the prison mail worker, a roly-poly Mexican we called Ramo, questioned as he looked over the letter he held. *"That's you, Bodie?"*

I sighed. "Yeah, it's me, bitch."

The envelope was flung onto my lap before he shuffled off down the row with his mail cart.

"Anything for me?" Rewind shouted from the top bunk.

"Nah," Ramo replied over his shoulder, not bothering to stop. His contempt was obvious.

"I think he's holdin' my shit," Rewind muttered.

"Why? You pissed him off too?"

"You got jokes, but shit ain't funny. My woman supposed to send me a picture with her ass all out."

I laughed. "You ain't got a woman, man."

"You don't know. That's why you got that old torn-up picture you be whackin' off to. That trick probably givin' that ass up all over H-town now."

"You're about to step right into an ass whippin', Rewind."

"Man, I'm just sayin'. Used to have four of 'em just like her, back when I was movin' some weight from here to Lake Charles. Where they at now? Two of 'em pregnant. *Ain't mine though.* One 'claim' she saved. The other one strung out on that 'heron.'"

"Whatever, nigga. You ain't moved no weight. Probably ain't had no bitches either."

"Think I ain't? My boys still doin' thangs in Inwood, over there off Antoine."

"Uh-huh." I'd tuned out Rewind as I turned my mail over to inspect it. It had been forwarded from my last "crib." When I saw it came from a correctional facility, I paused. When I saw the name of the inmate who'd sent it, I was overcome with disbelief.

Rewind was still talking shit when I walked out the cell. "Where you goin'?" he yelled.

"Get some air. It's startin' to stink up in here."

It was open recreation time, so I walked downstairs to our cell-block's TV area, where *Bad Boys II* was playing on the big screen. Gabrielle Union was taking her top off in the water to the elation of the front row. I steered clear of a large group of inmates belonging to Aztecas, one of the major Mexican gangs on the inside. Their tats were as recognizable as their reputation. Their competition was L.C., Los Camarilla, and the two groups had blowups on the regular.

I found a vacant chair away from any potential beef and prepared to open my letter. I didn't know my moms was still alive, let alone that she'd find me on the inside. She was a dope man's bitch from back in the day, when shit was less crucial. They were still usin' knives 'n' shit then. She had me young and wound up getting hooked on the product right after. That's when life got crazy and she started bouncing from jail to jail. My grams took me in when I was a baby and raised me as her own.

"She probably wants some money," I mumbled aloud to no one but myself. I removed the letter that had already been screened.

In some shitty handwriting, it read:

Dear Antoine,

    I don't know if this will reach you or if you will even want to hear from you momma. After you grandmomma died, I did not think I would find you. I heard about what you gone through and feel very bad. If you like, you can write me back. That would be nice. I'm not going anywhere. Hopefully, you will go somewhere good soon.

Love, Sherry, Your Momma

PS If you got some change you can spare, I'd like it so I can buy some things in here.

I sat numb to the words I'd read. I was about to stow the letter away and watch the movie when a few splatters of crimson spewed across it. After it registered what they were, I turned in the direction the blood had come from. The shit hit the fan as the inmate two seats over held his neck, which had just been shanked. A gang of bodies sitting behind him pounced like a pack of crazed hyenas to finish the job as the COs shouted for lockdown. Simultaneously, other fights broke out in the area. Niggas was going down as people took advantage of the confusion to even whatever scores they had. I was keeping my head low and eyes open when somebody was shoved into me. I fell to the floor, dropping the letter.

"My letter!" I shouted. I sprang back to my feet, punching the motherfucker stupid enough to grab at me. I went to snag my letter, but felt a shot hard enough to break my back. I fell to the floor in pain, knowing I wouldn't be getting back up under my own power. The riot team was on the scene. As I was shoved to the ground and ordered not to move a fuckin' muscle by the masked man in black, I watched my bloodstained letter get stepped on and lost in the shuffle.

Just another fuckin' day, I thought as I was yanked to my feet and hauled off to solitary.

II

AMELIA

"Miss, are you going to sing or continue to behave like a bloody mannequin?" the snotty European judge rattled off. The other two simply looked like they felt sorry for me.

"I-I'm gonna sing."

"Then sop up your tears. We don't have all day, Miss . . ."

"Amelia," I solemnly answered. "My name's Amelia."

I awoke from my dream, realizing I was crying. Something soft rested on my face. My eyelids were heavy, hard to open, but I put forth the effort, straining at first with one eye, then the other. The bright orange color assaulting me was startling as it didn't compute. I closed my eyes in panic. I tried thinking back, remembering dancing at the club. I strained to think beyond that, but couldn't shake off the throbbing in my head and soreness of my body. But why was I so sore? I opened my eyes again. After they adjusted, I saw that a throw was draped over me. My body was stripped naked.

Panicking, I sat up to find myself on Tookie's couch. I remembered Montez as he strolled in wearing warm-ups. He stopped dead on the dime when he saw me.

"Oh," he said, startled I was awake. He tried looking away, but his gaze kept returning to my bare breasts. My nipples hardened as if they had a memory all their own.

"Hey" was all I could bring myself to say. Suddenly modest and feeling a little creepy, I quickly wrapped the throw around my body. Everything came flooding back to me now. I remembered why I was so sore and other things that didn't bear repeating. I must've stumbled into the living room and passed out at some point.

"Um . . . good morning" fumbled out of his mouth.

"Is it?" I replied.

"I gotta get to class. Imma get Tookie for you."

He walked to the bedroom, the scene of the crime. I heard Tookie's voice as she answered whatever he was saying. Fastening the throw around me like a makeshift wrap, I made my way to the kitchen. I was fishing in the refrigerator for something to quench my thirst when he returned.

"Well, it was nice meeting you."

"You too," I said, not really knowing what to say in a situation like this.

He was walking out the front door when Tookie came running. She wore a striped sleeveless top and a pair of shorts that barely covered her assets.

"Hey, boy, you forgot my sugar," she yelled.

Catching himself, he leaned over and planted one on her. She squeezed his ass.

"Good luck on your test," she giggled, sending him on his way. He flashed a smile at her, then disappeared.

A hush fell over the room, both of us afraid to touch upon the topic. I found a glass in the cupboard and poured some cranberry juice. Tookie came over, leaning on the counter, but said nothing. After taking a sip, I waited to see how my stomach handled it. When I didn't throw up, I broke the silence.

"Have you seen my clothes?"

"Sure have. I washed and dried them for you."

"My top!"

"Relax. I used Woolite on cold. It came out fine."

I breathed a sigh of relief to which we both laughed.

"About last night," I volunteered. "Um . . . I don't normally do stuff like that. That wasn't me."

"Girl, who you tellin'?" Tookie blurted, her facial expression exaggerated. "You looked like a repressed nun who accidentally caught a flight to Hedonism. Child, don't even sweat it. I'm just happy to help you unwind."

I laughed, but was still nervous. "Yeah, I did. But that's beside the point. I don't roll like that. I shouldn't have been doing that with you. And your boyfriend."

She put both her elbows on the kitchen countertop, back arched. "Let me tell you something. Montez ain't my 'boyfriend,' " she said, making signs with her fingers for emphasis. "He's a sweet boy that's one of my interns. It was junior's birthday and I figured he had the same fantasy as most men. If he was my main man, I wouldn't have been sharing him. Believe that."

"Oh. Still, I just don't want you thinking—"

"*Thinking what?* Ain't nobody in this place a bigger freak than me. Ya know?"

"I'm just saying—"

"Will you shut up already? It's over."

I laughed. "All right! All right! It's over."

"You can tell me one thing though."

"What's that?"

"What happened to your man?"

"Things didn't work out between us."

Tookie eyed me. "He in jail, huh?"

My cheeks ran flush. "How did you know? Did Me-Me—"

She put her hand in my face to shush me. "Your cousin didn't tell me shit. You just got that look. Like you used to be one of them dope dealer women—all cutesy 'n' shit with big tits and a little body. Skinny heifer."

"My body ain't little," I shrieked.

"Hell, it is compared to mine. Look at you," she said, pointing for emphasis. "You barely fill out that throw of mine you're tryin' to rock. On me, that might make one pant leg."

"That's it. Now you're clowning me too much," I laughed. "I gotta get home."

"Well, I've cleaned and disinfected everything," she said with a hearty laugh. "Your clothes are folded nice and neat by the washing machine. Go on and get yourself together. I'll make some pancakes or something right quick."

When I returned clean and fully clothed, Tookie was flipping pancakes onto the plates. She juggled the task with the phone conversation she was carrying on.

"Yeah. Yeah. Uh-huh. Hang on, she's right here," she said into the receiver while looking at me. She shoved the phone at me.

"Who is it?" I mouthed silently, knowing no one should be checking up on me.

"Your cousin," she mouthed, gesturing for me to take it again. I began whispering, wondering how Me-Me knew I was there. Tookie rolled her eyes and physically placed the phone in my hand. "Calm your nervous ass down. We were talking and I told her you stopped by. She just asked to speak to you," she whispered. I took a seat at the small dining table and put the phone to my ear.

"Hello?"

"Hey, cuz" came from the raspy, strained voice on the other end.

"Me-Me?" I asked, not completely certain.

"Yeah. Don't laugh. I got laryngitis."

"Aww, I'm sorry to hear that. How's the baby?"

"J. R.'s fine," she said referring to her little boy, Joseph Reginald, who was no longer a baby. "Tookie said you'd stopped by. That's funny."

"Why?"

"Because I was about to call you anyway. I need a favor," she grunted, clearing her throat so she could continue. "I need you to bail your cuz out."

"How?"

"By filling in for me at Lullaby's. I need you to sing for me."

The boil of emotions almost swept me up. "I don't sing anymore. You know that, Me-Me," I said in as stern a voice as I could muster without sounding like a jerk.

"Amelia. Please. I can't do it. I know it's late notice but I can't find anyone else. Just one night."

"Cuz, I can't do it," I said low, trying to avoid Tookie's gaze. She finished the pancakes and put the griddle in the sink.

Me-Me hesitated. I knew she was dejected. I'd come across just the way I didn't intend. "Okay," she sighed. "I guess I'll keep looking."

"You want to talk to Tookie?"

"No," she strained. "Tell her I'll talk to her later."

I hung up and set the phone on the table. Tookie looked at me, shaking her head.

"What?" I asked.

She slid a plate of pancakes toward me, then plunked down the maple syrup bottle. "It's none of my business, but I never let that stop me."

"Go ahead. Let me have it. I'm an ungrateful, selfish little so and so."

"Child, I wasn't going to say all that. I don't know all the ins and outs of your relationship with your cousin. What I do know is that Me-Me is good peoples. She went to bat big time for you when you needed a job at Mirage."

"I don't sing anymore."

She chuckled. "I didn't even know you could *sang* until Me-Me said something. Ain't it just like getting on a bike?"

My bike had been wrecked, never to be ridden again. "I don't want to talk about it," I answered.

"Fine. Your pancakes are getting cold anyway."

As I sat there, I considered telling Tookie more. I didn't though. Instead what came out of my mouth was "I'm suddenly not hungry either." I excused myself, thanked Tookie for everything, then left.

12

IKE

"Wait, wait. Hold up a second," I protested. My assignment sheet had me working the solitary hold. "Why am I working solitary?"

Another CO laughed as he wrapped up his shift. He worked on the riot squad. "You missed the fun, Ike. We had to crack some eggs. Vato locos got crazy in the rec area."

Serena, not mindful of the men in the middle of dressing, came over. She heard my complaints. "Most of the hardheads are on lockdown until we sort things out. We got one of ours in the infirmary and one inmate dead. And it's lunchtime, so guess where that leaves you, Winters," she said, poking her finger in my chest.

"Lunch," I shouted as I took another tray off the cart and opened the slot on the cell door. In the three cells where I'd previously delivered food, I'd been cursed out in various degrees of Spanish and English. This one was quiet with the inmate simply taking the tray.

"Hey! Hey!" he yelled as I shut the door. I thought I was lucky with this one.

I lowered my head and peered into the window of the space smaller than eight by eight. "What?" I yelled back.

"That you, Winters?" the eyes glaring through the slot asked.

"Bodie?" His being on solitary came as a surprise to me. I reined in my curiosity.

"Yeah, man. It's me," he laughed.

"What you want?"

"A favor," he mumbled.

"I'm listening."

"There was a letter of mine. Did you see it?"

"I just came on shift, so I don't know what you're talking about."

"Aight, aight. Look here . . . I lost a letter in the rec."

My eyes were tired from looking into the hole. "If I come across it, I'll get it to you," I hastily replied. I began closing the door.

"Wait!"

I sighed. "What?"

"Come closer, man."

"This better not be some bullshit. I've got lunches to deliver." I leaned in so he could whisper.

"I need another favor. Can you get a message out for me?"

"With all this going down?" I shook my head. "Naw, dude."

"C'mon, bruh."

"Oh. Now it's 'bruh.' "

He cursed to himself. "I just want to get a message out to my woman. Tell her to call me."

I paused, hearing the other inmates on lock complaining about something. "That one on the picture you showed me?"

"Yeah. That's her."

I seriously considered it, pondered for a second. But thought better. He claimed it was an innocent call, but things were hardly like that. "Can't do, man. Catch her next time you get phone privileges. Whenever that will be," I said, taking notice of his current surroundings.

He banged on the door. "How much?" he mumbled, trying to regain his composure.

"I don't do that shit. I keep my nose clean around here."

Even though I couldn't see it, his sneer was visible. "That's probably why you're broke as fuck. Stupid motherfucker."

Broke and stupid. Those words stung unlike anything else he

could've said. I heard Deryn's voice instead of his. "I guess I could be rich like you. Huh, Bodie? You really got it goin' on in this condo of yours. Stupid motherfucker," I shot back with a laugh. I slid the small door shut, diminishing his rants. The screams subsided as I delivered the rest of their lunches. Bodie was just another inmate like the rest, I told myself.

13

BODIE

"**P**unk-ass bitch!" I yelled at the top of my lungs. I'd tired of banging on the cell door and gave it a final, futile kick. I was silly enough to think that maybe Winters was different from the rest of the COs. Shame on me. As I slumped to the tiny cell floor, I swore I'd pay him back. With nothing else to do, I ate my lunch, then fell asleep.

In the blackness that made up the depths of my mind, I heard him coming. I couldn't see anything, but he was there. Closer.

"Why did you do this to me?" he asked again.

"Leave me the fuck alone! I didn't kill you! If I did, you'd stay dead!"

From out of the darkness, a rotted hand grabbed my arm. "How do you know you're not dead too?" Abdel asked, his face equally rotted.

I screamed and yanked my arm free of his hand, only to realize it was a CO's instead.

"Boy, are you crazy?" CO Arnold asked as she squatted beside me. "Don't make me mace you in here." She held some of my personal property in her hand, apparently delivering it to solitary. I was still freaked from the dream, but shook it off and turned my focus to her. As pussy starved as I was, her full lips and bursting titties beneath her uniform were enticing, giving me thoughts—thoughts I didn't want to associate with her. A nigga had his limits and all these years without something to slip my dick into except my hand weren't making it easier.

"Bad dream," I explained, making light of it for her benefit. I jumped to my feet, stretched my arms.

"I can see," she said, nodding with a smile now. "Thinking about that vato you knifed in the rec, Antoine?" She took joy keeping me on edge.

I smiled back, fronting. "I ain't did nothin'. You wouldn't be in here alone with me if you thought that."

I watched her smirk, knowing she wanted to agree with me. "I don't know shit. That's for the disciplinary process to determine," she said.

I laughed at the way she said *disciplinary*. It sounded almost like *dick*liplinary. "I'm the only black man locked down with a shitload of Mexicans. *And I'm alive?* C'mon now. Why don't you go ahead and wrap this up and send me back to my cell? I got shit to do."

"Always the hard-ass."

"Just bein' me." I folded my arms and propped myself beside the cell door, as if expecting her to suddenly walk me out. She rose to her feet again, dropping my belongings on the floor. The letter from my momma wasn't among them. She got in my face, daring me. On the other side of the thick door, I could hear another guard. She wasn't stupid. Wouldn't be in charge if she were.

"Don't get smug with me. I could keep your black ass in here."

"Or?" I asked, picking up on the unspoken.

"Or you could cooperate and make things easy." I watched her grin from ear to ear. She ran her tongue across her lips, moistening them. I smiled for different reasons. Arnold was pathetic in my eyes, but held the power. Upon further thought, I guess that made me the pathetic one.

If I could've willed away the hard dick in my pants, I would have. I tried, but it seemed to grow and swell under her gaze. She gripped my shit and began stroking.

"Nice," she praised all husky like, her breath becoming shallow. "Now that's a good boy." She said it like I was some kind of dog instead of a man. I grunted, torn between wanting to punch her and praise her. Any other bitch, I would've had my pants down and her head bobbing.

I tried to resist even as my blood flowed like a mighty river, its natural course in a situation like this.

"Feels good, huh? You like it when I stroke you, Bodie?"

I didn't answer. She squeezed harder, more pain than pleasure.

"You want to put it in? Want to get this pussy? Don'tcha, boy?"

I mumbled. She slipped into my pants, kneeling before me. The touch of her soft hands sent me into overload as she pulled it out. I cringed as her thumbs played with my head, rotating across it in sensual circles.

"I can't hear you. Maybe you want to be sucked first? That's it?"

I tried to shake my head to the contrary, but couldn't as she prodded me. My hands moved from the wall, where they anchored me. On the back of her head, they rested. A gentle nudge was all it took to send those juicy lips sailing toward my heated dick. Just the graze from them and I wanted to explode. She played with the head, peppering it with smacks. She raised my dick up, taking my balls into the other hand, where she caressed them like fine jewels. *Fuck it,* I thought. Things weren't going to be better for a long time. I closed my eyes, preparing to experience the hollow pleasure.

"Argh!" I screamed as she suddenly scrunched my balls in viselike grip. I almost fainted as white-hot pain embraced me to the core before the numbness kicked in. Arnold let me go. She hollered for the guard to open the cell as I crumbled. The door snapped open on command.

As she stood over me, I could hear her cackle. "Don't think it's that easy, Antoine. I remember you playing all hard to get. Not so high and mighty now, huh? Heard you call me a bitch before too. Well, in here, you're my bitch. Please believe."

Tears rolled down my face as the door slammed shut, sending me into darkness again.

"How do you know you're not dead too?" Abdel had asked.

Because it would feel better than this.

14

AMELIA

I was starving when I got home. Maybe my stubborn ass should've had Tookie's pancakes, but I had to get away. Nobody would understand. I found some leftover pasta from work in the fridge and popped it in the microwave.

While it heated, I checked my messages. The first one was a collect call that had hung up. I knew who it was. I was still concerned about him, but didn't have much to say these days. No point in rehashing the what-ifs. I went back to the microwave to check my food. Still cold in the middle. I stirred it, then added a few more minutes. In as short a time, I'd second-guessed myself.

In my purse was a number I kept for certain situations. I fetched the phone, then made the call. While it rang, the microwave chimed. I was about to hang up when the person picked up.

"Hello?"

"Bodie gave me this number."

"Oh."

"He called for me. He said to call you to reach him."

The guard at his prison shouted something to his kids, then turned his attention back to me.

"He's not going to be able to call you for a while," he uttered.

"Why not?"

"Um . . . he's on lockdown. I can't get through to him now."

"Did something happen? Is Bodie okay?" I asked, prying more than I should. Maybe I was still more than a little *concerned* about Bodie. Like a batch of fire ants, some things are hard to shake off.

He chuckled and wheezed in the same breath. "Yeah. He's okay. Can't say that about the other guy. Some guy was shanked. Bodie's in solitary."

"Shanked?"

"Y'know. Stabbed. This Mexican was killed."

"Bodie did it?"

"Lady, I don't know. I wasn't workin' that shift." His kids screamed again, followed by probably his wife. "Look, I gotta go. Do you want me to get a message to him?"

"No. No message. Just forget I called."

"Suit yourself," he said before ending the call.

Two. Two people killed by a man I didn't think to be a killer. I guess I really was all wrong in the relationship I'd had with Bodie. Maybe the secret I'd kept to myself was for the best.

I went back to my pasta.

The phone rang just as I was taking a bite.

"What!" I hollered, stabbing my fork into the food, which had been warmed just right. I turned the phone on and answered.

"You really need to get a cell phone," my best friend mouthed off.

"Just another bill I can't afford," I said, speaking nothing but the truth.

"I guess I'll have to send you one."

"What did I tell you about gifts?"

"It's just a phone. Sheesh. If I didn't know better, I'd swear you were avoiding me."

"You're still in Miami?" I asked, changing the subject.

Natalia sighed. "Naw. Toronto. I had an appearance at an award show. Schedule's always full."

"Goes with the territory when you're a big star."

"I guess."

"What's wrong?"

"Nothing."

"Come on, Nat. Who do you think you're talking to? Spill it."

"My album dropped to number two on Billboard. Two. Can you believe?"

I fought back an outburst of laughter. A few years ago I would've wished for such a thing. Maybe, deep down, I still did.

"That damn Nelly," she muttered. *"But he's cute though,"* she laughed in the next breath. I let mine go too and joined in.

"I miss you, girl," I added, feeling that connection rekindled as if it were yesterday.

"And I miss you more. But I'll see you soon."

"What?"

She chuckled as if privy to a secret. "I'm performing at the Houston Rodeo!"

"Get the fuck outta here!" I screamed, almost falling out of my chair. When most people think of a rodeo, they just think of cows, horses and shit. The Houston Rodeo is actually a big event with people such as the Isley Brothers, Destiny's Child, Alicia Keys, and Mary J. Blige having performed there before. Natalia was now adding her name to the long list.

"Yep. I'll be down next week to finalize everything."

"You're coming home!"

"Yes indeed," she sighed. "And you know we gotta hang. Do it big, y'know?"

"Just let me know and I'll rearrange my schedule at work."

She got quiet. "You still at that restaurant? Mirage?"

"That's it."

A long pause again. "Why'd you let that triflin' nigga Bodie sidetrack you? You *know* where you should be."

"C'mon, girl. Let's not go there." The new developments with Bodie made this more of a sore subject.

"All right," she said. I imagined her throwing her arms up in frustration. "But you know it's true."

My agreement came wrapped in silence.

"I gotta run, boo. Makeup."

"I saw you on Leno. You've been caking that shit on lately."

"Fuck you," she chuckled.

"Fuck you too, girl. Bye."

I still had a grin as I stirred my cold-again pasta. I twirled my fork around and around, then did the reverse. I repeated this several times, never raising the food to my mouth. I bit my lip, thinking about how I'd handled things with my cousin. The phone was right there, waiting on me to make the right move. To do the right thing.

"Hello?" Me-Me answered, sounding more strained than before.

"It's Amelia." I hesitated. "I'll do it, cuz. When do you need me?"

15

IKE

"**W**hat it do, man?"

"Look what the wind done drug in!" my barber, Dre, shouted over the thumping Mike Jones ghetto chorus of payback for any brother on the come-up "Back then, hoes didn't want me. Now I'm hot, hos all up on me." I hadn't been to his shop on Gears Road in weeks. All the barber chairs were filled. Some of the men were mesmerized by the bootleg tape of a stripper performance on the corner flat screen.

"Man, don't clown me. I been workin'," I shot back at the large man, walking up to give him some dap.

"I can tell," he said, his eyes wide at the bush atop my head. The other barbers and patrons laughed in response. Today, Dre wore a matching burnt orange T-shirt and baseball hat, University of Texas colors, adorned with FREE PIMP C even though my man was free now. While he counted his money, his last customer was checking out his cut in the handheld mirror before getting out of the chair.

"Can you squeeze me in?"

"Tell you what," he said, pausing for dramatic effect. "My appointment's late and I can't let you leave the shop like that. I'll squeeze you in after the next one."

"Aight."

I copped a seat in one of the empty chairs, watching the full-bodied stripper wobble her ass cheeks directly in front of the camera holder.

"Damn, she's got some ass on her," I remarked, louder than intended. Most grunted in agreement.

"You should've seen the white girl that walked in front the shop today," Dre proclaimed. "Ass like a sister."

"Naw."

"I'm tellin' ya."

One of the other barbers joined in. "Something's in the water. That shit unreal. White girls' asses explodin'. Like booty Botox."

"It's all about genetics. Survival of the species." This was one of the customers, getting his goatee edged. His barber stopped so he could speak.

"What you mean by that?" Dre asked.

"It's simple," he said, clearing his throat. "With any species, the females have to attract the males . . . to keep the species going. Look at peacocks. You have to have something to catch the male's eye, make them want to mate with you. No matter what color we are, we're all the same species. So if white girls want to continue to mate, their body has to adapt to match the ass sisters and Latinas are packing. Get with the program or get left out."

The shop pondered what he'd said. Some nodded their heads; others smiled.

"What you is? A scientist or somethin'?" his barber asked.

"No, but I stayed at a Holiday Inn Express once."

We all laughed, one of the barbers hurling a towel at him.

Dre finished his cut, then pointed his comb at me. "Hop yo ass in the chair so we can fix thangs," he said.

Dre seated and draped me before fastening the pin around my neck. As he combed my hair out, he asked, "Your usual, bruh? Line the beard, edge it up and trim it down?"

He swiveled my chair so I could view myself in the mirror. I took a long look at my image before answering. "Take it off, man. Fade it up and make it close," I sighed.

"You sure?"

"Yeah, man. Goin' to a party tomorrow night for my woman.

Wanna look professional for her." In my head, I was calculating how much time it would take me to get to Al's Formalwear after this.

"Must be big for you to do that. Whose party?"

"The mayor's."

Dre quit what he was doing. "Damn. It's like that?"

"Naw. My boo works up in there. Her boss is the top house nigga."

"Oh," he quietly replied while applying his craft with the clippers. "You still at the prison?"

"Yeah," I answered, not sure what else to say.

He didn't say anything right off, just continued cutting. "What she think about that?" he eventually asked, as if no time had elapsed.

"She don't like it. But that's none of her business."

Dre chuckled. "Women. It's *all* their business. Well, going to those kinds of parties, you probably won't be there for long."

"I don't know about that."

"Shit. I do," he smacked emphatically. "Can I give you some of my business cards to pass out? Would you at least do that for a brother?" he joked.

As I held back a laugh for fear of Dre gapping me, I dwelled on what I was doing to reach out to Deryn. *I'm going to have a good time and won't ruin hers,* I silently told myself. It would be my mantra the entire night. And that maybe, just maybe, if some opportunities came my way, that I might be willing to listen. At least.

The freshly cut clumps of hair fell onto my shoulders en route to the shop floor. As Dre whistled a song to himself, I thought about the similar, mandatory cuts inmates received when they first arrived in prison. In a stupid fleeting moment, I wondered if by taking this step that I wasn't sentencing myself to something worse.

16

BODIE

Silence. Dead silence. In solitary, the still between the screams was the worst part. Seeing as I was in unwanted company, I kept my mouth shut and waited for the occasional curse or threat in Spanish that I hoped to overhear. Hearing others or having them respond to you let you know you were still alive and that you mattered in some kind of way. This was slow. Pathetic. Probably just what CO Arnold wanted. She was smart enough not to return. The bitch had it in for me bad. My sore nuts were a testament to that. The sad part was that once I recovered, I still finished off the hard-on she'd left me with. Like I said. Slow. Pathetic.

I didn't have my book, so I used my imagination once again to keep me sane.

I heard the whir of the Ferris wheel, tasted the salty moisture off Galveston Bay, felt the sun radiating on my chains and my cornrows. I was back on the Kemah Boardwalk, twenty miles outside Houston. Amelia was there with me, clutching the stuffed animal I'd won for her. I held her close as she was dizzy from the ride we'd just gotten off. With her bangin' little body so close, I was dizzy too . . . but from being under her spell. We each had that fire, but when we were together and things were going right, it was like napalm. Hot. Sticky. Explosive. Dangerous. None of my "friends" could measure up to Amelia. I wouldn't acknowledge it, but she was the one.

We were sharing a rare weekend alone, none of my business intruding on our flow. I didn't do shit like this for anyone else. The cutesy hand-holding and displays of affection were for weak niggas. Weakness, be it for your own product, pussy or people, could put you six feet under or sixty feet inside.

"This is different," she said, breathing in the sight and sounds of the afternoon crowd.

"But you like it, right?"

"Like it? I love it!" she gushed, before kissing me passionately. Our tongues played with each other, reminding me of what I had to look forward to when we returned to the room. "Thank you," she said as our lips parted.

"Anything for my girl."

I opened my eyes, still in solitary. "Anything for my girl," I mumbled with a smile. To hear her voice right now would do me so much good. I turned over on my side, reaching up to feel my smooth scalp. I still remembered the day they shaved my cornrows off my head, felt them as they fell onto my shoulders in clumps. Looked at them as they lay discarded on the prison floor.

17

AMELIA

"**M**elissa's told me a lot about you, Amelia," Neal, the big man, said, referring to Me-Me by her birth name. Lullaby's was his place. As large as he was, there was a gentle demeanor about him. Like a big cute teddy bear, but one that could snap you like a twig if he wanted.

"She probably told you too much," I replied in a playful jab at my cousin. As she perched atop a nearby barstool wearing a pink top and white cargo crops, I knew she couldn't talk much due to her laryngitis. She smirked at me while playing with the microbraids she loved so much. I stuck my tongue out at her.

"Feisty," he said with a chuckle. "Your cousin said you would be."

"Then she also told you I didn't want to do this. I don't sing anymore."

Neal hesitated, glancing at Me-Me. She cleared her throat.

"And I already thanked you, girl," she said. "You're a natural. Much better singer than me."

"Whatever," I mumbled as the stage caught my eye. My mind wandered. "Um . . . I'm doing this once. I can't promise how I'll sound."

Me-Me's eyebrow raised. She saw what I was looking at, then curled her lips. I hate her.

A beer delivery driver walked in, demanding Neal's attention. "It's late notice and I really appreciate it," he said, touching my hand. "Let me or Melissa know what you need and we'll do it. Rehearsal time with the band, wardrobe, free admission for your friends—just name it." He excused himself from the curved booth where we were seated.

Me-Me hopped down from her barstool to keep me company. I watched her, remembering the two of us growing up side by side in South Park. That was before my family moved to Missouri City and before Me-Me sprouted. We shared the same even caramel complexion, but Melissa Bonds was four years older and at five-eight, an equal number of inches taller than me. The former tomboy had "bad eyes," as our mommas used to say, and wore these dorky glasses on the tip of her nose. Since Neal had brought her to Lullaby's as the featured singer and his right-hand girl, she'd had laser eye surgery and had added an *oomph* to her stride. No longer an awkward giraffe, she was in command of her body. Maybe having her little boy, J. R., helped bring that on. I wouldn't know.

"What do you think?" she whispered, situating herself in the booth.

"This is nice, girl," I said as I surveyed the layout of bars, tables and chairs. Along the walls were framed, autographed photos of jazz greats along with press clippings, presumably about the food. I focused to remember Neal was a cook, first and foremost. My eyes skipped over the stage this time. I knew at night was when it would come alive, but saw the resting potential. The cook had done well. "This used to be an old dry cleaner?"

She nodded.

"Shit." A lot of time and money had been spent to make a building in this part of town look like this.

"Neal lives upstairs," she volunteered, pointing to make up for her lack of volume.

"Uh-huh," I said, cracking a smile. "Spend the night sometimes?"

Me-Me frowned up, folding her arms. I never was too sure about their relationship.

"Never mind then. I have a serious question though."

She signed with her fingers like a gun for "Shoot."

"Can I sing what I want?"

18

IKE

"**What?**" I asked as the Acura zoomed down I-45. I was triple black tonight—black man, black tux, black car. Tight. Deryn, a real mouth dropper in her gown, kept glancing my way, then smiling to herself.

She toyed with her hair, fresh from the beauty shop, in the visor mirror. Either she wasn't satisfied or she was simply nervous. Call me crazy. I would've bet on the former. She finally answered me. "You look . . ."

"Suave?" I offered, feeling pretty good about myself. I'd had reservations about cutting my hair, but with the tux on, it fit. I looked . . .

"Professional," she answered. Her smiles weren't as much for me as they were about me. Professional. As in employable.

I turned up the volume to Ludacris' new joint before commenting. "I always look professional, just not your idea of it."

"Please. You look good tonight, Isaac. Let's not make an argument of it." Her smile was discarded in an instant, flung out the sunroof, where it was caught by the night air. In the rearview mirror, I imagined it hitting the truck behind us, smashing its grille.

"I can do that."

"And would you please switch the station? I'm not in the mood for that mess."

I remembered a time, not long ago. Deryn was chasing Ludacris through the Underground in Atlanta for his autograph. We were taking a break from school. Different people then. "It's your car," I answered as I found something more to her liking on Majic 102.1.

The mayor's party was thrown at the Hilton Americas, next to the convention center. The Toyota Center, where the Rockets played, was within my sight. *What I wouldn't give to see T-Mac and Yao instead*, I thought to myself. From the types of cars that lined the entrance, I expected flashing cameras and reporters everywhere. We valet parked with the rest of them, then followed the parade of guests inside. As I led Deryn by the arm, I paused to admire the lobby.

She laughed.

"C'mon. Act natural," she said, eyes ablaze with a mystical twinkle. "You haven't seen anything yet." She prodded me along to the ballroom.

I entered the room, expecting to see where it ended, but it set in. "Whoa."

The hundreds of people gathered for the black-tie affair would've been enough for a boy from the hood like me, but the room that held us was so damn . . . big.

"Mayor Nelson started to hold it at the Four Seasons, but Marshall convinced him to have it here," Deryn volunteered. "Forty thousand square feet makes a big impression on the donors."

"Yeah," I mumbled as I spied the light show dancing off the walls. "Me too. And I ain't got shit to donate."

The mayor's guests, people with serious stroke in this town, gravitated toward Deryn, flowing around her like planets in orbit. If they came near, they were trapped by the elegance she displayed and confidence she exuded. She laughed their laugh and knew their jokes before they spoke them. I was simply her moon, trying to avoid a collision.

I didn't know this woman. I'd chosen to instead look at her through the lenses of the past. Maybe this was where her disdain for me came from. Bitterness toward a lover comfortable with being left alongside the road, waving like some fool in her rearview mirror as she sped away.

We worked our way to the center of the black-and-white hive, slowing to smile and nod. I saved the extra nod for the blacks and Latinos working the room, letting them know I "got it" even though I wore the tux like a mask tonight. Reserved tables for Mayor Nelson's circle were in the shadow of the stage. The band had begun playing KC and the Sunshine Band. Do a little dance. Make a little love. Donate tonight.

"Maritzah, this is Deryn," I heard as Deryn's boss finally reared his head. I was just beginning to think the night might not be so bad. I turned to see him, his wife in tow, as he gave Deryn a kiss on her cheek. We were content nodding at each other. Marshall Patterson was my size, about a shade lighter, and with NBA teeth—those kinds you know he paid for after he got some money. While most of the men sported black tuxes, the prick rocked a white dinner jacket. It was almost as pale as his wife, a tall redhead *down for the cause.*

"My, such a lovely dress," she said as she studied Deryn from head to toe. I heard a slight accent, like she was from overseas or something. "Marshall always raves about his assistant and how well she dresses."

Deryn played the role, spinning half a turn. I took pride in that I'd bought the shoes. "Thank you. It's Allen Schwartz." *Never heard of him,* I thought. "And yours?" she asked.

"Nicole Miller," she replied. I'd heard of that one. Celebrating my trivia knowledge, I grabbed a flute of champagne off a passing tray. I was taking a sip when Deryn introduced me.

"Maritzah, this is my fiancé, Isaac."

The redness descended from her hair into her cheeks. "Oooooh, he is a cute one!" she gushed. She rubbed her hand up and down the sleeve of my jacket as if I'd like it. People in these settings were different. "So when is the big day? Details, woman," she playfully demanded.

Our eyes met. "Um . . . nothing's in stone yet. We'll see" was Deryn's weak reply. Marshall's forehead crinkled.

"We're just trying to decide on the proper venue," I offered in my best voice. "With Deryn's work schedule, it's so hard to plan anything."

Maritzah beamed to life. "Well, I'll have to get on my husband here about that. Have him give Deryn some time off." She rubbed his arm briskly now. It was my turn to smile.

The silly chitchat came to an end when the band stopped. We watched as the mayor brushed by us to welcome everyone. The band helped him onto the stage.

"Hip replacement," Deryn whispered to me as we clapped.

He wasn't long in addressing the hundreds of people. I only managed one more glass of champagne before the end. He concluded by thanking his generous contributors. They responded by laughing, causing a loud rumble that echoed through the ballroom like we were in a cave. The band kicked it off again as Marshall helped his boss from off the stage.

Deryn and I sat at one of the reserved tables and shared a plate of finger food and more champagne. She quietly filled me in on some of the people, old and young, who made her job so interesting. This was her first time doing this and I was grateful to be included.

"What?" she said, noticing how I was lost in her hazel brown pools. I hadn't said anything for a sec.

"Thank you," I said.

"For what?"

"Dragging me here. For sharing some of your life with me. This ain't bad." I kissed her hand.

She smiled tenderly. "No more champagne for you."

Somebody had to ruin things. "Mind if I borrow your fiancée?" her boss, the secret agent double-oh-dick, asked. He didn't wait for me to answer. He tapped her on the shoulder and spoke to her in hushed tones. She nodded.

"Marshall has some business associates I need to provide figures to. I'll be right back."

"Fuck that shit," I blurted out. "Can't you wait until Monday?" If Marshall heard me over the "Achy Breaky Heart" cover the band was now doing, he didn't show it.

She grasped my arm firmly and leaned over by my ear. "Stop drinking, Isaac. You're getting tipsy. You know I work beside these people."

"Go. Go do your job then," I said, dismissing her. She looked like she wanted to say more, to shoot back like she normally did. Marshall tapped her on the shoulder again. I would get it later.

My bladder called on me before Deryn did. I excused myself from the people nice enough to converse with me, going in search of a bathroom.

The nearest bathroom was just out a side door. I made my way past the conversations, hustling to drain my bladder. One of the hotel staff grabbed me as I entered.

"Sir, you're going to have to use another restroom."

"I just need to piss."

"Somebody just threw up all over the floor in here. There's another one on the left down there," he directed.

I thanked him, then stepped quickly.

The bathroom was empty, making my hard piss even louder. I let out a howl of relief as I hovered over the urinal. While washing my hands, I splashed the cool water on my face, snapping me to attention. I grabbed a gob of paper towels, drying off, while I stared at the man in the mirror. Deryn was probably back at our table by now. I looked at my watch, wondering how much longer she wanted to stay. Then I ran out. In the hall, I decided to take one last look in the mirror. It felt as if some paper from the napkin was on my face. Turning around, I darted back inside the bathroom to check it out.

Where it had just been silent except for my responding to nature's call, that had changed. A bump startled me at first, followed by several banging sounds, then a woman's moan. I fought back an out-

burst, realizing I hadn't been alone. Someone was in the handi-
capped stall on the end. As I suspected, there was a little towel lint
on my eyebrow. I flicked it off and smoothed the brow down, ready
to leave them alone to get their freak on.

The woman moaned again. I could hear the whoosh of air as she
sucked on her lip. I was curious now. That curiosity brought my attention to the pairs of feet visible in the bathroom mirror. I blinked,
trying to focus before saying, "Fuck it," and turning around for a direct look. I knew I had to get back to Deryn, but I stayed locked in on
the shoes—the black sandals the woman wore.

The stall door shuddered from their act. I saw his hand as he
gripped the top of the thin metal partition. "That's it. Tear that shit
up, Daddy," she gasped. I watched the man's shoes as they took one
step forward, their intertwined shadows playing on the stall floor,
unaware they weren't alone. I felt the veins throbbing in my head. It
suddenly became difficult to breathe. My pulse raced in sync with
theirs.

"Fuck me harder, Daddy," my woman chanted to her lover as her
toes curled, feet writhing around in the shoes I'd bought her.

19

BODIE

I did pushups in the dark to pass the time. They couldn't keep me in solitary much longer. Especially since I didn't do shit. But that's how it is. We usually get busted over the things we had nothing to do with to make up for the shit we got away with. Some kind of universal balance. The world's way of saying, "Catch ya later, motherfucker."

"C'mon, man. We gotta go," Aaron said, peering outside at the street through the window blinds. His paranoia was always worse when it came time to take a trip down I-10. My body was doing pushups, but my mind was elsewhere. My mind was back on the outside. Years ago. The last big blowup I'd had with Amelia . . . before everything went wrong.

Ro sat patiently, looking almost asleep, waiting for me to give the order. The rest of our crew had gone out the back door to their cars parked around the block.

"Calm the fuck down," I barked at Aaron. "We're going in a minute."

He shook his head. "Bitch don't need to be here," he mumbled under his breath.

"Who the fuck are you talkin' to?" Amelia shrieked. She'd shown up at my house unexpectedly. I'd given her enough money to go shopping with Natalia, so I didn't plan for this. Not planning for things is when you get shook.

Aaron didn't acknowledge her. Instead he looked at me, apologizing with a facial expression, before pressing on. "I don't like sittin' around like this."

"You ain't sittin'," Ro commented as he decided to take a more active role. He moved around in his chair and glared at his brother. "You standin'. Let's go outside. Give them some time."

The Fontenot brothers hobbled outside, Aaron's mouth still running. The door was barely closed behind them when Amelia lit into me.

"So you just gonna let him disrespect me?"

"He didn't mean anything by it." I waved my hands in front of me, clearing some space.

She pushed my hands aside. "Bitch. He called me a bitch, Bodie. I know what I heard. Where I come from, that's disrespect."

"Aaron's stressin' right now. Y'all Southside women too sensitive. Used to them soft niggas pamperin' ya 'n' shit," I growled. I looked at my watch. "Whatcha' doin' here anyway? You ain't got shoppin' to do?"

"That's not all I do. I ain't one of your little hos."

I laughed. Bad move.

"Think I don't know? Go ahead. Lie to my face."

"I ain't goin' there with ya. We'll talk about this later. What do you want?"

"Did you shop my demo?"

"That's what this is about? Man—"

"This is important to me, Bodie! You said you would make some calls."

"And I did."

"When? Last year? I thought you were my manager."

"Shit. I am, but I got things to take care of."

"Like what? Riding around with those dumb asses out there looking for trouble? Too busy being a dope man? You're going make another of your 'runs'?"

I ran up on her, slammed her against the wall. She was too frightened to speak, but refused to cry. I liked that about her. She was strong. I needed someone like that by my side. I loosened my grip, then spoke forcefully into her ear. "You need to keep my business out your mouth."

"I hate you," she muttered as her heart rate returned to normal. "I hate you, Bodie."

"I'm sorry."

"If you were, you wouldn't have done it," she said, sliding away from me. I tried to kiss her, but she wouldn't have it. My lips touched nothing but weave with a spin of her body.

The horn honked outside. "We'll talk about things later," I offered.

Amelia hurled a scowl in my direction. "Were you ever serious about my singing?"

"Shit yeah. I told you Imma help you. You just gotta let me handle some things. Just be patient. Work with me, boo."

I looked into her eyes as the horn honked again. I couldn't read them. Outside, Aaron's mouth could be heard. Amelia spoke one final time before leaving me to my business. "I came by because I had good news. I wanted to share it with you. Me and Natalia auditioned for *U.S. Icon* and we made the cut. We're going to the next round, Bodie. See. I'm doing it on my own."

I'm doing it on my own.

"Yeah. You are," I answered to someone who wasn't there as I did another pushup in my cell. Universal balance.

20

AMELIA

"**D**oes this look okay?"

Me-Me nodded. We were upstairs, in Neal's crib over Lullaby's. We'd been there all day, just catching up on things. Earlier, she'd prepared me this special tea she used before each performance.

"You don't think it's too much?"

"Not what I would wear," she uttered. She'd been following doctor's orders. Her speaking voice was returning. "But it works for you."

I looked in the mirror at the black halter dress I'd bought at Nordstrom. Don't know how I got it for only fifty dollars without it being clearance, but I'm not complaining. For this onetime event, I wasn't breaking the bank. The top of the dress had the sophistication Me-Me liked, but the shredded hem at the bottom was all me . . . if things were different. "Thanks . . . I guess."

"Cuz, you ready?"

I chuckled, then answered flatly, "No."

"You rocked the rehearsal. It's like you haven't ever stopped."

"It does feel like that. Kinda."

"Amelia?"

"Yeah?"

"What happened to you?"

"What do you mean?"

"Growing up, I liked to sing, but never took it seriously. It took Neal to literally drag me where I'm at now. But you . . . you always had it, girl. Don't let that shit with Bodie handicap you like this. Go down there and tear it up. Even if for just one night."

"Just one night? Somebody singing Luther up in this bitch?" Tookie had decided to join us. After getting off early from Mirage, she'd rushed right over. She'd just come upstairs to check on us. "Damn. Amelia, I'm strictly dickly, but if I weren't, I'd have to jump ya. Me-Me, you did right. Lil bit's h-o-t."

I laughed at the compliment as only Tookie could put it. Me-Me had spent hours on my hair and makeup, teasing as many ringlets and curls as she could from the short patch atop my head. I hadn't felt sexy in a long time.

"Um . . . before I do this, can I ask a favor of y'all?"

"Sure," they answered almost simultaneously.

"Can we say a prayer together? Natalia and me used to do it before we performed. She's not here, but . . ."

"Nothin' but a thang," Tookie said with a smile.

"What she said," Me-Me said, hunching her friend.

We took hands in a circle and bowed our heads.

Neal announced to the crowded club that Melissa, the one they'd come to see, wouldn't be able to sing tonight. I stood silently by the band, listening to the moans of a few. I imagined some would storm out, but it didn't happen. Me-Me stood offside, staying in the shadows so as not to attract attention. Tookie was seated at a table near the front, having endeared herself to the two gentlemen seated there. They both gave me encouragement when our eyes met. I drew a deep breath, then let it out slowly, as if in a Lamaze class. No baby was being born of my body tonight, just one of my voice. Hopefully, it would be a healthy baby.

"But I have some good news for those of you that came out," Neal orated as he brought the patrons back from the edge. He held the mic, pausing to wink at me. "We have another talented member of the Bonds family, Miss Amelia Bonds. She has so graciously decided to perform for you tonight. I don't know. After hearing her at rehearsal, I'm thinking that maybe I should've charged y'all more."

I laughed along with the club at Neal, more from nerves than from amusement. The trumpet player gave me a nod, signaling things were about to jump off. I was fascinated at how different Lullaby's looked at night, the life it took on. My eyes fixed on the neon trails and accents across the ceiling, watched as they fed the energy and emotion of the place from the large picture windows that looked out onto Elgin, across the club and straight into me. The building tension nourished me, left me feeling like a junkie getting his first hit in years. I could have overloaded and cracked, but this was what I was born to do. I smiled.

"So without further ado, I give you Ameeeeeeelia Bonds!"

The horns kicked off as the band went into Keyshia Cole's "I Just Want It to Be Over," something more funky and up tempo than what usually went down here, but Neal already told me I could do what I wanted. I grasped the mic like a bandit and parted my lips to hit the opening verse, "Over and over . . ." *They ain't ready for this shit*, I thought.

Over the next hour, I ripped and roared, taking my captive audience on a journey of reawakening—from Cheryl Lynn's "Got to Be Real" to Mary J. Blige's newest. I pushed and commanded with my voice, pulling emotional responses from the audience they weren't prepared to give. I looked over at Me-Me to see her dancing in place, hands raised and clapping uncontrollably. This I remembered back when we were kids in church.

By the time I took a break, everyone in the place was restless. They clamored for more, clapping and chanting my name. I wiped the sweat from my brow and, after a quick glass of water, took to the stage again. The band wanted to know what number I was going to do. I told them this I had to do alone.

Neal dimmed the lights, encasing me in a soft, intimate glow. The club grew silent. I closed my eyes, taking me back to the day at the Four Seasons I stood before my judges.

"And what do you plan on singing for us, Miss Bonds?" the European judge asked, impatient with my crying and staring at his watch. The former eighties singer looked more medicated in person than she did on TV. Neither one could care less what I was going through.

I opened my eyes to the here and now. No judges. No fear. No disappointment. No failure. "I'd like to sing something personal to me," I whispered to the audience. "I'd like to sing a little number called 'Ain't No Sunshine,' by Bill Withers."

I stared into the darkness surrounding me then began my a cappella rendition.

21

IKE

"Isaac, stop! You're killing him!"

I ignored Deryn's shrieks. I mean . . . *what would you do?* Marshall couldn't answer as I was holding his head down in the toilet. He tried reaching up to grasp my arm, but I just tightened my grip on his neck. I felt his forehead bang into the porcelain again. It was small satisfaction for the blinding white rage consuming me.

Amazing how different Deryn's voice now sounded, like straight jackrabbit fear. The promise of ecstasy it carried vanished as soon as I kicked the bathroom door off its hinges. Her dress was hiked over her waist as she bent over the toilet, lust evident even on her upside-down face. Her thong was slid to the side. The man who was supposed to be simply her boss seemed comfortable, at home deep in the pussy. His pants were dropped to his knees. He stopped his pumping and tried to say something, as if there were a logical explanation that he could come up with. Fuckin' politician.

I punched him in his ribs, felt the familiar cracking sensation. He groaned with the first shot before my next sent him bouncing off the tiled wall. His busted lip sprayed the wall in a fine red mist. Lacking the support from his dick, Deryn fell over the toilet. She was barely to the floor before she began pulling her dress down. Her thong she'd pulled aside was still twisted and out of place.

She sat there, iced with fear, as she came to realize just how serious things were. She could've left me at home and spared me the pain and humiliation. Marshall tried mumbling something. He looked like he wanted to cry. He was still available to transfer some of my feelings to. I jabbed him hard in the nose, never taking my eyes off Deryn.

"This what you wanted?" I asked. "Want me to kill him? You know I can."

"No," she begged. She'd edged herself into the corner of the stall. "Please. Stop." Tears formed, then rolled freely.

"Bruh . . . I'm sorry. Let's . . . let's stop this now." He paused from his stammering to spit. His hand held the side I'd destroyed. The dinner jacket wasn't quite so white anymore. "We can work this out," he uttered from a mouth that didn't sound quite right.

"*Bruh?* Man, you don't know me." I grabbed his throat and yanked him into the air. As I plunged his face into the toilet, I yelled over his garbled, frantic screams. "You wanna work this out?" I laughed sarcastically, knowing his life was in my hands. "Naw. Naw. You wanna work my woman out."

As Marshall gurgled, Deryn rose to her feet. She screamed again for me to stop. When I felt his body going limp, I yanked him back by his collar. As he coughed and floundered on the floor of the stall, I glared at the woman I was supposed to be in love with. The looks between us transmitted wasted history—homework in the dorm, making love in my truck, trips to Galveston, the way she comforted me when my pops died, the celebration we held when she first got her job. All of that drifted up, dispersed like the smoke from a candle after it's been snuffed out.

"I hope your raise was worth it," I said before I stepped over a traumatized Marshall and walked out. Deryn called out once, but I never answered. Most people were still in the party when I came out the men's room. The band was playing "The Macarena." Where else would they be?

I waited impatiently for the valet to bring Deryn's car around, then sped off after tipping him. As I drove, running stop signs and red lights, I weighed my options on where I was going this time of night. I was a hurt little boy at the moment, so it only seemed logical to run to my momma. I'd sleep there for the night and cool off before I did anything rash.

It took minutes to take me from Deryn and Marshall's pretend world to the familiar Third Ward environment in which I'd grown up. Deryn was there too in those times, but she'd made it clear that it was a chapter closed, never to be revisited. Exiting I-45 onto Scott Street, I cursed to the full moon that I was still thinking about her no matter how hard I tried to put her out of my head.

On Elgin, my eyes were drawn to the string of cars parked in front of Lullaby's. It looked like something out of Miami the way its colors radiated. My momma wasn't lying. Like the mayor, our own ghetto celebration was going down, I thought proudly. There was even a stretch limo to spare, its driver having a smoke as I drove by. Catty-corner from the former dry cleaner now turned fancy, glowing night-club, I could spy the edge of the dilapidated apartments where Deryn used to live with her crazy momma and seven brothers and sisters. I took the long route to my momma's, driving down Elgin past them, before looping back around onto Rosalie Street.

When I came to my stop, I had to negotiate past a small group of women to park. They looked inappropriate for the neighborhood, dressed as they were in expensive jeans and designer tops. Beautiful they were, but not from this stretch of Third Ward. I took a deep breath, then exited the Acura.

"Can I help you?" I offered, closing my door while thinking of what I was going to tell my momma.

Two continued walking, but the third stopped. Seeing me in my tux, she got the others to stop.

"Are you looking for something?"

"Nah. We're going to Lullaby's," she answered. My eyes now focused on all the other cars lining the block.

"Damn, she was right," I gasped. I remembered my momma's words.

"Are you comin'?" one of the others asked.

"No," I chuckled, grateful that somebody apparently appreciated me. "I've had enough tonight."

"Suit yourself," she followed up. "They have this girl Me-Me singing that's off the chain. You should check her out sometimes," she offered as her final act. My Deryn stupor was subsiding enough to appreciate how fine she was.

"I'll think about it. Thanks." I dismissed the lovely ladies with a wave, then hopped onto the house porch. Before knocking, I tried to arrive at a story for disturbing her at this time of night. Just as I was about to knock and pray, a couple walked by. I put my hand down, curious now.

I hopped off the porch and decided to follow the crowd around the corner. I had to see what this Lullaby's was about. My life was ruined, but maybe they had good drinks.

I found my tux was a little too much for the place, but no one seemed to mind. If anything, it probably got me a few looks, like I was somebody important. This "Me-Me" the girls were talking about was already performing when I arrived, singing her ass off. I had to snag a spot near the bar in the packed house, but could still take in the show. I ordered a beer, but the bartender took his sweet time, mesmerized like everyone else in the club at the hot number rocking the spot like she was on a mission from God.

"Damn. That's Me-Me?" I asked of him when he finally brought my beer. I'd forgotten about my change. The caramel-colored woman with the wild, sassy hairdo was incredible in her fiery passion. Her banging little body was wrapped in a black dress with these frayed ends that whipped about with every gyration of her hips.

"Naw, dawg. Her throat fucked up. That's her cousin . . . Amelia. Bitch foine." He adjusted the toothpick in his mouth so he could crack a gold-toothed smile.

When the singer took a break, I had a chance to observe the crowd in this place. I had to give it to him. The owner had done a great job turning an eyesore into an attraction. People could complain about the noise and stuff, but I had to hand it to him for doing something positive in the hood. The three lovelies who'd encouraged me to stop by stood near the door, still holding out for seats with a good view. Not too far from where I stood was the probable owner of the limo outside. An older man, almost as overdressed as me, sat in a booth with an entourage of flunkies and boppers. Like a cat stalking its prey, he stroked his salt-and-pepper goatee as he watched the singer's every move. Before long, I was doing the same. Why did she seem familiar? I knew I had never met this woman before.

When she took to the stage again, the lights dimmed. Everyone quit whatever it was they were doing and focused their full attention on the dynamo in their midst. She was going to sing a cappella for her next number . . . "Ain't No Sunshine," a favorite of mine.

As her unaccompanied voice rang out, she unknowingly blew on the dying embers of my soul. Sometimes a spark is all it takes.

22

AMELIA

I finished it. I'd accomplished what I was unable to do during that audition for *U.S. Icon*. My throat felt tight, probably from trying too hard tonight. Lullaby's was enveloped in silence. I didn't know what to make of it. Rather than wiping my eyes, I let the tears stay. Years ago, they were from sadness, failure . . . rejection. Tonight, they were bred of relief. I stared beyond the stage into their eyes, wanting a sign, but not really needing it this time.

The place erupted, shaking the stage. I almost tripped as I took a step back. People stood from their seats, barking, cheering, clapping, whatever worked for them. Whatever I was expecting to come of tonight, this was far from it. One of the men, a stocky fella in a sport coat, began leading the chant for me to do another song. Some of the other people in the club joined in. As Neal had the house lights raised, I scanned their faces, feeling the genuine appreciation for my performance. It filled me, made me want to please them, but I was done. Out of all the clubgoers, my eyes locked on a man by the bar. His tux caught my attention at first, followed by the warm smile that rested on his lips. He held a Budweiser in his hand and raised it in my direction. I reciprocated his warmth with my own before taking a bow.

Beside the stage, Neal had approached. He mouthed to me, asking if I had anything left. I shook my weary head, finally allowing my hands to remove the tear remnants. With more grace than I expected of him, he sprang onstage to rescue me. After a quick hug and an "Atta girl," he took the mic.

"Let's give it up one more time for the lovely fire starter, Amelia Bonds!" he urged the crowd. They enthusiastically complied. I took a final bow before Neal cued the DJ to begin spinning. I thanked the band for backing me, then quickly left the stage.

Me-Me and Tookie ran up, assaulting me with hugs and kisses.

"You did it, girl! You tore this motherfucker up!" Tookie proclaimed.

"I'm speechless," Me-Me joked in her hoarse voice. "You were the shit!"

"Uh-huh. I know that look. Don't even think about stealing my best employee, bitch," Tookie said as she waved a finger at my cousin, her best friend. "Imma have her singing at Mirage when she brings out the dessert trays."

"Whatever, you two," I dismissed with a laugh. "I was just helping out."

"Those tears say something else," Me-Me observed with a smirk. "Welcome back, cuz."

I didn't get a chance to respond as other people in the club were coming up to offer thanks and praise. They were quickly eclipsed by two large, no-neck thugs, who surged forward. I thought they were going to hit me. Instead, they parted to make way for someone, shielding us from everyone else.

"Amelia, long time no see," the older man in the Italian suit proclaimed like we were old friends or something. I remembered him, but never under that description. He smoothly entered the arena created by his monsters, stroking his goatee all the while. He looked to give me a hug. When I didn't respond, he planted a kiss on my cheek.

"Hello, Mr. North," I addressed him with a calm smile. Jason North was the head of On-Phire Records. His was one of the labels Bodie had arranged for me to audition for back in the day. I recalled the rejection from them, same as the rest that Bodie had hooked up for me.

"You were sensational, my dear. Simply sensational." Something about his manner made my skin crawl.

"Thank you. It's been a while."

"Couldn't tell. You mean to say you haven't been practicing regularly?"

"No. Not at all. I haven't been singing at all."

"That makes this showing more impressive. So . . . is Bodie still your manager? That is his name, right? Bodie."

"Yes. He was my manager." I paused. "But I'm no longer pursuing a career."

Jason chuckled. "You should be. You were simply a fill-in tonight and you owned this place," he remarked as he cast a passing gaze on Me-Me. She, along with Tookie, was held at bay by the human walls. "Something to consider, don't you think?"

"Didn't you pass on me?" I snapped, tiring of this game. With him, memory lane was nothing but a street in a bad neighborhood.

He looked at his bodyguards, laughing. They laughed back as part of their job requirement. "Times change. People change. You're a prime example."

"What does that mean?"

"When Bodie brought you to us, you were just a kid in the world. You had the pipes, but no experience behind that stuff you were singing. No pain. No emotion. But now . . ." He paused. "Now you've got something different in your voice. Maturity. Yeah. That's it. You're drawing from a different place. It worked for Mary J. And we can make it work for you, my dear."

"What are you saying?"

"I'm saying I know talent and potential when I see it. You're off the charts. The On-Phire family is interested. Very interested. We can take you places, Amelia."

"Whatever happened to Cracka Jack? Or how about Yrgna? That were your acts, right?" I asked gleefully, referring to the white rapper out of Kentucky and the backward bitter rapper diagnosed with dyslexia. Both of them flopped.

"Just a few unfortunate mistakes. Labels take gambles. Some pan out, some don't. What's before me is a sure thing."

"Well, I'm not sure. Thanks though," I said, blowing him off. I turned away without further comment and motioned for his body-guard to step aside.

"We'll talk later," he assured me. "Oh. By the way, where is your manager these days?"

"I don't know," I lied, frowning at the bodyguard, who stood his ground.

Neal had returned from the stage. Probably summoned by Me-Me, I thought. He placed his hand on the bodyguard in front of me, motioning for him to step aside. They matched each other in size, making for an interesting stare down. Without looking away, he spoke. "Jason, I told you about starting mess up in here. That ain't gonna play out in my house."

"Neal, you know me. I was just talking business with Amelia here. We go back."

"And it looks like she ain't interested, so let it be."

"We'll talk another time, my dear," he said, giving in, but not giving up. He motioned and his monsters relented, dispersing in the crowd. "Neal."

"Jason," Neal replied in kind. His chest was heaving, as if he were ready to come to blows. "You all right?" he asked me.

"Um . . . yeah. How about you? You look more worked up than me."

"I'm straight," he asked, suddenly regaining his calm persona. "I know Jason from my ex-wife. They knew each other back in New Orleans. He comes in here to check out acts. I'm supposed to be a good host, but he gets on my fuckin' nerves," he said. "Oh. Excuse my French."

I laughed. "Thanks for coming to my rescue."

"Shit, Melissa would kick my ass if I didn't. Looked like you were holding your own anyway. I just hope you enjoyed tonight as much as it seemed."

"I did. Really."

"Good." He beamed. " 'Cause we'll have you back anytime you want. And I mean that. I know how it is about dreams."

"Yeah. I think you do," I offered, seeing something genuine in the big teddy bear's eyes. "Thanks," I said as I kissed him on his cheek.

"Go on," he urged. "Mix and mingle with your new fans. Live it up. We'll talk later."

"I think I need a drink first."

Neal winked. "Just tell the bartender what you want. Everything is on the house for the 'fire starter.' "

I chuckled. "Fire starter. I like that."

When I made it to the bar, I asked the bartender for a Long Island iced tea. The man in the tuxedo was still there. I stood right behind him. He didn't notice me, but I wanted him to. He wore a close, crisp haircut and his body appeared to be in shape. It surprised me that none of the single women in the place were on his arm. There was a strong presence about him mixed with a little bit of roughness that reminded me of Bodie.

Bodie had been the last man I'd slept with. Way too long, I thought, feeling that perhaps the night's emotions were getting the best of me. Perhaps sex was on my mind after that wild night with Tookie and Montez. As he sat there drinking another Budweiser, he held the neck of the bottle between two fingers, rotating it. He was lost, deep in thought. His body was all that was here. I decided I wanted to meet all of him.

"Did you like the show?" I asked directly. I came out sounding like some dingy school girl in my delivery.

He almost dropped the bottle when he realized I was talking to him. I watched him come back to the now . . . and me. That pleased me for some reason. "You were off the chain," he blurted out, fumbling for words.

I watched him grimace, probably wishing he'd said something smoother. It made me laugh. "Thanks," I replied. "I'm Amelia."

23

IKE

I took her hand. It was soft, so warm to the touch. I wondered what the rest of her might feel like. As horrible a night as I'd had, this wasn't the place to be thinking like that. Something with her familiarity made me too comfortable.

"Pleased to meet you. I'm Isaac, but everybody calls me Ike."

"Which do you prefer?" She slid the barstool closer, then hopped atop it like she had time on her hands. The gap-toothed bartender handed the "foine bitch" her drink. He cut his eyes at me, egging me on in his stead.

Whatever, I shrugged. She looked even more amazing up close.

"I think I'll call you 'Ike' then."

I drifted back to Deryn, hearing her call me Isaac as she complained about something. "Good. I'd prefer that," I stated.

"Then why didn't you say so?"

I shrugged. "Because I'm a pushover."

"I don't believe that."

I took another drink of my beer. "It's a free world. Believe what you want."

She didn't comment. Rather, she turned around so she could watch everyone. Some smiled. Some tried to discreetly get her attention. A heavyset sister and a taller one, standing by the owner of the place, waved. She grinned and waved back.

Without looking at her, I spoke. "Earlier, I meant to say you were awesome."

"Thank you." She turned to sip her drink on the bar. "So what do you do?"

"I guard folk."

"Security?"

"You might say that," I answered, fudging the truth.

Amelia glanced over at the booth occupied by the big shot. "You're not with Jason and them are you? I mean . . . you're wearing a tux and they're not, but . . ."

"Who?" I asked.

She breathed a sigh of relief. "Forgive me. That guy over there got on my nerves."

"Him?" I asked for clarification. "He's been watching you like a hawk since I got here."

"Oh?"

"Don't worry. I'll protect you," I said smartly.

"Like in *The Bodyguard*? I loved that movie. Would you be mine?"

We shared a laugh.

"Seriously though. It's none of my business, but I get a bad vibe off him. You should steer clear." Even as I spoke, I sensed his eyes on her.

"And you're an expert in these things?"

Another swig of beer. "You might say that."

"I see," she said, now imitating me with a swallow of her own drink. "Is that how you got that blood on your shirt? Being an expert?"

I looked down, noticing the few drops dotting my white shirt. The flesh was scraped from one of my knuckles. I slid my hand off the bar before she noticed that too. "Just a little accident," I offered.

She smiled, choosing to remain in the conversation.

"This ain't a pickup line, so don't take it that way. But do I know you?"

She tilted her head playfully. "I don't think so. Where are you from?"

"Right here. Third Ward, baby," I proclaimed. "My mother lives around the corner. And you?"

"Mo City."

"Uh-huh," I offered as the two of us sized each other up off what we thought we knew.

"I lived in South Park first though," she further volunteered, as if that additional info would alter the equation forming in my head.

"Hmm. I don't know what it is, but it seems like I've seen you before."

"Houston's a big place. Could be from anywhere," she offered. "I'd remember you if I'd seen you though."

Was she feelin' me? Was my game that 'on point'? My throat tightened. I suddenly felt warm. She looked down to play with the shredded ruffles on the end of her dress. As she moved them about, the smooth skin of her thighs played a game of peekaboo.

"Is this the only place where you sing?"

She burst out laughing. A private joke. "Shit. This is the first time I've sang in a very long time." She finished her Long Island. "It's been a long time for quite a few things," she muttered into the glass of ice.

As her cubes settled, I felt something rising in me.

"I've had my one-drink minimum, so I think I better get away from this bar. Thanks for your company, Ike."

I wanted to reach out, grab her. "You can stay. I'm enjoying this," I said, trying to conceal my desperation. She had done a lot of good for me in such a short time.

"I have to. They're waiting on me," she said, referring to the two women from earlier. When I looked at them, they threw on fake smiles. "If I don't go back, they'll think I'm trying to hit on you."

"And you'd never do something like that."

Amelia smirked. "Naw. Never. Maybe we'll talk again."

"I hope so," I conceded.

She hopped off the barstool, sashayed a step or two, then returned. "Question."

"Answer."

"Are you involved? Any baby momma drama? Figured I'd get that out the way."

We laughed those nervous laughs that echo a first kiss. I'd shared a laugh like that with Deryn once.

"No," I said, speaking the truth of something discarded in a bathroom stall. "I don't have anyone."

"Uh," she grunted matter-of-factly before leaving me to view her ass winding through the crowd. Every shoulder or waist it brushed against was anointed by its firmness. I was a sinner in need of a little private redemption right about now.

"Let me have another beer for the road, man."

"Toldja," Goldy snorted. "Bitch foine."

"She fine, but she's no bitch. I've had experience with bitches."

For just being nosy, I was somehow still there when two o'clock rolled around. Closing time—the witching hour when the tricks decided if they would treat. At this time of night, people only had a few options—fuckin' or Frenchy's. The one thing a pair of fine legs and the fried-chicken joint over on Scott Street had in common was that they'd both be open all night.

I milled toward the front door with the rest of the crowd, thinking it was only going to be worse waking up my momma now. I was looking for Amelia when she grabbed my arm.

"Where are you going?"

"Home," I said absently. "Why?"

"Can I cop a ride with you?"

"Sure. You're not limo riding tonight."

She gave a fake laugh. "Don't get it twisted. My cousin is helping clean up. My friend is going to pick up one of her 'toys.' And I am tired. I just want to go home."

"Mo City?"

"Close. I stay in Stafford now," she said, referring to the area just west of Mo City. If I were returning to my home on the north side, I'd be crazy tired.

"I can do that," I said.

"Nice car," Amelia said as she rested during the drive.

"Thanks," I replied, wondering if she could tell it reeked of a woman's touch instead of my own. I halfway expected my cell to be blowing up, but it wasn't. Deryn's attentions were elsewhere, probably as they'd been for quite some time.

"Get off here," she instructed me as I exited US59 onto Kirkwood, where her apartment was. She brought her hand to rest lazily on my own. Her wrist, cooled from the AC, rolled back and forth over mine. I flexed my fingers and grazed my knuckles against hers.

"How'd you know I wasn't some kind of psycho?"

"I didn't," she admitted. "I gambled."

After giving me the access code to the gate, Amelia instructed me to a vacant parking spot near her unit. I turned the car off, then lowered the radio. A ballad from Natalia, one of H-town's hot new singers, was playing. She stared at the radio.

"Want me to turn it back up?"

She giggled before taking a stretch. "No. I'm just thinking about something."

"Guess I should walk you to your door now." I was spent. The night's emotions, both good and bad, had bled me dry. Our hands, which had been in constant contact on the armrest, separated.

"Yeah. That sounds like a plan."

Every step of the way, I imagined how soft her bed might feel, how she might taste. I wanted to know if I could make her sing. I'd already decided against that action, so I kept a safe distance between us.

"Are you still the bodyguard, Ike?" she asked. She'd noticed my actions.

"Nope. Just one tired nigga," I joked.

We arrived at her door. "Sorry I made you drive way out here then. Want to sleep on my couch? The bed pulls out." Her eyes were open wide, everything hidden revealed.

Yes. "No, I'll be all right. I have to go," I abruptly answered. It wouldn't be right for me to do *whatever* while using Deryn's car.

"Think we'll stay in touch?"

"If you'd like."

She reached in her purse. "Give me your hand."

I complied.

She scribbled a number on the back of it.

"This your cell?"

"Nope. Home. Can't afford a cell."

I laughed. "Mine's about to be cut off."

She laughed. "Call me before it does?"

"Definitely."

We kissed. Not one of those wild ones. More tender than tense.

"You're like a dream, Isaac," she said as our lips broke contact.

"Can I tell you something?"

"Uh-huh," she whispered. We were about to move up the scale.

I clenched my fists. "This ain't me," I muttered.

"What are you talking about?"

"This tux, the car. Hell, even the haircut. This ain't me. You've probably got your mind set on a certain type of man. I just want you to know that I might not be that type." The dormant dog, silent guide in times of weakness for all men, was cursing me to high heaven.

She was puzzled by my revelation. The eyes, large with the moment just minutes ago, shrank. "Remember when I said I gambled?"

"Yeah."

"Jackpot."

"Huh?"

"Honesty," she answered. Her smile returned. "Thank you, Ike. Now go get some sleep and call me when you can."

I sped for my momma's, knowing I was broke until payday. I would sleep outside her house until morning came.

24

BODIE

"Wake up, Campbell."

"Shit. Let me sleep."

"Get up," he said, poking me. "Now."

"What time is it?"

The CO laughed. "It's morning."

"Y'all lettin' me out?"

"Get your stuff. You're outta the hole."

"For real?" I strained my eyes to look at him for the first time.

On the labored walk from solitary back to my cell, I felt every sore knot on my body. At my count, it was a week. Or was it two?

"I told y'all I didn't have nothin' to do with that shit in the rec."

He didn't say shit at first. Most were bursting to talk about something. His time came. "They got to the bottom of it quick. Two days," he volunteered, eyes straight ahead as he escorted me along the quad.

"No shit?"

"Aztecas. Retaliation for snitching. Somebody got time tacked on because of him."

"Then why in the fuck did they keep me in there?"

He felt uncomfortable saying any more. "Orders."

"That bitch Arnold," I guessed.

He held back a smile. A lot of people felt that way about her.

"Anything else I missed?"

He passed his hand through his greasy, stringy hair. The Confederate battle flag flashed on his forearm. "Somebody called for you."

"A dude?"

"No."

"What she say?"

"She didn't leave a message. Just said to forget she called. I don't like being called at home. Tell her. My girlfriend thought it was my ex-wife. She flakes out on shit like that."

"As soon as I get to a phone, I'll take care of it." Amelia still cared. She hadn't given up on me. How could she? No matter what we said, we were meant to be together. "Thanks," I offered to the redneck.

"Thanks, my ass. I'm late on a child-support payment. Take care of it." He shoved me along before anyone thought we were too cozy.

Cells were open on my block when I returned. As I carried the few belongings that kept me company, most of the other inmates ignored me. I was alive and stuck here just like them. No better, no worse. Some inmates joked with one another. Some smiled, all the while planning business arrangements back home, revenge or just the next batch of shit coming in through the mail. I ain't gonna lie. I used to take a hit or two out there, but hadn't touched the shit since being inside these walls. Maybe if my head had been clearer at the pawn shop . . .

"Bubba" left me on my own at the base of the stairs. I slowly ascended, looking out toward the rec area, where I last saw my momma's letter. Walking along the railing, I saw my open cell door. Every other cell was open too, but I half expected mine to be shut— something closer to my recent circumstances. Nearing, I heard Rewind's loud voice sprinkled with others. Not knowing what was up, I took the stuff I carried from my stint in solitary and balled it around my hand. I was prepared to defend myself if someone had ideas. I peered cautiously, spying four hardheads talking the usual bullshit. Rewind was there, lying on my bunk like he'd swallowed a stupid pill or something.

"You still alive, celly?" he teased for his friends, dudes he probably knew for some time. Under most circumstances, I would have waited for them to clear out, but I was too tired for games. I entered the cramped space, eyeing them suspiciously. I grazed the shoulder of the one closest to me as he tried to hide a tiny plastic bag in the waistband of his pants. I paid him no mind. Rewind still hadn't moved when I walked up to my bunk.

"Are you gonna move?" I asked. I didn't have to speak the *or* of the conversation.

His boys waited for his response.

"We was tryin' to have a talk, man." Rewind still hadn't budged. The stringy motherfucker instead flashed a smile. He was testing me and trying to man up for his audience. "Can't you take a walk or sumthin'?"

"Naw, man. I'm tired. Now get the fuck up out my bunk."

My celly squinted, his cold eyes suddenly darkening. Everybody knew about his temper, but I could stomp a hole in him if I chose. When he finally moved from his spot, I took a step back. With Rewind, you never knew what he might have in his hands.

"Man, you gonna let dude talk to you like that?" One of them had to instigate. I guess they looked up to him as some kind of leader or something.

Before shit got crucial, I spoke. "Rewind knows me and him cool. So just watch what you say before things get funny up in here." I looked at Rewind, deciding I didn't want to give CO Arnold any excuse to toss me back in the hole. I extended my hand to give him a pound. "We still cool. Right, celly?"

"You been away in solitary. I know what that does." He pounded his fist on mine. "We cool still. Imma go somewhere else so you can get your head back on straight. We'll talk later."

The way he ended it, I knew my dealings with him would be different from this point forward. I heard his boys teasing him before they cleared the cell. Man, in solitary I'd gotten used to sleeping without one eye open.

With no more company, I got comfortable on my bunk once again, propping my feet up. While watching the doorway warily, I glanced at the wall near my head. Amelia's picture, as old and battered as it was, always gave me comfort.

It was gone.

"At least she called," I muttered to myself, too weary to pitch a fit.

25

AMELIA

I put away the photo like I should have long ago. It was of me and Bodie. He didn't want to take the picture with me, but on that day at the Kemah Boardwalk, I had my way. I looked back on the years a final time before stowing it in the nightstand drawer on the side of my bed. With the sun creeping through the bedroom blinds, I digested what had unfolded.

If Ike had spent the night on my couch, he would've found his way to my bed. No doubt. And this morning, he would've seen the picture. Maybe it was a sign that he was a better man than I expected. I wouldn't have wanted to explain my history to him. I was wound up from spreading my vocal wings again, but the note on which last night ended was more intense. I'd fooled myself, thinking it was just about the dick as I flirted effortlessly at Lullaby's. The damn boy had to go and surprise me with some substance. I liked him.

As I pulled the sheets back to finally start my day, the reminder was dried onto my thighs. My nectar had flowed heavily as I'd pleasured myself to sleep. I gave Ike my number because I knew it would be *when*, not *if*, he called. *When* couldn't come too soon.

I set about cleaning up my place. I did the extra touches as if I expected company soon: vacuuming under the coach, wiping atop the refrigerator, scrubbing that lip on the toilet—which I hate doing—

breaking out the good sheets. When I finished, I jumped in the shower before I ate.

As the steamy mist bathed me, I indulged myself. The shower head was my microphone. Where I'd only caught myself humming these past few years, today I broke out in full song. On the other side of the shower curtain was an entire arena I blessed with my best rendition of Alicia Keys. Amid the cheers and chanting of my name, I halted midnote. The phone. I postponed my concert for another day, quickly turning off the water.

A snatch of a towel and I was off, running to where I'd last left the phone. It wasn't there. I'd moved it when I was cleaning. I waited for another tone to guide me. Dripping on the carpet, I grabbed it before my answering machine picked up.

"Hello?" I offered. I knew Ike wouldn't wait too long to reach out. There was a pause. "Hey."

"You're out of solitary." I didn't mean for it to come out so . . . quick.

"Yeah. I'm 'free.' Didn't know you knew about that," Bodie chuckled. His voice was lifeless, drained. "Didn't know you cared."

"I do. Still." I tried to reclaim my distance. Emotions ran deep, hard between us.

"Good. Thangs like that keep me goin', y'know?"

"Bodie . . ."

"Want me to stop?"

"Yes. Please." I felt the spot at the base of my neck, touched the faint lines of the rose and the writing etched below it. I went back to last night, wondering if Ike had seen it as he walked me to my door. I remembered he couldn't have. The strap from my dress had covered it.

"Got somebody? Some nigga hittin' it? Is that why?"

I felt guilty for no reason. "No," I denied flatly. "Things just aren't like that between us anymore. S'all."

"Whose fault is that?"

"Yours."

He laughed. "Ouch. If only you knew."

"I guess I won't. You never tell me anything. Remember?"

He paused. I heard him move the phone from his ear, then put it back.

"What was his name?" I asked.

"Huh? Who?"

"The Mexican. The one you killed. This time."

"Girl, now you trippin'. I'm tired as all hell and managed to get this call through. *And you wanna trip?* You know better than to say shit like that."

I felt his anger rise. We brought that out in each other too often. "Why'd you call? Is there something you want?"

He countered. "You called me back when I was in the hole. You didn't have to."

"I know."

"You still love me, baby."

"Bodie, I'm not going through this with you."

"You don't have to say it. I know." Damn him for being so cocky. Damn me for simply being.

My doorbell rang, startling me. I realized I was still in my towel. No one had called for me to buzz them in through the gate. Like most, they could've piggybacked behind a resident.

"I have to go."

"Me too. Will you come see me again?"

"I don't know. I'll see."

"Bring another picture. I lost your old one."

I grimaced. Just as I'd kept one of mine, so had he. That was such an old picture of me. "I'll see," I repeated.

"I love you. Never will stop."

I closed my eyes. "I know."

As I hung up, the doorbell rang again. Free to speak, I yelled, "Just a minute!"

I hurriedly threw on some underwear, shorts, and a tee. My hair was drooping from the shower, but I tweaked it with my fingers.

Instead of Ike, I opened the door to a large man in black. Equally black sunglasses hid his eyes. Stoic in his demeanor, he filled the entire doorframe, reminding me of Jason North's people from last night.

"Are you Amelia Bonds?"

I hesitated, considering whether I should lie or not. He seemed too cordial to be with On-Phire Records. I moved on. The big man still looked like he could be a bodyguard or something. Ike was in security. Maybe this was one of his employees. "Yes," I chose to answer.

"I have something for you." From behind his back, he produced a small, wrapped object.

"Who is this from?"

"Can't say, ma'am. I have my instructions."

Sounding so official, it has to be Ike, I thought. I took the object from his hand.

"Have a good day, ma'am." Not waiting for me to open it, he walked off to a waiting black Escalade. He got in and it sped away. I looked around to see if anybody was watching, then returned inside.

I carefully peeled back the paper, exposing a tiny cell phone. I finished freeing it, then closed the door behind me. A tiny note attached told me to hit the speed dial on 1. Getting into the game, I eagerly complied.

"Bitch, I toldja you needed a cell."

"Nat!" I shrieked. Natalia loved the dramatic.

"So you like it? I know how you are, so I got *just* a cell. There's a new Sidekick you would've loved, but I behaved."

"I told you I can't afford this."

"There you go again," she yawned. "You'll be able to pay me back soon enough since you're singing again."

"Wait! Wait!" I exclaimed. I was flustered. "Who told you? Were you there?"

"Word travels fast, boo," she said coyly. "Heard you rocked it. You could've told me before you did it. Could've had all kinds of press coverage set up."

"It wasn't like that. I was doing Me-Me a favor."

"Suuuuuuuuuure," she drawled. "How many times did you re-hearse that?"

I laughed. "I can't accept this phone."

"Well, just try to give it back when I see you."

"Where are you?"

"Um . . ." she said, "I think I'm over Ohio right now. But I'll be there in a few days. You better be ready to live it up."

"Whatever."

"Met anyone last night?"

"Damn. You're all up in my business from thirty thousand feet."

"Uh-huh. Must have," she noted.

I didn't know how much her "eyes" at Lullaby's had observed, so I volunteered the minimum. "Spent time talking to a bunch of people."

"Whatever," she offered this time. "So how did it feel? Taking the stage again?"

"Wonderful. Magical."

"Uh-huh." She was listening, but something was distracting her. The schedule of a star. "Look, my publicist says I gotta call in to a sta-tion in L.A. right now. We'll talk some more about thangs."

"Believe me, I know."

"Enjoy your phone. It's got unlimited minutes. Put it on speaker for phone sex, bitch."

Before I could comment, she hung up on me.

26

IKE

"**B**oy, wake up!" she screamed while tapping on the glass with her key chain. I was startled from my bad sleep. It was daylight. The sizzling Texas sun was already beaming down through the windshield. My tux reeked of funk and sweat.

I turned the key in the ignition to lower the window. As it came down, my momma ceased her tapping. "Dang, Momma. You scared me. What you doin' out here?"

She leaned through the window, probably looking for a liquor bottle. I wasn't buzzing anymore, just tired. "I came outside to get the paper, Isaac. I should be the one asking that question. Come inside, boy."

I picked the cold from my eyes and wiped the drool off my cheek. I didn't like my momma seeing me like this. I straightened out my jacket, then reluctantly joined her in the house. It wasn't like I had somewhere else to go.

The TV was tuned to the local news. My momma was having her morning coffee on the couch with her guest, Mr. Vernon. I said nothing, instead stood around, while he pretended he'd just come by for an early-morning visit. He'd been here all night, but wasn't going to admit it. He was a good man, so I didn't stare him down too hard.

"What's up, youngster?" he asked, offering a kind word.

"Nothing," I answered. I could've sat down, but my leg was still asleep.

"Doesn't seem like nothing." My momma was ready to put me on blast. "Boy, what's going on with you?"

"Can we talk about it later?"

"Suit yourself. You're the one sleeping outside in your girlfriend's car. You want something to eat?"

"No. But something to drink would be good." I had a bad case of cotton mouth.

She took a sip of her coffee, now turning the pages of her morning *Chronicle.* "You know where the kitchen is. Help yourself."

I found a warm can of 7-Up in the cabinet. Filling a glass with ice, I poured the fizzing soda. I returned just as Mr. Vernon was leaving. He nervously gave my momma a kiss on her cheek, then departed.

"Where's he going?"

"Something came up," she answered. "Come. Sit."

I joined her, taking my tuxedo jacket off. I was going to owe some money when I brought it back. "I didn't mean to run him off."

"He'll be back," she assured me. "Now . . . about you. When did my boy start sleeping in cars?"

I took a long drink from my glass. "It was too late when I came by. I didn't want to wake you up." I didn't tread on the Mr. Vernon issue.

"Uh-huh." She continued flipping the pages of her paper. "Didn't you go to that party last night with Deryn?"

I sighed. "Yes."

"What in the hell happened?"

"Things got out of hand."

She flipped the paper to the front page, then threw it down in front of me. "Marshall Patterson. That's Deryn's boss, right?"

I glanced at the story. Some bullshit about him being "mugged" at the mayor's party by an *unknown assailant.* I looked away. "Yeah. That's him."

"Do you know anything about this?"

"Shit happens?" I offered.

"What did I tell you about that mouth?"

"Sorry. I'm still trippin' over sh-stuff."

She put her arm around me. "It's on the news too. Blood of Jesus, that man looked awful. They say there are no witnesses."

I didn't comment—simply picked at the skin on my knuckle. She knew. When I realized she was now looking at Amelia's phone number, I turned my hand away.

"Baby, where's Deryn?" she asked.

I leaned back, resting my head on her shoulder. As much as Amelia had helped, I hadn't fully defused from the Deryn situation. I answered, "Home, I guess."

"Is that why you're here?"

"Yes."

"Do you need a place to stay?"

"Probably. I need to bring back Deryn's car first. Get my truck."

She found some old clothes of mine and allowed me to get cleaned. She didn't push for answers about Deryn, sensing how uncomfortable it made me. She just knew her son was hurting. How do you tell your mother that you caught the love of your life getting hit from the back by her boss?

I didn't want Deryn to be home when I returned her car. She was there though. I knew it as soon as I tried to open the front door. The key went in, but stuck. I tried taking it out and reinserting it. It didn't work. She was quick. Like an old friend, my rage returned to comfort me. I banged on the door.

It didn't take her long to answer it. It would have done my ego good if she looked as wrecked as me. Instead, she was beautiful. She looked subdued in her camisole and cropped pants, but nowhere near the humbled, remorseful person she should've been. I came closer.

She raised her hands defensively. "Don't even think about touching me. I'll call the cops."

"Please. I think you've been touched enough," I answered. I went around her, pushing the door open. I dropped the Acura keys on the floor at her feet. I looked around, surveying for any sign of Marshall. All her late nights at work ran through my mind. "Why'd you change the locks?"

"Because I don't want you here," she snapped.

"It's my house too."

"No, it's not," she asserted. "The house is in my name. I pay the mortgage."

"It's like that, huh?" I smiled to spare her the satisfaction.

"Yes, it sure is. You embarrassed me last night. That was despicable, what you did."

"What I did?" I yelled. "Did Marshall's banging your head on the toilet give you fuckin' amnesia?"

"Isaac, you broke the man's ribs. You tried drowning him in the toilet. He could've pressed charges. I'm not going to discuss this with you."

"Were you ever? Or were you going to keep playing me for the fool? You're fucking him behind my back and have the nerve to talk down to me. You fuckin' ho. I loved you." Loved. Past tense. I used the word as a weapon instead of my fists.

"And I'd love for you to leave. I want you out. Get your things and go." My weapon was dull, inflicting no damage at all.

She picked her car keys off the floor. Leaving me to pack, she strolled to the back patio with the cordless phone in hand. "And get that piece-of-shit truck out of my driveway. It leaks oil," she muttered as an afterthought.

Deryn stayed away as I hauled my belongings through the house. Throughout our time here, she'd made it apparent which things she claimed as hers. Those items I was uncertain about, I simply left. I should've seen it coming, but I'd been blind. Blinded by the past and by my own stubbornness.

Carrying out my last box, I foolishly walked onto the patio. Deryn was sitting in one of the lawn chairs. She carried on a conversation with someone like it was just another day. I tried biting my tongue and walking away. "You really don't have anything to say? Not even some bullshit excuse? You are a piece of shit." *Tried.*

She paused from her conversation and covered the mouthpiece. "I'm trying to enjoy my day. Just go, Isaac." She went back to her call.

As I turned to leave with box in hand, I hooked my foot around one of the lawn chair's legs. With a harsh, sudden whip, Deryn tumbled onto the deck. My momma raised me to never hit a woman. Since my arms were full, I didn't offer to help her up.

Against the backdrop of Deryn's curses, I dropped my stuff in the bed of my truck and left. As I backed up, I looked at the oil stain in the driveway she complained about. It would be clean soon, no doubt. Scoured away like every other thing in her new life she couldn't stomach or that didn't fit.

In my rearview mirror, I saw the black Acura, just where I'd parked it. I had room to maneuver around it in the driveway, but imagined ramming it instead. After backing into the street, I shifted my old truck in drive, taking one last look before rolling down North Bambridge in a cloud of smoke.

27

BODIE

"Your lawyer wants to see you," the CO said as he led me to visitation.

Until he'd opened his big dumb mouth, I just knew it was Amelia instead. When she got off the phone, somebody was there. I knew it. And it was fuckin' with my head.

I entered the room, checking the different tables for my attorney. It wasn't until the CO gestured that I saw him. The man casually smiled, then motioned for me to come over. I eyed the guard suspiciously. He played dumb, so I walked over to see what was up.

The weasel in the sport coat started to get up. I motioned for him to stay seated, knowing this wouldn't take long.

"You ain't my lawyer."

"True. But I am *a* lawyer," the man I'd recognized as Jason North admitted. "Please. Have a seat, dear boy."

I pulled my chair back and copped a seat. "Make it quick. I have a busy schedule."

He laughed. "What? Basket weaving?"

"What do you want, Jason?"

"I see you remember me." Jason North, the face of On-Phire Records, had this air about him. Like he tried to play he was down when what he was really doing was looking down. Can't hate though. He knew music. On-Phire had struck gold with AK, whose shit I jammed back in the cell. Nigga was dead and still going triple platinum two albums later.

"Yep. But you're wasting my time and I still don't know what you want."

"Can't I just be concerned about you?"

I grinned. This nigga wanted to play games. "What's up with Melvin? Does he know you're here?" I questioned. Melvin was the real motherfucker in charge at On-Phire. I had a prior "business" relationship with him, my New Orleans connection in the pipeline back in the day, which is how I got Amelia an audition with them years ago. Unfortunately, they'd slept on my boo just like the rest. This clown before me was the one to break the news. And he did it with a smile. Amelia cried the whole ride home. *I should break his face for old time's sake. They can't tack much more time on,* I thought.

"Melvin had an unfortunate accident last year. Before the hurricane forced my label to relocate. I'm who you need to be talking to."

"Accident?" I was listening now.

"Yes. It's a dangerous world we live in. I'll miss him."

"I'll bet." He'd killed Melvin. Damn. Never thought he had the balls. Something else to stow away in my head. I continued. "Now . . . what do you want? I ain't no singer and I ain't no rapper."

Jason's eyes narrowed. "But your girlfriend, Amelia, is, my dear boy."

"Watch that *boy* shit."

"Understood. You're still her manager these days?"

"You could say that." I had Amelia sign some paperwork back in the day, a formality to get me in the door with some of the labels. "What about her? She don't sing no more."

His eyes narrowed again. "But she does, my dear boy. Either that or it was the best lip-synch I've ever seen."

"You must be talking about one of her tapes."

"Nope. No tape. Live. Saw her out here matter of fact. Just the other night. She sounded sensational. Looked sensational too," he said, licking his lips. He brought his attention back to me as if re-hearsed. "You are a very lucky man."

My brain hurt. I wanted to beat him, wanted to ask him a million questions about Amelia, wanted to be free. Free. I couldn't speak. Nothing to shut him up. I was reeling that she hadn't shared some-thing as special as that with me. Maybe she was sharing with some-one else. I clenched my jaw.

He sensed my confusion and jumped on it like the vulture he was. "She didn't tell you," he uttered, a fact not a question. "Oh well. I guess your current situation has you out of the loop."

"Why are you here, man?"

"Maybe you should talk to her about opportunities."

"With you?"

"Of course." He stroked his goatee, proud in how he'd spun his tale to get to this point.

"Why now? I still remember that shit your punk ass said."

"Antoine, this is a business. Houston is fertile ground these days for fine, sexy singing sensations. Beyoncé, Brooke Valentine, LaToya Luck-ett. That girl from *U.S. Icon* that's blowing everyone out the water."

"Natalia," I muttered, hurting at what I'd cost myself and my baby that day by going to the pawn shop with them.

"Exactly. Natalia is queen over everything right now. But they're positioning her for the pop world. Even from your prior experience, you know it's all about the *product.* I figure a rival from the same town, but with greater range and a harder street vibe, could take the crown. Know anyone like that?"

"You realize they're best friends?"

"Of course. I do my homework. All the better." He smirked.

I shifted in my chair. I picked one of the millions of questions floating around in my head. "What made you change your mind? You coulda' signed her back in the day. Easy."

"Something's different about her now. She's ready. I could tell with just the little bit I heard. Do I have *you* to thank for that?"

I ignored his smart aleck question. "If I talk to her . . . what's in it for me?"

"Now we have a dialogue, dear boy. It certainly took you long enough. I thought you were more direct. You know I'm a lawyer, right? Well, I had the chance to review some of your case."

I went to say something. He raised two fingers off the table to pause me.

"I have ways. In my humble legal opinion, I saw a lot of circumstantial evidence. You didn't help either by playing the mute in court. They were probably just dying to give you lethal injection."

"Fuck you."

He continued. "Nevertheless, I might be able to assist you. Get things looked at again by a—no pun intended—*crack* legal team. Maybe something was missed by your awful lawyers. Maybe you remember something more about that day . . . or someone."

"Time's up."

"If you say so. I have appointments and a celebrity pool party to attend to anyway. But just think how good things could be with the right management team behind Amelia. Of course, you would be on that team."

"You should be in here more than me," I realized aloud. "I'm done with this."

Jason stood up, adjusting his sport coat. The yellow diamonds in his On-Phire medallion glistened as it swung from side to side, blinding me. "If you decide to get in touch with me after you talk with your client, just let him know," he said, referring to the CO who had delivered me here. "He's one of my many talent scouts on the inside."

I watched the dangerous man leave, refusing to get up from my seat until he was gone. North was heading back to the world beyond these walls. Free.

Nothing was ever free.

28

AMELIA

He called, I reaffirmed, smiling to myself like a silly fool. As much as my mind should've been on seeing my best friend today, it was stuck on my new friend. He called.

It was a typical sweltering day when I drove my Hyundai to Hotel Derek, located just across the interstate from the Galleria. I parked, then hastily entered the swanky, sophisticated world it offered in its bosom. Picking my mouth up off the floor, I gave the false name provided to me at the front desk. The concierge eyed me up and down, determining if I belonged in the boutique hotel. Satisfied, he gave me a room number for the imaginary person, but told me I'd find her at poolside.

Modern crimson lounge chairs lined the crystal blue waters of the pool outside. I took in the decor that reeked of "Miami-ness" as I walked toward the canopy housing Natalia. A white linen curtain was pulled down for privacy.

When I walked up, I spotted her. Natalia was in the middle of a Pilates class, so she didn't see me. I silently stood by while she finished on the mat with her instructor. From the thinly built woman's voice and tone, she obviously wasn't from Texas. I didn't know accents, but guessed Australia as she kept repeating something about strengthening Natalia's "power plant."

Sitting in one of the nearby chairs, a brawny, bald brother in a wife beater, baggy jeans and Timbs chatted constantly on his cell phone. It wasn't until Natalia barked at him to keep it down that I ceased being invisible. He stopped midsentence, checking over the top of his sunglasses to see if I posed a threat, then went back to whatever had him so excited. Some bodyguard he turned out to be.

When Natalia was finished, she rose and attempted to shake the wrinkles out of her linen outfit. Not an ounce of the chubbiness I remembered in her waist and hips was there. Even though she'd just been flailing about on the mat, the extensions in her ebony hair looked as if she'd walked off a magazine cover. I applauded to get her attention.

"Girl, how long you been there?" she shouted as she ran over for her hug. Her tiny bare feet bounded lightly, caressed by the ground's noontime heat. She'd had a dancer's training.

"A little while," I answered, squeezing her tightly. "Your bodyguard saw me."

Natalia tsked. "Girl, Owen ain't my bodyguard. He's my personal assistant."

Owen snapped his cell phone shut. "Ahem. That's your personal assistant that just got Special K on line to do your next video," he tooted triumphantly in a high-pitched voice that didn't quite sync with his appearance.

"Owen's on his shit," she admitted. "Owen, this is my girl Amelia."

He'd already jumped back on his phone. He waved with the tips of his fingers. I imitated his gesture. Nat laughed and nudged me along to one of the tables, where we took a seat. Her Pilates instructor had packed up and was jetting off to her next appointment. Posted on opposite ends of the pool like two centurions were two real bodyguards I hadn't seen.

"You ever stay here before?" Natalia asked, seeing I was still in a daze.

"No . . ."

"They have great mojitos." The poolside waiter was upon us, at the ready. "You want one?"

"Uh . . ."

"I know it's kinda early, but what the hell? Two mojitos please," she rattled off without hesitation. "Oh. Wait. Owen, you want a mojito?" she yelled. He nodded, phone still at his ear. "Make that *three* mojitos, sir." As fast-paced as her life had obviously become, she still had some of her Southern manners.

"Nat, do you ever slow down?"

"Girl, please. These babies they keep turning out with a pacifier in one hand and a recording contract in the other won't let me. Now if you'd get off your ass and have my back—"

"Here we go again," I laughed.

"So," she said, finally catching her breath. "You tore it up at Lullaby's?"

"I dunno."

"C'mon, girl. This is me you're talkin' to."

I grinned, finally looking her in the eye. "Yeah. Maybe just a little."

"See! That's my girl. I knew it!" She high-fived me as we cackled.

Our mojitos were delivered in a gust of wind—service like I'd never seen or delivered for that matter. The cool, minty mixture was strong yet soothing as it went down.

"You're looking good, Amelia. Refreshed."

"About damn time, huh?"

"I didn't say all that."

"But you wanted to."

"So true," she admitted. "We gotta get you back in the studio. My treat."

"Slow your roll. I want to take my time. Get my feet wet."

Natalia snickered at a thought. "Got anything else wet lately?"

"Nat!"

"Hey. Just askin'. Need me to hook you up with one of my associates, pretty lady?"

"Nope. That won't be necessary."

"Hmm. You got me curious. I know Bodie's ass ain't goin' anywhere. You got off your *thoinga thoing* and found somebody worthy of you?"

He called. "Too early to tell and way too early to talk about," I answered.

Nat knew not to push as she pinched me on the wrist. "Keep your damn secrets."

Owen came over, his mojito long gone and cell phone temporarily shut. He reminded Natalia of her commitments for the rest of the day—she was in town to promote her appearance at the Rodeo, but she blew it all off for me.

"Feel like shopping? I know I do," she remarked, cutting off Owen with a wave of her hand. "Let's go to the Galleria," she said over his strenuous objections.

"Natalia! Can I have your autograph?"

"Take a picture with me," the other young girl demanded as she forced her way past the first one. Nat told her bodyguards to go easy on them and politely honored both their requests. The three men were so professional in the way they'd handled the mob forming outside the MAC cosmetics store. Watching them in action, I thought about Ike and the way he'd carried himself when we'd met.

Natalia dressed down in sweats, sunglasses and a ball cap, but that just seemed to make her stand out. We'd made it through several stores on the first level as the bags on my arms showed, but a teenage boy ruined it when he yelled across the mall at her. People of all ages, sexes and races loved my girl. Her bodyguards had kept their distance, but now had to step up.

"I knew this shit would happen," Owen muttered. While he watched the spectacle, he had put up his phone. Of course, Nat had also shoved her bags into his arms so she could greet her fans. He wasn't too thrilled. "Be prepared for things like this if you get serious," he offered.

"Uh-huh," I said, unsure how to react to his remark. Camera

phones began clicking as people, needing to convince friends and family, found the means of more proof.

"Can I have everybody's attention?" Natalia announced. When the buzzing died down, she continued. "I hope y'all come to see me at the Houston Rodeo. It would mean a lot to me because I wouldn't be here if not for all of y'all. I want to represent for Houston."

People in the crowd cheered. One person let out an on-cue "We love you, Natalia!"

"Not bad," Owen admitted. "When we started with her, she used to stutter and break out in a sweat."

Her security was preparing to shuttle us to another store when Nat raised her hand for one more announcement. "One more thing. I can't forget to introduce y'all to my best friend and Houston's next big hit . . ."

No.

". . . my girl Amelia! Amelia, say hi."

I looked like the dorky new kid, put on the spot on the first day of class. With my arms full of bags, I shut my hanging mouth and smiled awkwardly into the blank stares. In their eyes, I was a weak Gayle to her Oprah. I hadn't been force-fed to them by MTV or BET, so I had no importance in their world. I'd be lying if I said it didn't sting just a little. My pride said to show them, *make* them mine like I'd done the crowd at Lullaby's. This wasn't the place and I was that person for only one night. The clock had struck twelve and my carriage was a pumpkin again. I just kept smiling instead and moved through the crowd onto the shopping experience.

I left Hotel Derek after transferring the bags of stuff that Nat had bought for me over my objections from the limo to my trunk. The Galleria shopping spree was unexpected, but I was so happy to be spending time with her that I was a pushover. Lord knows I couldn't afford a quarter of the items I'd picked up.

Owen had twisted Nat's arm, getting her to agree to fulfill the evening's commitments. I could've tagged along, but told her we'd catch up tomorrow after I got off work. She had plans for us to grace

Scott Gertner's SkyBar over on Montrose for a big party. *Scott*, as she'd referred to him, was going to let her drop a few of her new songs on the crowd.

As I moved up the freeway onramp, I used the first gift Nat had provided. I nervously dialed the number Ike had left me during our earlier conversation. It rang.

"Hey, it's Amelia. Um . . . *are you busy right now?*"

He'd called.

Now I'd called.

29

IKE

Mr. Vernon handed over the key to the place once we unloaded my stuff. I could've done it on my own, but my momma had insisted.

"I did the roof last month," he boasted to make small talk. Right now, I was appreciating the faint traces of cold air sputtering from the vents.

"Thanks, Mr. Vernon. I owe you. And my momma."

The tan two-story brick double on Truxillo Street was one of her lease properties in between tenants. Partially furnished, the bottom unit was right on time for her pitiful son. My temporary home was in a better part of Third Ward, no ditches lining the streets and remnants of the rich history from its heyday still obvious to the trained eye.

"That's what we're here for, boy. Both of us," he offered. "Your father was a good man. Helped out a lot of people around here. I don't want you to think I'm disrespecting his memory."

"You mean about the other morning?"

He nodded, embarrassed to admit he'd spent the night at my momma's. I had the feeling he'd wanted to clear things when he volunteered to help me move in.

"I'm okay. Really. If I wasn't I'd tell you."

"Good. 'Cause I love your mother. I hope you're all right with that."

What was I supposed to say? I didn't respond. Simply put a stack of my clothes down and wiped the sweat off my brow. I looked at the temperature on the thermostat. It hadn't moved much since we turned it on. "This thing ain't coolin' much," I reflected.

"Imma send somebody to check on that air, youngster. The last tenants complained about it, but your mother thought they just wanted to get out of paying the rent." He chuckled. "It probably just needs some freon."

"All right then," I said as I shook his hand and sent him back to report to my momma. I still had to at least unpack the basics. Arnold wasn't too happy when I called in, so I was sure to catch hell when I went back to work.

In what was going to be my bedroom for the near future, I picked up a scrap of paper where several numbers were scrawled. Most had been scratched out, products of failed guesswork. With Mr. Vernon professing his love in the middle of my hurt, perhaps I needed a distraction. The number that beckoned seemed to be more of a craving.

"This better be the right one," I cursed as I sat on the bare mattress and took another shot at dialing. All the rest had been on the fly and met with no success.

"Hello?" I recognized the voice, full of bass and brashness that I'd wanted to raise several octaves like my own personal instrument.

"Hey. It's Ike."

"You finally decided to call. I was beginning to wonder if you'd forgotten about me," she teased. She knew better, but wanted to hear me say it.

"It ain't like that. I smeared the ink before I had a chance to put it down. I've been guessing. The numbers have been all wrong until now."

"Persistent. I like that. Whatcha' doin?"

"Unpacking. Moving." I heard Deryn coolly telling me to leave.

"Hmm. Let me guess. Your condo?"

"Hardly," I said as my face contorted. "Something temporary."

"I'm glad you called."

"Really?"

"Yes." Her voice warmed. "I was thinking that maybe we could see each other again."

"I'd like that."

"You sure you don't have a girlfriend?"

"No," I blurted. "And you? Anyone you're connected to?"

She paused. "No. No connections. I've been disconnected for a long time."

"Good."

"Ike?"

"Yeah."

"I would love nothing better than to talk some more, but I'm literally running out the door. My best friend's in town and I have to go meet her."

"I understand."

"Do you really?"

"Huh?"

"Most people say that, but don't really mean it. Do you mean what you say, Ike?"

Women. "Yes. I do, Amelia," I answered formally.

"Good. Good," she purred. "Can I call you back later?"

I quickly gave her my cell number.

My cell phone rang in my ear only minutes later. I was still on the bed, but was lying down. The place was still warm. I brought my watch to my weary eyes, realizing it was, in fact, several hours later. I'd fallen asleep. I'd succumbed to the heat and exhaustion and not known it.

"Hello?" I said before my voice mail picked up.

"Hey, it's Amelia." I sat up at attention. "Um . . . *are you busy right now?*"

"No. I'm not doing anything." That was the truth. Boxes were still strewn about from earlier. My reflection in the dresser mirror reminded me of a haggard old man. Had Deryn sapped that much out of me?

"I'm over by the Galleria. Anyway, I was wondering if . . . maybe you needed some help with your stuff."

"I didn't have much to move, but thanks anyway."

"Boy," she huffed.

"What?"

"Can I come by? I want to see you. Is that blunt enough?"

"Oh," I gushed, feeling like a dumb ass. "I'm sorry."

"Don't apologize. Say it's okay to come by," she laughed. "Somebody's a little slow today."

"Sure, Amelia. I'd love the company."

"One more thing."

"What's that?"

"Directions."

"Oh. Yeah."

After coming off like I was on some shit, I figured out where Amelia was and gave her directions. It wouldn't take long for her to arrive. I bounded off the unmade bed and scrambled to make my new surroundings look semipresentable.

I'd just showered and doused my shirt with some cologne when a Hyundai slowed in the street out front. Unless they were checking out the FOR LEASE sign on the front lawn, it was Amelia.

I spied through the window blinds, watching her park, then walk up the driveway. She hurriedly worked her sandals, causing the white cropped pants she wore to swish back and forth. From my hidden vantage point, they appeared sheer. A revealing distraction. I separated myself from the window before my thoughts headed south too.

When she knocked, I took a second to compose myself. I'd been in my relationship with Deryn so long that I couldn't remember the last time I'd had a female guest. I'd already seen how she looked, but was taken aback when I swung open the door. Amelia wore a rose-colored tunic whose mesh revealed hints of her caramel skin underneath. Hints can be frustrating when only the answer will satisfy.

She looked up into my eyes, all smiles. She appreciated being in my presence. It was definitely mutual. "Hey, you," she said.

"Hey, yourself," I answered. As we hugged, I inhaled the fresh, fragrant scent from her hair. It made me comfortable and aroused, if such a thing makes sense.

"Not bad with the directions."

"You probably found your way in spite of me. Want to come inside?"

"Thought you'd never ask. It's hot out here." She brushed against me and came inside.

"It's hot inside too," I remarked, commenting on the AC problems.

She looked at me, grinning. "We'll see about that, Ike."

I granted her a VIP pass into my war-torn world.

30

BODIE

"C'mon, you got it, baby."

I grunted, pushing harder as he urged me to dig deep. He smiled, satisfied at my effort.

"Another one. You got another one in ya," he encouraged as I lowered the weighted bar down to my chest. My muscles burned. Hitting the weights was my only alternative to deal with the frustration I felt. That or kill a motherfucker. My girl was singing again. My girl was getting on with her life. My girl had shut me out and I had to hear it from somebody like North.

"Another set, man," I barked when I was finished.

"You sure, young buck?" the old-timer asked. He was a lifer for shit done before most of us were fishies in our daddies' sacks. This ten-by-ten area—this was his church. As big and swole as he was, we were just passing through, allowed to play with the dumbbells and weights at his discretion. Me? I'd come for a sermon.

"Put on some more weight."

He looked at me as if I were crazy. When he saw in my eyes that I was, he added plates to the bar. "Suit yourself," he sighed as I took the bar in my hands and picked it up.

I managed through two reps before straining on the third. By the fourth, he pulled the bar away from me and placed it on the weight-bench stand.

"You tryin' to kill yourself?"

"Might be," I said, looking up at him, the vessels in my forehead throbbing. "If this place don't get me first."

"That ain't no way to talk, young buck."

"Shit's fucked-up, man."

"Then why don't you do something about it?"

"Too many choices and none of them good. Kinda like what got me in here."

He laughed. "We all can say that."

I sat up on the weight bench and looked at him for a second. I was for keeping my business to myself, but just let it go. "I'm losing the only thing that fuckin' matters to me. And I can't do a thing about it."

"Then fight for your shit, young buck. Whatever it takes. Don't go out like no punk."

As I showered, letting my aching, overworked muscles relax, I ran over all the options available to me. I had to be out there with Amelia to make sure nothing went wrong. She needed me even if she wouldn't admit it. She'd always need me.

Twelve years is a long time. I thought about how much money I had stashed and how much longer it would last. I was out the game, so no new income was flowing on the inside. When it was gone, so was whatever clout I had with the guards. Back in my cell, I made one of my many moves.

I made a signal to the CO pointed out by Jason North. He walked over and pretended to tie his shoe when he got close. Without looking at him, I spoke.

"Tell North I'll help him, but he's gotta help me with my situation."

He didn't speak. Simply stood up again, continuing on his rounds.

Next, I found a way to get to a phone. Some more paid dental work for someone's kid courtesy of me. These calls had to be quick, so I didn't waste time.

"What it do?"

"Nigga, it's me."

"Can you talk?" Aaron grunted.

"Quick."

"Shoot."

"Somebody's messin' with my slab."

"Nah, man. Ain't nobody touched that car," he said, referring to Amelia. "I done told you that already. We took care o' that."

"Then maybe you been slippin'. Something ain't right with it. I can tell."

"Naw, man. I—"

I cut him off. Sometimes he just didn't get it. "Watch my slab, bruh. You know what my Lac means to me."

"Aight. Aight. Imma check out things again. Make sho nobody been under that hood."

I saw Jason North's smile in my mind. "Just make sure it's on the low."

"That's me. Always discreet 'n' shit. I'll roll by the garage. Make sure it's waiting on you with no fingerprints in that candy paint."

"Good. Do that."

I hung up, then had the CO dial one more number, trying even his bought-and-paid-for patience. CO Arnold was roaming around here today and had them all on edge. My nuts still throbbed, in a bad way, at the mention of her name.

That damn answering machine of Amelia's picked up. She knew who it would be, but I decided to leave a message this time. I had to see her, look into those eyes and make sure that ass was still mine. Like I'd told the old-timer, I wasn't going out like a punk.

31

AMELIA

Ike's long workout shorts accented his ass as he gave me the tour of his abode. It was hard to judge the place as it hadn't been lived in yet. No revelations or insight into the man in whom I had more than a passing interest. In his bedroom, it was uncomfortably hot, the kind of sticky heat that can coax clothes off a body. As dampness gathered on both of us, an awkward pause was all that indicated similar thoughts. We didn't stay long enough to test it. Too early in this game boys and girls liked to play. After a quick showing of the freshly made bed and an empty dresser, he halfheartedly led me away to the kitchen at the rear.

"I'm a little warm. Do you have something to drink?"

"It's the air. It needs to be fixed." He leaned into the refrigerator, his bare arms looking toned and muscular. "I'm just getting up to speed. All I have is grapefruit juice from my momma's and Budweiser."

"I'll take a Bud if you'll have one with me."

He turned his attention from its sparse contents to me. "You sure?" he asked.

"What? I hate grapefruit juice."

"Suit yourself." He popped the caps on two bottles and we toasted.

I turned up the bottle, which amused him. "How goes the security business?" I asked.

He shook his head. "Not so good, as you can tell. By the way, I'm more of a guard than I am in security."

"Guard. Bodyguard. Whatever. I don't know the difference, so don't ruin the illusion for me."

"I'm not one for illusions. Too many delusions lately."

"Are you always this upbeat? Or are you just trying to knock me off my feet?"

He put his beer down on the counter next to the sink, then folded his arms. "I'm coming off something that went bad. Real bad. I think you should know up front."

"Honest Isaac," I sang. Not too sure if he liked that. "And how do you know I'm not as well?"

"Are you?"

"No. My thing went bad long ago." I walked over to the window, where I peered at the backyard. His eyes studied me as if I were an ancient map. As sheer as my white pants were, my thong was the big red X signaling buried treasure. I lingered in the window longer, hoping he'd stake his claim on the booty. "I think you were delivered to remind me of that."

"I remind you of a bad thing?" He raised his shirt, flashing his stomach and chest, to wipe the sweat off his face. It was my turn to stare at his display.

"No. You remind me that it's over. Behind me."

"And how does that make you feel?"

I raised the cool bottle to my temple. "Happy," I answered. "It makes me feel happy." The condensed drops on the outside dripped down my camisole, providing brief satisfaction. Looking down, I could see that my breasts were beginning to protrude through the damp mesh.

"Damn, it's hot in here," he remarked.

"Not any better outside. Probably breaking a record."

"If I had a pool, I'd invite you for a swim."

"But I didn't bring a bathing suit."

"You don't need one," he joked.

"Even without the pool, I'm pretty wet," I joked in kind. "Every-where."

His eyes widened, then he sheepishly smiled. "Want another beer?" he asked.

"Sure."

He opened the door again, cool air escaping. As he fished two bot-tles free, I scrunched into the tiny opening alongside him.

"Mmm, this feels good," I proclaimed, as our bodies came in con-tact under the refrigerator light. "But we can't stay in here forever. Anywhere else you want to take this?"

Ike turned into me, our lips barely apart. You could smell the sex rising hotter than room temperature. "We could go out . . . some-where."

I threw away my restraint. I kissed him wild and wanton, differ-ent from the night he brought me home. In between our mouths merging, I spoke. "Where . . . you wanna . . . go?"

"Nowhere," he answered, sucking my tongue as if he were a pro. He left the bottles in the fridge and grabbed on to my ass. I gasped at the quickness with which he moved. It had been so long since I'd been taken, so long since I'd wanted to be taken. His fingers dug into my cheeks as he hoisted me up to him. As his lips canvassed my ear-lobe, he panted, "Anywhere."

I wrapped my arms around Ike, wedging him firmly between my thighs. "You're not going to leave on me again, are you?" I asked se-ductively. He moved away from the fridge, carrying me with him. Before he kicked the door shut, I snagged one bottle of beer for us to share. Secure, I bit into his neck, as he carried me out of the kitchen.

The heat had driven us crazy. We banged and bumped down the hallway, grinding against each other like crazed animals, en route to his bedroom. He lowered me onto the mattress.

"Last chance," he advised as he stood over me.

I took off my sandals, then drank from the bottle, my lips linger-ing on its lip. "Take it," I offered, smiling. "Take it like you can't live without it."

I was startled as he snatched me up and carried me on to the bathroom.

Seeing where he was going, I went with it. I turned the shower knobs on as he turned me on, running his hands viciously over my body. He was hard to control at this point, wanting me to no end. I handed the beer bottle to him. He took a swig in a failed attempt to hold his true thirst at bay. As the water sprayed down, I stepped in fully clothed.

Ike stared at me, astonished, as the water streamed down my body, soaking me through and through. The cold water was a shock at first, making my nipples rise further. Beneath the wet, clinging mesh, they jutted like succulent berries. He kicked off his tennis shoes and stepped into the bathtub to join me beneath the intense rush.

Water splashed off our intertwined bodies onto the bathroom tile. My top came off, then his, our tongues lapping at every curve and crevice. I took the beer from him and had one last taste. I handed the bottle back to him. He gazed at my skin, my shoulders, my breasts with reverence. As the waters rushed over us, he turned it up, then hurled the empty bottle across the bathroom, shattering it on the wall.

"Scared?" he asked, looking into my eyes.

"I ain't never scared."

We kissed again. His muscles were tight to the touch as I dug my nails into his chest. I felt his hands as they traced the curve of my lower back, sliding into my pants. They felt so good on my ass that I cooed. I hurriedly unzipped them, allowing them to fall in a soaked clump. His hand found its way to the front of my thong, where he massaged my throbbing clit in tiny circles. As he took my breast into his mouth, I reached into his shorts, reminding me of how good the hardness could be. With each tug on his dick, he sucked harder, making me erupt in a flow of warm juices. I tugged until his shorts came off with his underwear, massaging his head with my thumb. My legs were becoming weak as the eruptions came more and more frequent. He inserted two fingers inside me.

"I . . . Ike, yessssssssssss," I hissed as I felt my eyes flutter.

He pushed me against the shower wall, startling me. "Scared now?" he grunted.

"Only if you break another bottle," I said as cocky as could be.

"How about if I break you?" he said, kissing my neck. His fingers had sped up their assault of my insides. I craved the dick.

"Break me, baby," I purred, pussy primed for whatever Ike could spring on it.

He went down on his knees. I reached overhead and grasped the showerhead. Unsure if it would hold, I pulled myself up and spread my legs for him to feast.

He reached up with his hands, cupping my ass as if to form a seat, as he thrust his tongue like some spear into my conquered territory. Water flowing down upon my head and Ike's face entrenched between my legs, I moaned in three different octaves as chills broke out all over my nude body.

"I can't take it no more. Put it in, baby," I pleaded. I was out of breath and could barely speak.

As he allowed me to lower myself, I turned my ass to him. He came closer. I felt his dick first, then the rest of him as he pressed up against me. Not even an inch separated us, but it was the many inches that I had to have.

I gasped as I felt Ike enter me, not expecting it to feel so tight.

"Are you okay?"

"Mmm-hmm. Just keep it comin'."

I went onto my tiptoes with the first upward thrust of his manhood before rocking my ass back onto him.

"Damn. This is good," he panted in my ear.

I moaned in ecstasy at the filling feeling. "Is it? Is it good?" I managed to ask.

"Mmm-hmm," he replied this time as our bodies began moving in sync. He wrapped his arms under mine and held on, riding the ass. It felt like the water came down harder as I came.

My eyes misted as Ike's powerful body pressed me against the shower wall. My ass cheeks quivered as he dared to go deeper and farther into my pussy. I coated him with every probe, free as I hadn't been in oh so long. I braced myself as he went harder and harder, exorcizing the demons for both of us.

"Fuck me harder," I urged tearfully. "I want to feel you." He obliged, until releasing all he'd been holding since opening the door. I reached back, holding him steady as he spasmed.

Spent, the two of us descended to the floor of the bathtub, where we held each other beneath the unyielding stream.

32

IKE

"Do me a favor?"

"Sure," I said. At this moment, there was nothing I wouldn't do for her. A fluke. An incredibly wonderful fluke that I held as we spooned. I hadn't felt this level of intimacy in my bed since I don't know when. There was always an agenda with Deryn.

"Next time, have something else to drink."

I ran my fingers through the damp curls atop her head, not believing what had transpired between us. There was haunting familiarity about this woman too that I couldn't shake. I stopped at the rose and letters in dark ink at the base of her neck, curious. "You didn't like the beer?"

"No," she laughed. "You're lucky I hate grapefruit juice more."

I tickled her, finally able to enjoy the drop in temperature, inside and outside. As she wiggled about across the bed, I glared at the tattoo again. "Who's Antoinette?" I asked.

"I was wondering when you were going to ask."

"Yeah. Well, I was kinda busy earlier," I joked, images of water cascading down her back as I penetrated her still fresh in my head.

As she lay on her back, she playfully pushed me with her foot. "That's my middle name."

"Oh," I answered. It was no longer important. Her nude form was intoxicating. The view of her middle as she arched her legs was more urgent than her middle name. Her eyes cut to my dick, hardening by the second.

"Think my clothes are dry yet?"

"Maybe." I'd hung them outside. I didn't have an iron, so they were going to be wrinkled.

"You're being kind of quiet. All these one-word comments. You're not feeling regrets, are you?"

I blushed. "Naw. Nothing like that. I'm just a little in shock. I mean . . . things right now are so different than where I was recently. And that's a good thing. Back then, you couldn't have told me that. I just never figured a woman like you would . . ."

"Would what?"

"Y'know." I slid on the side of her, hiding my emerging erection. "You're this big star and I'm—"

"Please. I'm just a waitress who got her 'sing on' the other night, so don't get it twisted. *And what has you so down on yourself? Did she fuck you up that bad?*"

"Yeah," I sighed. "But I ain't no punk."

She kissed me gently. As she pulled away, a tiny giggle escaped from her lips. "You sound like somebody I know," she muttered. "Always trying to be hard."

"That's this person in your past?"

"Yep." She rolled onto her stomach, surveying the bedroom as if decorating it with her mind. Women. Her delicate feet danced about in the air as she arched her back. Her peach of an ass was as tempting as it had been in the shower. "Long in the past. Do you have a cigarette?"

"I don't smoke. Didn't think you did either."

"I really don't. Just feel like I need one after what we just went through. Whoo." She fanned herself. "Too long."

"He was your last?"

She smiled, amused at the nerve of my question. "Yes . . ." She caught herself. "Well, except for this one surreal night I don't care to remember. Going on four years. I was starting to feel like a virgin again. So don't think this shit is normal for me."

"Whatever." I smirked.

"Boy, I mean it!" She pounced atop me, graceful yet powerful. I marveled at her big smile, her kind eyes. "Don't make me break a nail."

"All right. I believe you," I said, laughing as I shielded my head from her playful slaps. "Damn. A nigga can't joke?"

"Is that what I'm feeling? *A joke?*" She maintained her position, crouched atop me. Her warm pussy resting on me was like a snake charmer. It was playing a melody, not of sound, but of scent and touch. I began to rise, my dick swelling with each pulse. Her eyes begged me to explore her again. I was loving it and wanted to love her. Things ain't supposed to go down like this. Not this soon. But life doesn't always toss you a script.

It was my turn to laugh. "Yep. A joke. Just wait till you hear the punch line."

She tilted her head back and closed her eyes, hips quivering as I slid into her moistness again.

Whoever let Amelia go was a fool.

"Did you see anything?" Arnold asked.

"What are you talking about?" I asked as I went on my shift.

"Don't play dumb, Winters. Weren't you at that party with your little girlfriend? The one the mayor held?"

"Oh. That," I calmly replied. "I didn't see anything. I left early."

"Hmph. Thought you might have some dirt. Are most of them people as freaky as they say?"

I paused, deciding to have some fun. "Freakier." When I thought about Deryn and Marshall, it didn't sting as much.

Arnold burst out in laughter. "Whooo. That's what I thought. Them rich people got too much money and way too much time on their hands. Nothing but freaks and pervs." The two other COs politely laughed along with her.

This coming from someone as twisted and sadistic as you, I thought. "Well, guess I need to get a move on."

"All eager to go on shift, ain't ya? Must've been these days you took off. Haircut all fresh 'n' shit. Did your little girlfriend give you some too?" she teased.

"Why you gotta go there?"

"Because I can," she reminded me, pulling rank. "Let me make sure your uniform is in regulation." I watched her pretend to inspect my uniform, from the blue stripe down my pant leg to the patches on my shoulders. As she touched the TDCJ patch on my right arm, she spoke to where only I could hear. "Y'know, you could assist me with some paperwork in my office . . . for a few hours. It would be easier than dealing with those animals."

A few hours. Serena never quit. She parked her lips as if tempting me to kiss them. From what I'd heard around here, she liked putting them to other uses. "I wouldn't be doing my job then, now would I?" I answered, trying not to piss her off too much. I gently passed her, exiting the locker room.

"Winters!" she yelled. I stopped in my tracks.

"Yes?"

"You're doing shakedown today."

"I'm working the laundry," I replied, confused by her statement. "I saw the roster."

"Things change. The newbie quit on us last night. Said things are too dangerous around here. Enjoy," she taunted.

33

BODIE

I read because I was tired of doing pushups. As I finished the book on Malcolm X, I was saddened by a man cut down right when he could've saved so many of us wayward people. Peoples maybe like my moms and now me. I guess that's how it is—forces always at work to stop any real change. On a personal note, I wondered when I would hear from Jason North about maybe getting out of here. Putting the book to rest on my chest, I looked at the bare wall absent Amelia's picture.

"On five!" came the familiar call. One more shakedown. Our cell was searched twice as much as the others. Rewind kept MFs on their toes.

"Where's Rewind?" CO Winters asked, by himself this time. Stupid move on this block.

"Hell if I know, boss," I muttered. I placed my book on the bunk and stood up, ready for the routine.

"How you been, Bodie?"

"You mean since you left me hangin' in solitary?"

He threw a sharp glance my way; then his face softened. He smiled. "Yeah. I guess."

"I'm aight. Ain't seen you around here in a minute. Took you that long getting your hair cut, huh?"

Winters laughed. "Naw. Just had some business to take care of."

"Fo sho?"

"Look, man. Sorry about how things went down in solitary. I'll try to find that letter for you."

"Mighty big of you, man. Why you actin' all nice 'n' shit? Need some info or sumthin'? 'Cause I ain't no snitch."

He went through Rewind's shoes thoroughly. "Things just looking up in life for a change, my man. S'all."

My turn to laugh. "Must be some bitch."

He didn't answer, but his face gave it away. He kept searching, shaking my *Str8 Dime* magazine to see if anything was hidden in the pages.

"Wish I could say the same. I gotta get out of here, man. My girl singing again and I'm sittin' in here with my thumb up my ass. Can't have her back like that, y'know."

He looked at the blank spot on the wall. "Oh yeah. Ole girl you had up there? What happened to the picture?"

"Probably that bitch Arnold. Oops, sorry. Don't mean to talk about your boss."

Winters shook his head. "It's okay. We do it too," he muttered. He'd moved on to my mattress.

"You'll never hear me say this again, but for a CO, you ain't as bad as most."

"Thanks," he chuckled. I don't think he cared one way or another what I thought about him, but he did a good job of faking it. He picked up my book. "Finally finished it?" he asked.

"Yeah. Just now."

"I hope you learned something from it."

"Maybe. I learned that if I get outta here, I'm gonna do right by my girl. Try to get right like your woman got you all of a sudden."

He put the book down on the bed. "You're serious."

"Damn straight."

"Good for you. It's never too late."

He poked around Rewind's bunk, almost at the end of the shakedown. As he peered up through the bed frame, he asked, "So what's your girl's name?"

"Amelia, bruh."

His eyes grew big as if he'd found something under Rewind's mattress. I waited for him to pull something out, but he didn't. When he looked at me, it was like I wasn't there.

"All clear in here," he mumbled.

"You all right, man?"

"Yeah. I'm fine," he said, all distant. "Close five!" he yelled before he'd cleared the cell. The door clanged shut and Winters was gone. Looked like the nigga had diarrhea and I had the strange feeling I'd just been the one shit on.

34

AMELIA

"*Hey. I need you to come see me. You can't just cut me off. You're my heart. Come see me. Okay? We got things to talk about. I love you, girl.*"

I'd come home from Ike's to this message left on my answering machine. I'd gone from feeling like a new woman to being slapped by feelings I kept trying to bury for good. The onset of guilt made me nauseous.

"Damn you, Bodie," I muttered, placing my finger over the DELETE button. It hovered there, but I never pressed down. Instead, I went to prepare for work, where the tortured mood lingered.

The evening at Mirage was a blur of rushing dinner orders, crashing plates and demanding customers. I took solace in that it kept me occupied. Tonight, I would be attending a special get-together for Natalia at Scott Gertner's Skybar and Grille. On one of our breaks, I convinced Tookie to come along. She and Montez already had plans, but she just decided to bring him with her. He wouldn't mind because what Tookie said goes anyway.

"I work with one celebrity, but now I get to hang with *another*? What did I do to deserve this?" she teased.

The elevators opened to the packed penthouse nightclub, treating us to the sounds of Scott Gertner and his band. I put on my happy face, wondering if Ike might show. I'd called him a final time before coming here, leaving a message just in case. He'd said he'd be at work, but a girl couldn't help but wish. I don't know why I suddenly needed his reassuring presence, but it was wrong to be slipping into those dependent habits I'd had with Bodie.

Hearing the music, Tookie began gyrating. Montez, not used to the spot, tried to be cool. After telling the woman we were with Natalia's party, we were ushered past the line of paying patrons and over to the reserved section of tables. Outside the windows was a breathtaking view of downtown Houston that even Montez had to acknowledge. "Damn, this place got it goin' on. How come we ain't been here before?" he remarked as we passed the main bar.

"Uh . . . because it's out of your college budget," Tookie cracked back.

Scott, who owned the venue with its two terraces and intimate, sexy atmosphere, was entertaining as we wound our way to the reserved section upfront. He shouted out a scantily clad Natalia, who had traded in her mojitos for apple martinis this evening. As she sipped, she winked, enjoying the attention from the master of ceremonies. A man in designer jeans and a black T-shirt knelt beside her, eagerly scribbling in a small notepad as she spoke. Seated next to her was the ever-present Owen, who acknowledged us first. His cell phone earpiece was firmly wedged in place.

"Hello, Miss Amelia and friends," he uttered, standing up to greet us.

"Owen, this is Tookie and Montez," I introduced over the band.

"Pleasure," he said facetiously. "Order whatever you want tonight. Natalia wants you all to have a good time."

Montez, hearing what he said, took the initiative. "Y'all got some Cristal?"

"Boy, are you even old enough to drink?" Owen chided. Me and Tookie laughed at Montez' expense, then took a seat at the other reserved table. It took me a second to realize four of the other tables were Natalia's party as well because I didn't recognize a single face.

"Uh . . . Amelia, can you give them our drink orders? 'Cause me and Montez want to check out the terrace."

"Sure, girl. I got ya." Tookie patted me on my shoulder and the two of them were on their way. As I sat there alone, images of me at Lullaby's came to mind. Neal had called me the fire starter that night. As I tapped my fingers on the table, I imagined being called up in here to perform and the crowd's reaction. A hostess came to take our drink orders, snapping me back to reality.

Scott and his band took a pause for the cause, cuing the DJ to begin spinning. Some Bobby Valentino sent the ladies to the dance floor with men in tow. Tookie and Montez would be out there soon if they weren't too busy. As Scott walked past, he gave Natalia a hug and made her promise to do a number or two with his band. Owen was listening and smiled intently. He saw me watching.

"I see you. Don't worry. Your chance will come. But not tonight. This is Natalia's show," he said, answering a question I hadn't asked. I was too flabbergasted to say anything. I guess that's why she paid him. He said and did what she couldn't. And he wasn't about to let things as silly as friendship or talent steal his mistress' shine.

As Natalia continued speaking with the notepad man, she finally realized I was there. She cut a smile at me and waved. The man writing took note, pausing from his scribbling, to point at me. He said something. Natalia nodded, then laughed. He grinned as he went back to jotting.

Rather than get flip, I tried to engage in a civil conversation with Owen. "Who is he?" I asked.

His eyes trailing a well-dressed man in a suit, Owen spoke. "A reporter. He writes for *Str8 Dime* and a couple of others. Y'know . . . gossip, inside news. He's doing an interview with your girl."

"Does the business ever stop?"

"Nope," the large man giggled. "Something you should think about."

I looked at him strangely. "What do you mean by that?"

"Nothing, girl."

I eyed him silently for another second. "You don't like me much, do you?"

"Girl, please. I don't have a problem with you. Like I just said . . . it's always business."

A noise came over the place. Over the beats of the Kanye West song, people were talking. Natalia and the reporter noticed it too, looking toward the entrance. And then he came through the crowd.

"Perfect timing," Owen mumbled.

Penny Antnee, the Miami rapper whose album *Money Well Spent* lived on the Billboard charts and who had a cameo on Natalia's album, strutted past the autograph seekers. This was a place used to celebrities, but that didn't stop the buzz he caused. His eyes locked on me and he granted me a rare smile.

As he walked over to join Natalia and her interviewer, I had to ask, "Are they?"

"Puh-lease." The tone in which he said it told me to leave it alone.

Tookie and Montez returned, sweaty from their dance and whatnot. I was glad as I'm sure Owen was tired of entertaining me.

"Who's that?" Tookie asked as she figured out which one was her drink.

"Penny Antnee," Montez answered. "Your girl knows Penny Antnee?" he asked me.

"Yep. Natalia knows everyone."

"I heard that," she said as she came over to our table. Back where she had been seated, Penny was dealing with the reporter. "Ain't he fine?" she remarked.

"Sure is," Owen answered, giving me that same look from before.

"Ditto," Tookie answered before Montez hunched her.

"Nat, these are my friends Tookie and Montez."

Natalia entertained them, telling them too much about me in the process. I was quick to add my version whenever I could.

"Is he your date?" Natalia whispered about Montez.

"No," I answered. "He's with Tookie."

"You're disappointing me, boo. I thought you'd bring someone."

"Well, it didn't work out that way."

"I'd offer you Penny, but you're not his type."

I'd taken the hint. "That's so noble of you."

"Hey. Anything to get you off Bodie."

"I'm over him," I blurted out.

"Since when?"

"Recently. And I mean it." Scott and his band had taken position in front of us again. He nodded at Natalia.

"I don't believe you," she said. "But we'll talk about it once I do these numbers." She began to get up from the table.

I tapped her on the arm. "What were you saying about me earlier?" I asked.

"What are you talking about?"

"The reporter. I saw you look at me and say something."

She smacked her lips as Scott announced her to the crowd. "Oh. That? Nothing. Just business."

I thought about what Owen said as she accepted her applause. It's always business.

35

IKE

I wanted to beat Bodie, drag him around the cell and make him tell me it was a joke. That would've been a lie. I knew it to be the truth as soon as her name escaped his lips. I'd been with his woman. *No, my woman*, I reminded myself as I sped along in my raggedy truck, trying to get it over fifty miles per hour. Not sure if I could say that either.

I should've seen it, figured things out. But Amelia looked different now. Besides, I had Deryn. Why would I pay that much attention to another man's woman? Yet there I was. Remembering the smile, those eyes, how fondly he spoke of her. The familiarity dangling right in front of me at Lullaby's should've been a warning. Houston was too big for something like this to happen. But it had.

I looked at the time, desperate to be somewhere. I'd told Amelia I probably couldn't make it. Skybar had been somewhere Deryn liked to go, but when my work schedule allowed, my bank account didn't. I stopped at an ATM en route, knowing I might be overdrawn next week.

People were already leaving when I arrived. I parked my truck down the street. As I passed a wave of beauties, I checked for Amelia, but she wasn't with them. Just some girl named Kelly telling her sister Shenita that she needed to calm down. That just made Shenita angrier as she ripped into curse words I barely heard on the inside.

Sweet girl, that one, I thought sarcastically as I ignored them and entered the building lobby.

As the penthouse elevator opened, I questioned the departing passengers.

"Is Natalia up there?" I asked, remembering everyone would know Amelia's friend.

"Yeah. She still there, man," answered a yawning, gap-toothed brother in front of his thick-in-the-hips woman. "But you ain't gonna have a chance with her. Just go on home." His woman laughed. I blew him off, waiting for the elevator to clear so I could go up.

On the way up to the penthouse, the elevator operator refused to look at me. He kept his head down, intent on the numbers flashing by as we rose.

"Pretty busy tonight?" I asked nervously.

"Yep. You're kind of late, ain't ya?"

"I certainly hope not," I replied, thinking beyond his intent. In the mirror, I looked at the shirt and slacks I'd hastily tossed on.

I stepped off the elevator into a late-night jam session. Most of the club had cleared out, leaving a group of about twenty wilding out before the band. I thought for sure the singer blessing the mic was Amelia, until a note wasn't quite right. The fire I'd felt, the synergy with the crowd at Lullaby's, was missing. I was tempted to leave, but ignored my inner coward. I'd come all this way not planning on punking out. Walking over, I saw her.

Natalia.

Amelia's friend was singing, as I suspected. She was a polished professional from her moves and mannerisms. The tall, thin beauty whipped around in barely there navy garb more scarf than dress. Not bad at all. My initial opinion was that Amelia was a better singer, but I was probably a little biased.

A thick sister who wasn't partying with the rest looked like she'd had a few too many drinks. As she turned her head, we recognized each other. She was one of Amelia's friends from Lullaby's. I decided to approach her.

"Are you all right?" I asked as I braced her from tipping over.

"Sheeet. I'm havin' the time of my life. This place has the best drinks I've ever had. I just need a little weed now and I'll be set," she gushed without throwing up. I figured she was going to live. "Ain't you that dude Amelia left with the other night? That motherfucker in the tux?"

"Yeah. That was me. She still here?"

"Yep. She over there with Montez. He wanted to dance, but I need to catch my breast . . . I mean *breath*," she giggled. "Guess I could catch my breasts too. Go see her, man. She'll be happy to see you."

Through the moving bodies, I saw Amelia's face as she danced. She looked happy. A tall, locked dude got a little too close and her expression changed. I headed toward them.

"Hey!" her friend shouted over the music. Nobody else noticed. "What's your name?" she asked.

I held back a laugh, figuring it might make her go off. "Ike," I answered.

"Ike? Sheeet. Well, she ain't no Tina, so don't get no ideas. I stay strapped."

"Yes, ma'am," I replied with a wink. This was a fun bunch.

Amelia didn't see me at first. I gazed upon her as if for the first time. With what I'd just learned, it might have been the last time. I cataloged every detail of the moment. Her halter dress looked as if silk were spun over her body. Her glittered skin twinkled beneath the shifting strobes. When I looked for her smile, it was missing. That dude with the dreads again.

I think she was telling him to back up. I'd been enough places to know when somebody was overstepping his bounds. He was saying something back to her when she saw me. Nothing else mattered from that point on.

And I was certain.

No other way to explain it.

"Ike!" she screamed, running and hurling herself into my arms. I spun her around and she held on for dear life, not out of fear, but longing.

"Surprise," I breathed into her ear, her perfume enthralling me. The way she tenderly stroked the hairs on the back of my neck was special.

The remaining gathering was small enough for us to draw attention. Natalia paused in the middle of her song, humming one of her verses instead, as she squinted through the lights.

"I thought you weren't going to make it."

"Me too. Couldn't let you down."

"Thank you . . . for not letting me down." What I had to tell her might change her opinion. As we talked, that guy Montez or whatever returned to the drunk lady, but not before scowling at me. The young motherfucker thought I'd ruined his game tonight. The problem was that he didn't have any.

"I didn't interrupt anything, did I?"

"Hell no. You were right on time." She kissed me, lips ablaze with strawberries washing over my tongue.

Applause rang out as Natalia finished her performance. We were about to have a seat, but Amelia had other plans.

"C'mon, I want you to meet my friend," she said, taking me by the arm. "She doesn't believe you exist." More people knowing about me wasn't going to make this any easier.

Natalia was accepting congratulations from people before they left for the night. One guy looked like the rapper Penny Antnee.

"Nat," Amelia hollered. "This is Ike. My friend," she said, squeezing my arm.

Natalia's eyes lit up as her mouth curled into a wide grin. "Well, it's about damn time," she muttered. Natalia gave me a big hug. A real star hugged me. *Me.* Like she knew me. Damn. "We've got a lot to talk about, Ike," she said, sticking her tongue out at Amelia. "But first, we have to take a photo. The photographer from the *Chronicle* has been here all night and I'm sure he wants to go home."

A scruffy-looking white dude with curly hair shrugged his shoulders. He raised his camera, ready to wrap it up. Before I knew it, we were all huddled up beneath the lights—the owner of the club, me,

Amelia, Natalia and the guy I was just realizing really was Penny Antnee. Damn. By the third shot, Amelia was snuggling next to me. Can't say it wasn't welcome. I held her close until she was pried from my arms by Natalia. Girl talk.

I didn't really know any of the other people and thought it too childish to ask Penny Antnee for his autograph. *Maybe I'll ask him if he'll go by my old gym. Talk to the kids,* I thought. Just then, his handler got off the elevator. It was time for him to go. No more photo ops, I presumed. Yawning, he quickly exited before I could speak.

Having some time to myself, I walked out on one of the terraces. The faint breeze kept the humidity from bothering me too much. I leaned over, marveling at the gigantic glass-and-metal monoliths of downtown, where I never dared tread.

Amelia, bruh, I heard Bodie say.

Maybe that's why everything had gone so wrong in my life.

I never dared.

The metal doors scraped as someone else came outside. A large, muscular brother who I hadn't noticed stood on call. He never approached or said a word. Just kept watch for something. Minutes later, Natalia came outside. He leaned over and she whispered in his ear. He nodded, then returned inside. She came over, her mane of curly hair bouncing freely.

"Amelia's not out here," I voiced.

"I know. She's in the ladies' room. I came outside to meet you."

"You threw a nice concert tonight," I complimented, straining not to stare at her visible cleavage.

"Thank you," she gushed. "But that wasn't a concert."

"Sorry."

"To see a concert, you have to go with Amelia to the rodeo next week. Yours truly is headlining." She chuckled. "Just a few years ago, I couldn't afford a ticket to see Beyoncé."

"Oh. Well, I'll see if I can make it."

"No, boy," she said, swatting me on the arm like I was an old friend. "I want you to promise me that you'll go. I got the tickets covered if that's what you're stressing over."

"I don't—"

She cut me off. "My girl has some things she needs to put behind her. Some bad shit. I don't mean to bring it up with you . . . a stranger, but I saw how she reacted to you. I know when Amelia is on someone. I saw it with that piece of shit."

"You're talking about her ex?" I held my nerves in check, not sure what to make of her.

"Yep. He was no good for her."

"And how do you know I am?"

Her nose wrinkled, then she cocked her head to one side. "What do you do, Ike?"

"I—I'm a corrections officer." My eyes locked on hers, begging to let everything out. I could tell she was reading into it.

"Like I said, he was no good for her. That man ruined my girl's life," she continued, pretending as if what I said didn't register. "You'd be doing me a favor if you ensure she's moved on. Ya dig?"

"Yeah. I get it," I quietly answered.

"Amelia said you do some kind of security work. From the ones I deal with, the pay looks to be pretty good. Probably better than what you're making," she hinted. "I'll have my assistant, Owen, see what contacts we have here in Houston."

"That's mighty nice of you."

She cut a smile I had trouble deciphering. "Anything for my girl. How about you? Will you do anything for Amelia?"

"Yes."

"Good. So promise me you'll go with her to the rodeo. Then you'll get to see me give a real concert."

"What were you and Nat talking about?" she asked. Rather than taking Natalia's limo home or leaving with her heavyset friend, Amelia chose to ride with me in my truck. She slid under my arm on the long bench seat as I drove. It wasn't the Acura, but she seemed okay with it.

"The Houston Rodeo. She invited me."

"Damn. I was going to ask you. She's always jumping the gun." She paused, watching the road. "So what did you say?"

I reflected on my conversation with Natalia. "I said I'd go."

"That's what I want to hear. Is your AC fixed yet?"

"Not yet. Probably tomorrow."

"You're coming home with me then."

At Amelia's, I sat on the sofa, surfing through the different TV channels while she showered. A new episode of *Busted* was coming on, so I kept the channel there out of perverse curiosity. Amelia emerged from the bathroom wearing a cotton pajama set. More for comfort than seduction, but she didn't have to work the latter. Her slender legs smelled of fresh lotion.

"I thought you were going to join me," she pouted.

"Thought about it," I remarked. "But I remembered our last shower."

"It's just not the same without broken bottles, huh?" She bent over, and when our lips touched, we enjoyed the newness of it all. "Mmm, hold that thought," she commanded before dashing into the kitchen.

While Amelia fumbled around, a redhead on *Busted* was talking about why she thought her husband was hittin' something on the side. She had a funny accent. Definitely not from Texas.

"Ice cream and . . . *wine*?" I asked, seeing the bowls and glasses she bore.

"Indulge me. I put up with your beer." She sat beside me, handing off my share of her strange treat. "It's Chunky Monkey," she advised.

"With wine?"

"Yep. Spent way too much time here alone. See what you can discover?"

"I guess," I said, digging in. The strange mix wasn't half bad.

"Watching *Busted*?"

"Yeah. You watch it too?"

"Sometimes. I just wait for the fight."

I laughed at her for admitting it. Amelia wasn't what you would expect from just looking at her. A good thing in my book. Looks weren't everything. Having someone you could kick it with was more important. Bodie had it all in her. Not to dwell, I turned my attention back to the TV.

The scene had switched to surveillance of the lady's husband. His face was covered up, but I could tell he was either black or Hispanic. It took me a little by surprise seeing as his wife was definitely neither of those. Images were shown of this dude with the other woman, her face blacked out too. It was them having dinners at fancy restaurants. Going to Hotel Derek during lunch and coming out hours later. Kissing after leaving work at city hall.

City hall.

I drank deeply of my wine.

"This is getting good," Amelia remarked. She shoved some of her Ben & Jerry's in my mouth even though I still had some in my bowl.

The show went live. The woman, who I now remembered, was in tears after being confronted with what she suspected. Things were about to get heated. I instinctively moved my hand over the remote.

"Just like a man. Always hogging the remote," she teased. I left it alone.

I sweated out the next few moments, denying yet demanding the train wreck to come. The husband thought the wife was away in Europe visiting her people. He was busted with his dick in Deryn's mouth when Maritzah and the cameras stormed into the lavish hotel room. Of course, they covered things with those pixels, but you could tell from the motion. I put my bowl down.

"What's wrong?" Amelia asked.

"Nothing. I'm just full."

"Was there something you wanted to tell me earlier?"

"Oh. Yeah." Maritzah slapped Marshall, who ran into the bathroom like a coward and locked her out. The cameras then turned their attention to Deryn. With a sheet wrapped around her, she ran down the hall screaming for them to leave her alone. Pitiful. Embarrassing. Sad.

"That was one of the funniest ones I've seen. Now what did you want to talk about?"

Deryn had disgraced me enough and now I'd been delivered from hell. An angel by the name of Amelia had offered me her hand. In the now, I felt her hand tighten in mine as if a sign. I heard Natalia, loud and clear. Bodie didn't deserve her. I wasn't quitting.

"I just wanted to say that I want you to be happy."

She set down her glass and pulled me to her. Embracing me, she spoke. "You're so sweet. And I am happy."

"I'm not in the best shape financially, but—"

"I've lived that life. I ain't like that anymore. I don't want your money, Ike. I thought you knew that by now."

"I do. It's just that a woman should have certain things."

"Ike?"

"Yeah."

"Shut up and make love to me."

Dare was all I thought as we undressed each other.

36

BODIE

I was working laundry detail when the CO responded to the squawking on his radio. He'd received orders to escort me. I dumped my large bin in the wash, then left with him. Time to see my lawyer again.

"What took you so long?" I asked as I pulled the chair out, taking a seat.

"I run a business, Mr. Campbell," Jason North replied. He'd moved up from his condescending *dear boy*. He continued. "I have a list of priorities. It's up to you to determine where you fall on that list. Don't you think?"

"Stop the bullshit."

He smiled coldly, then folded his arms, looking intently at me from across the table. "Are you committed then?"

"Yeah. But I ain't beggin'. I gotta get out of here."

"First things first. Can you deliver your *girlfriend*? Are you absolutely certain the contract's binding?"

"Yes."

"Then where is it?"

"Somewhere."

"Not with that sham of a lawyer over in Sharpstown, I hope. I think he's about to be disbarred. Ethics violations, I believe." He paused to analyze my reaction. "No wonder you're in this country club," he tsked. He snapped a loose thread off his blazer. I wanted to snap his neck.

"Like I said, it's somewhere. Now when you gonna get me outta here?"

CO Arnold walked by our table. North flashed his plastic smile. Once she was out of earshot, he hissed again. "When was the last time you talked to her?" he asked.

"The other day," I said straight-faced.

"And?"

"And I'm working on it."

"Good. I need this done soon."

"You almost sound desperate."

"Not desperate. Opportunistic. Make no mistake about it. I know talent and so do others, so it's in my best interest and yours to get this done. Amelia is beginning to get exposure."

"What's she doing?"

"If you're on speaking terms, you would know. Maybe I'm dealing with the wrong person." He sighed, checking his manicured finger-nails. "Maybe I should talk to that guy friend she's getting cozy with."

I lurched at him. "What?" I shouted. The COs reacted, quickly swarming around us. I kept my hands palms down on the table. I contemplated how much damage I could do before they took me down. Jason didn't flinch. Instead he waved them off, claiming I was merely reacting to some family news.

"Please. Sit." He gestured.

"Who the fuck are you talking about?" I spewed.

"Check the paper, dear boy. Some guy probably trying to replace you as her manager . . . maybe more. That's twice that he's popped up. They make a cute couple. Definite chemistry there."

"Naw. Naw. This ain't happenin'. It ain't goin' down like that." I punched my fist into my palm.

"But it is. Time to put up or shut up."

"How do I know you're not making all this up? Maybe you're ma-nipulatin' things, man. You're good at that."

"Don't play games with me, Mr. Campbell. You may not take me seriously, but you should. I'll get a team on board to review your case, but you better have something for me soon." He thumped his ringed finger on the table for emphasis.

"I'll get you Amelia," I reassured. And if North fucked me over, I'd get him. "I'm through here," I yelled at the CO as I motioned for him to take me away.

37

AMELIA

My pussy and thighs ached with satisfaction. Ike had feasted on me last night as if he were possessed. Knowing he had to be to work, we lay lazily on my bed. The ceiling fan whirred overhead.

"Don't go," I pleaded.

He put his hands on my breasts, tweaking my nipples to rock hardness between his fingers. I gasped, wanting him to take them in his mouth and fiercely suck, but he didn't. "I don't want to, but I need my check," he said, a galaxy away.

"Ever thought about quitting?"

"Someone else used to suggest that," he said with a chuckle. He released his grip on my breasts. The woman he never mentioned was in the room with us. Just like I never mentioned Bodie. Maybe I would tell him all one day. I'd cast my ballot last night as he loved me to no end. By this morning, he'd won the election . . . unanimously. Ike turned toward me, then continued. "I've thought about doing security details. Maybe gain some financial independence for once in my life."

"Natalia knows some firms out here that might have some work. I'll check with her." He looked away, then came back to me. Something about Natalia amused him, but he didn't let on. "Thanks. I'm not used to someone looking out for me like this," he said. "Y'all two must be pretty tight."

"Yep. Nat's my girl. Sometimes she can be overprotective."

"Yeah. I noticed."

"*Uh-huh.* What were you two talking about at SkyBar? I mean, besides the rodeo."

He rolled onto his back. "You," he answered. "She was just checking me out."

"I figured that." I sat up in the bed. Ike smiled, admiring my body. I'd missed that. We were alone again.

"What do you want out of life, Amelia?"

"I don't know. Been lost for so long, y'know?"

"It's not waiting tables. That night at Lullaby's makes it easy to figure out. Why'd you stop singing?"

"Stupidity. Poor choices."

"What's stopping you now?"

"Fear. Doubt. Both."

He stroked his hand along the small of my back. "Whenever you're ready to take that step, I'm here. I won't let you down."

The way he spoke to me . . . it was strange, as if he truly knew me. And it didn't scare him.

"Thank you," I uttered. I draped myself atop Ike and kissed his forehead.

"Naw, I should be saying that," he said. His fingers gripped my ass, pulling me firmly against him. I felt the warmth radiating between our legs, my wetness returning. I brought my lips across his nose, then to his waiting mouth. I drank him in, taking his tongue.

"You can thank me when . . . I'm . . . done."

I moved to his neck with my kisses, then passed over his firm chest, biting at his nipples the way I'd wanted him to do me earlier. Ahead of my mouth's advance, I reached between us and gripped his dick. It was already hardening. As I stroked, it snaked to life, throbbing with each vigorous caress.

"I . . . I have to go. Work," Ike sputtered as my lips moved to his waist. I grazed the hairs just below his belly button and blew. His breath had become deep, labored. I took his balls in hand, gently fondling them between my fingers. I lowered my mouth onto the head of his dick, licking it wildly while darting my tongue over his sensitive spot at the tip. As my lips sealed tightly, I began sucking on his moistened shaft. He gasped as I took him in my mouth and deep throated, determined to impose my will.

"Damn. Amelia. Mmm. Do that shit," he panted as I worked him to orgasm in my mouth.

Following another interlude, Ike was gone, rushing off to change for work. I tuned the radio to 97.9 The Box and decided to wash clothes and do a little straightening up. Natalia was to give an interview to the Madd Hatta Morning Show on her way out of town, so I didn't want to miss it. As I separated my whites, somebody knocked on the door. I turned the volume down and they knocked again. Maybe Ike had left something in his haste, I thought as I ran to the door. Maybe he wanted a repeat. I devilishly looked forward to the encore.

"What it do?" he said. My mouth dropped.

"Hey," I replied, recovering from the surprise. I stepped outside, partially closing the apartment door behind me.

"You don't sound happy to see me," Montez muttered.

"Uh, *hello*," I nervously joked. " 'Cause I don't know what you're doing here. Did Tookie send you? Is she okay?"

"Naw, she aight. I just came by to check on you."

"You just saw me last night. And . . . and *how'd you know where I live*?"

He laughed, sending his dreads whipping back on his head. "We came by that night. Remember? My birthday. Me and Tookie followed you here. Before the club. Before we went back to her place—"

"Yeah, yeah. Right," I said, cutting him off before he went any further.

"I wanted to make sure that guy didn't mess with you or nuthin'."

"Ike?"

"I dunno. I guess. That nigga you left with."

"That's sweet of you, but I'm okay as you can see."

"Yeah. You're okay all right." Montez licked his lips. When we'd danced at SkyBar, he'd come on a little strong. I ignored it, blaming it on the alcohol and his immaturity. "You not gonna let me in?"

"I don't think so," I replied. I scanned the commons of my complex, wishing for a neighbor to be outside or something. *"Does Tookie know you're here?"* I asked.

"This ain't about her. And she don't have to know either. I'll keep quiet." He tried to enter uninvited.

"Boy, get back." I pressed my hands against his substantial frame and pushed. He barely budged. I retreated to my doorway, where I made another stand. "There's something you need to understand. That stuff that went down was a onetime thing. Now . . . my friend's coming back and I need you to leave."

"Just let me come in for a second. Let me talk to ya." He tried to put his arms around me, tried to pick me up. I took a step back and hurled my balled fist at his eye. He yelped, holding his hand to his face as he staggered back. "What the fuck is wrong with you?" he bellowed.

"Boy, if you try that shit again, I'll blind you," I cursed. "And if you don't go right now, I'm going to tell Tookie about this. I don't think she'd appreciate your being here."

He blinked, smarting from his eye irritation. "Crazy bitch," he muttered, shaking his head as he took leave. I ran inside, locking the door behind me.

When I was sure Montez was gone for good, I breathed a sigh of relief. No way I could've held him off if he'd persisted. Natalia's laughter on the radio alerted me. I quickly turned it up, cursing that I'd missed most of her interview.

"Now I've been hearing rumors about some kind of beef, Natalia," Nnete, the show's cohost, probed. Nnete was also in charge of the entertainment news.

"Girl, I don't know what you're talking about," Natalia teased.

"Okay! Okay! Play dumb. An anonymous source at SkyBar last night

claims another H-town singer was in attendance. What's goin' on, girl? What's really hap'nin?"

"You got me. Yes, that is true. My girl Amelia was in the house. Y'all need to be on the lookout for her."

I heard her loud and clear, but moved closer to the radio. How was my name coming up? Why?

"Now we're getting somewhere! So y'all two are tight?" Nnete continued.

"Of course."

"No beef?"

"Of course not. We came up together."

"That's funny. 'Cause my anonymous source claims this Amelia is signed to the On-Phire Records. What you think about that? Can you confirm that for us? What's the deal? Is your so-called friend the new princess of On-Phire? All of H-town wants ta know!"

"What is she talking about?" I screamed at the radio.

"Girl, that's between her and On-Phire. I'm not privy to the negotiations, but I'm sure Jason North and them will take care of her," Natalia said coyly.

"It ain't true!" I yelled. As the interview continued, I furiously dialed Natalia on her phone. I needed to clear this up *now*.

38

IKE

An old Monte Carlo with a candy paint job was parked behind me, making it hard to back up. The driver appeared to be looking for an address or something. I barely squeezed by, showing my displeasure at the man I could barely see due to the sun in my eyes and the window's dark tint. Not even the loud music coming from the trunk ceased. Looking at my watch, I let it go and simply sped away.

The ringtone, John Legend's latest, alerted me. I picked it up, answering as I knew who it was.

"Missing me already?" I asked Amelia.

"Actually . . . yes," the woman who was not Amelia coolly replied.

I almost wrecked, hearing the woman's voice, foolishly concerned about her until I remembered the betrayal. Amelia made it easier to stomach, but seeing her on *Busted* ripped open those wounds before the whole world. A blacked-out face can't hide reality. It was real— her sucking Marshall's dick in that hotel room. It was real—her fucking Marshall in the bathroom. It was real—her betraying me in the illusion that doubled as our life.

"What do you want?" I asked Deryn.

"Just to talk."

"Can't. I'm late for work. Remember? That job of mine you hate. Gotta keep the pennies flowing since I don't have a home anymore."

"Where are you staying?"

"None of your fuckin' business. Now what do you want?"

"You left some things." I wanted an apology, not an inventory.

"Doesn't surprise me. I'll get them when I can. Like I said, I'm busy."

"You certainly didn't waste any time getting over me." Her comment struck me as odd. She couldn't have known about Amelia. No one did. "Stop by whenever," she sighed.

"I thought you changed the locks," I shot off.

"I'll be here."

Silence carried over the tenuous connection between us. "I gotta go," I said simply to break this up.

As I sped up to take Beltway 8, my truck shuddered. Steam shot out from under my hood as I pulled over to clear traffic. "Aw, c'mon now!" I remarked, marveling at my bad luck.

"You're late,"

"I know. Sorry, Martinez," I offered. "My truck broke down."

"Yeah. Right," he replied with a half laugh. "Just because you're out partying it up, don't make the rest of us suffer."

Martinez pissed me off. I still had a busted water hose and a sweaty uniform to prove my innocence. On the beltway, a Good Samaritan had been nice enough to take me to AutoZone; otherwise I'd still be baking in the sun. "I got no time for riddles. If you got something on your mind, spit it out."

Instead of speaking, he pushed his way past me in a hurry. On the locker room bench, where he'd just changed, lay a folded newspaper. I slid it closer, eyeing the society column, curious as to what set him off. Surveying the photos, I expected to see something about Deryn and Marshall. If it was obvious to me, others had to have recognized them on *Busted*. Oh well. You reap what you sow. I flipped the folded *Chronicle* over to look at the remaining entertainment articles.

Nothing about them.

Just my grinning mug staring back at me.

Stunned, I snatched the paper up before anyone else saw it. Sure it was clear, I looked at it again. The photo from last night had already surfaced.

The caption read:

**Singing sensation Natalia and up-and-comer
Amelia celebrate at Scott Gertner's SkyBar with
rapper Penny Antnee and friend.**

"And friend," I laughed to myself at the title I'd received. Even this level of notoriety was bothersome, but I guess that's how it would be with Amelia. Still, this wasn't the part of the paper Martinez would normally look at. Somebody else had seen it.

And stirred things up.

"There he is," Serena sang as she entered the locker room. She'd been waiting for me to arrive. "Didn't know you had it like that, Winters. Or is one of those girls your cousin?"

"Just some friends," I calmly replied as I stowed my stuff in my locker. If I let her know her prying got to me, she'd never let up.

"What did you say your girlfriend's name was? Deryn?"

"Yeah." She must've asked somebody. No way she would've remembered.

"Hmph. Funny name, but I don't think she's in that picture," she ribbed. "Does she know you were there, Winters?"

I slammed my locker shut, tired of Serena's button pushing. "Can't you mind your own business?"

"And can't you come in to work on time? Or do I need to write you up? Want to try me?"

"You can—"

"Can what?"

I seriously entertained answering Arnold's question, walking out the door and into the life that could be with Amelia. Except I wasn't relying on what-ifs. I couldn't. Things were just too shaky to throw caution to the wind.

"Nothing," I surrendered. "You can quit all the threats. I got work to do."

"You most certainly do. How's a double shift sound? 'Cause that's what you're looking at."

"Guess I better get to work then," I commented dryly.

I left Arnold to her usual mindless rants. Checking the schedule, I hoped I wouldn't cross paths with Bodie. I hadn't done anything, but the feeling in the pit of my stomach was too fresh to keep under wraps if I saw him. What was once his was now mine.

For better or worse.

39

BODIE

I paced about the gymnasium floor beneath the basketball goal. The cell phone, smuggled in here courtesy of the CO on guard, rang repeatedly.

"What it do?" Aaron answered, not knowing it was me.

"You better be watching her," I muttered.

"Bodie?"

"You know."

"Perfect muthafuckin' timing, man," he gushed.

"Why? You got some news?"

"I'm checkin' the Lac like you asked."

"Fuck the code. I'm on a burner. We can talk."

"*You sho?*" he asked. I sensed him wondering if he was being entrapped. He relented. "Aight. Aight. I've been watchin' that bitch."

"Hey—"

"Sorry, bruh. Didn't mean nuthin'."

"Where's Ro?"

"At home, I guess."

"He ain't with you?" Aaron was reckless. I needed Ro. He would get things done.

"No," he huffed. "And I don't need him for this. I caught this dude leaving Amelia's crib. Gonna take care of him real soon."

"You sure she with a nigga?" Jason North's taunts came roaring back.

"Yeah. She was. Saw him leavin' her apartment. Spent the night." He offered further, "Must be hittin' that right."

I banged the cell against my head, enraged at the images conjured up by Aaron's words.

When I placed the phone back to my ear, Aaron was speaking. "Bodie? Still want me to get Ro? He tryin' to clean up. All saved 'n' shit."

"No. You're right. You don't need Ro for this. Fuck that nigga up. Take care of him."

Aaron cackled as if we were back at the pawnshop. "He just got took."

The CO who had provided me with the burner cleared his throat. In response, I immediately threw the phone down and kicked it over to him. He was just retrieving it off the gym floor when CO Arnold entered.

"What you doin' in here, Bodie?" she asked me rather than her subordinate. He was still playing it off as if tying his shoes. I watched the burner slide up his pant leg before I spoke.

"I was about to shoot some hoops."

"Without a basketball?"

"That's why I've been waiting for you. I thought that's what you were bringing. Balls."

"Keep testing me, *Antoine*. And I'll make sure you don't see your visitor."

"Visitor?"

"Got you attention, didn't I?"

Arnold personally escorted me to visitation, ignoring my questions along the way. True to form, she delighted in my misery. By the time I entered the room, I was thoroughly frustrated.

My visitor, who had sat demurely in wait for me, calmly rose from her chair.

I gasped in disbelief. "Baby?"

"Hello, Bodie," Amelia answered.

40

AMELIA

I lied. "I have to work late."

Ike paused. "That's cool. Looks like I will too."

That made me feel a little less guilty. Like going to hell at twenty miles per hour instead of fifty.

"So maybe we can hook up tomorrow?"

"Can't wait to see you again," he remarked.

I lied.

But it's for a good cause, I told myself.

If things went accordingly, it would be the second and final lie that would leave my lips for Ike's ears. I could think of better things escaping my lips when it came to him. I pulled into the parking lot of the Shop N Go for gas and directions to the new prison. I hadn't seen Bodie since he was at Huntsville and frankly I was scared. Before I exited my car, I checked myself in the rearview mirror. For visitation, I was dressed very conservative—one of the few interview suits I owned. Never interviewed much for jobs. Singing and Bodie were my life. Unfortunately, that wasn't necessarily the order.

I played with a stray curl, needlessly concerned with how it looked. It shouldn't matter, but there I was. Thinking about Ike yet making sure I looked pretty for Bodie. Some jacked-up shit.

I'm not that girl, I voiced as convincingly as I could before going inside to prepay.

* * *

In that moment that I saw him, I hated that I stuck around. As fatigued as he seemed, his eyes radiated determination. He was ruggedly handsome in his white uniform despite whatever he'd been subjected to. I tried to block out thinking of him like that and how he used to set me afire. When he saw me, I watched those same flames ignite in him. His look was so intense that tears welled up in his eyes. I stood up from my chair, considering backing off and running away.

"Baby?"

"Hello, Bodie," I said, trying to sound as even as possible.

Despite the guard's objections, Bodie closed the distance and kissed me.

And I responded. Like a fool, I let old instincts guide me. With his arms around me, I felt the years melt away. Despite the pain and troubles he'd caused me, I was happy he was all right.

The guard, an attractive woman with a rough manner, saved me by separating us.

"Antoine," she called him. *Something no one called Bodie.* "Want me to cut this short? 'Cause I'll end this right now." I glanced at her longer as she smacked her lips and rolled her eyes at him. Bodie cut her down with his own stare. I could only imagine how hard things must be on the inside. Bodie always had a healthy sex drive. I wondered if he had thought about her in that way. Or had been with her. I quickly shook off those unhealthy concerns.

As I resumed my seat and Bodie took his, it was the guard's turn to size me up. The smile she gave was one of recognition. *Can't be,* I thought. I'd never met her before. She didn't strike me as the type to eat at Mirage either. She walked over to another guard, leaving me to guess.

"I knew it," Bodie smugly admitted. "You're still my heart." He rested his hand on his chest and held it there.

"Bodie—"

"I know. It's hard, baby. Relax. Just let me look at you for a second." The second felt like hours. That curl, out of place earlier, felt enormous. My lips suddenly felt dry. I fidgeted in my chair. Finishing his assessment, he stated, "You've changed."

"Yes. I have. I'm not that girl," I reaffirmed more for my benefit than his.

"It fits you. I hope you got another picture for me. You're finer than before."

"Thank you," I answered, uncomfortable with his compliment. "How are they treating you?"

"You know I don't talk about that shit."

"I'd forgotten."

"Anything else you forgot?"

"Like?"

"You been singin' again."

"Just a little. Nothing important."

"That's not what I hear," he scowled. There was more there than he was saying. Bodie. Always with his secrets. I couldn't talk though.

"I didn't come to argue. I came to be civil," I said like I'd rehearsed.

"*Civil?* You sound like my do-nothin' lawyer. How you gonna be singin' and not tell me about it? Huh? We had plans, baby. Now I gotta find out like I'm a nobody. It's Natalia, huh? She told you to shut me out."

"Look. I didn't come here to talk about singing. And Natalia had nothing to do with it."

"Then who did?" he inquired, his fingers thumping on the table with each word.

"Sharin' all your joy with somebody else? Somebody new?" he accused.

"You don't have any right to go there," I shot back. Anger replacing the other confused feelings I'd been swept up in.

"I go where I want. When I want." He didn't blink. If not for these walls surrounding us and the guards that lined them, I would've believed him.

"Bodie, why you gotta be like that?" I pleaded. "This isn't how this was supposed to go."

"Things is crazy out there, Amelia," he said apologetically. The way his tone kept changing was unnatural. It was like he was under duress. "You need me."

"No. I don't. And I'll be fine. That's why I came—"

"Look. Just hear me out. Okay?"

I paused.

"I know some people that can help you . . . and me. I can look out for you."

"I don't need you looking out, Bodie. I'm not that girl," I recited again.

"Bullshit. You call yourself seein' someone? You know you're my girl. Ain't no one else havin' you."

"Okay. Now this is getting crazy. I ain't your property, Bodie. You need to quit with the meaningless threats and move on."

He smiled. Cold. "Meaningless? You act like you don't know me no more."

I bit my lip to keep it from shuddering. A deep breath soothed me before I summed it up. "It doesn't matter. It's been over. It *is* over. I just needed to tell you to your face so I can get on with things . . . permanently."

He shook his head, mumbling to himself, "Don't do this. You don't mean it."

"I wish you well, Bodie." I began to push my chair away from the table.

"On-Phire Records has a deal on the table . . . for you. Right now," he blurted out.

I froze. Then it was my turn to lose it. "Never. I'd have to be crazy to fool with them. First, Natalia's buggin' on the radio. Now you? Lord, what is wrong with people? They got to you? In here?"

"Baby, it ain't like that. North 'n' 'em can do things for me. I can be there to make sure everything's on the up and up. Like old times."

" 'Old times,' " I parroted just so I would hear it. My eyes became misty. "I remember the old times. I remember watching your arrest on TV. Watched the cops slam you down. Watched your trial from the back of the courtroom. I've seen too much, Bodie. My eyes are tired. My heart is tired. *This*"—I motioned at the space that separated us— "this is tired. I can't breathe your air anymore."

"Imma make you forget all of this. I can make it work with North. I'm gonna get it right this time. You. Me. We're gonna be on top of the world."

"You still don't listen. I just came to say goodbye."

"Say it then," he challenged. "And try to mean it."

I'm not that girl.

My mouth froze, but my body didn't. The young Amelia stayed, but the woman I was going to be from this point forward chose to leave. As hard as it was coming here, it was harder turning my back on him and walking out. Bodie was too tough to break down, despite whatever turmoil he was in. He just sat there and watched me. Silent. Always my rock.

Funny thing about rocks is, they can wear you down. They can also be used to kill.

As I sped away from the prison, I wept uncontrollably. I needed Ike's comfort. I wanted to see him, but he was working. Like I was *supposed* to be.

My cell phone rang. I almost ignored it, but pulled over to answer it. Maybe it was Ike with a surprise. Maybe he'd gotten off work early.

I cleared my throat, then spoke. The voice on the other end was frantic.

"What happened to him?" I asked for clarity.

They told me. Again. The panic began spreading to me.

"No. No. I'll be right there," I said, frantically speeding off to Memorial Hermann Hospital.

Later, I would recall it.

Something Bodie said back at the prison was secreted away in my subconscious. *"Meaningless? You act like you don't know me no more,"* Bodie had uttered.

41

IKE

I didn't have to pull the double shift like I thought. Arnold was fucking with me. I wanted to share that with Amelia, but she had to work. Not quite sure where I was going when I left the prison, except to put as much distance between myself and that place as possible. Things were escalating. Bodie. The other COs knowing about me and Amelia. Things were way beyond my control.

I stopped at the Shop N Go to double-check the water hose on my truck. I was determined not to have a repeat. As I raised my hood, I saw a car like Amelia's at the gas pump. She was nowhere around here, thank God. Guilt and paranoia were my new buddies. The driver must have been inside paying, so I put my mind back on the inspection. After checking the hose and ensuring I'd put it on correctly, I left.

As I was on the north side of town, I did something reckless. I did what had become so natural to me when my shift was over. I went home.

In and out, I told myself. Just a quick stop to get my stuff and I'd be on my way. Now if Marshall was there, I'd just come back at another time. Deryn was his. At least until his wife found out along with the rest of Houston. I'd be a liar if I said I wasn't curious how Deryn was handling things. Curious is different from caring.

Deryn's car was in the driveway looking like she hadn't gone anywhere. She had said she'd be home. I parked behind her and cautiously exited. When my truck was running, I thought I'd heard something. I ignored it and paid the price when I opened the door. Just before the impact with my stomach, I heard the sounds of feet running across the grass toward me.

"Oomph!"

I let out a gust of wind as the shoulder drove into my gut. I fell back inside the cab of my truck and braced myself.

"Sorry," stated my assailant. A heavyset kid I remembered from the neighborhood. The football pass meant for him had landed in the bed of my truck. Of course, he missed it and found me instead. My uniform frightened him. He probably thought I was a po-po. His friend stayed across the street, free of the confrontation.

"It's aight, little man," I said to the boy already over half my size and at least my weight. Reaching in back of my truck, I fished out his football and made him "go deep." He caught this one even though I threw it wobbly. It gave me a brief smile before I went back to the mission at hand.

Without me knocking, Deryn opened the door. She'd been watching from the window.

"What did they want?" she asked instead of greeting me. She wore those damn Burberry pj's that I hated. Definitely hadn't been to work. In spite of her attire, her face was flawless. Weeks ago, this would've been a welcome sight. Of course, she was never home for me.

"Just having fun. Throwing the football around," I answered.

"Oh," she said, accompanied by a smack of her glossy lips. "They hit the house with that damn ball earlier."

"Must've messed up your nap," I offered with a false smile. "Sick?" I asked, acting ignorant to her recent troubles.

"You could say that. It's good to see you."

"Where's my stuff?" I said coolly. I closed the door, adding to the chill.

"No hug?"

"You're buggin'. Besides . . . I might catch something."

"You sure came by quick." She avoided the bait. If I came looking for a confrontation, it looked like I was going to lose out. "I thought it would be weeks before I saw you."

"Or maybe never," I sighed, surveying the home that was once mine. My eyes scanned for traces of Marshall. "I suddenly had some time on my hands. Now where's the rest of my stuff?"

"Upstairs."

I paused to look her in the eye. The garbage can outside would be pure Deryn.

"I didn't have time to do anything with it," she admitted with a shrug.

I looked in the direction of the stairwell. Remembered our last encounter there. "Is it okay to go up and get my shit? Since this is *your house.*"

"Yes. And in case you're wondering, nobody's up there. Marshall and I are through."

"Hey. None of my business." I shrugged smugly before bounding up the stairs. Pretending was hard, but I gave it my best.

The bed we used to sleep in was perfectly made, not a wrinkle atop the comforter. I wondered if Deryn had even slept on it. No time to dwell on the unimportant, I grabbed the remainder of my clothes from the closet. Having more than I thought, I placed the bundle on the bed. She always could make it back up. Having time to think, I remembered the work gear I'd stored beneath the bed. I got down on my knees and began pulling items free.

"Deryn! Got any boxes or garbage bags?" I yelled to her downstairs.

"No," she calmly answered from just on the other side of the bed. I was startled that she would follow me up. I peered at her over the top of the mattress, then returned to my scavenging.

"Into singers now?"

Damn. I didn't know so many people read the newspaper. Maybe they just looked at the pictures. I put the remainder of my things on her bed and stood up. "I'm not discussing my private life with you."

"Does she know you're broke?"

"Money isn't everything to some people. You're pretty pathetic. You know that, right? I could laugh, but for some reason I don't feel like it. Oh. I know why. 'Cause I don't give a fuck anymore."

Deryn smiled. Her manicured feet glided across the carpet to my side of the bed. That familiar look of trouble was there, but somehow softened.

"That's not it, Isaac. It's because you still care for me."

"And why would I?"

"Because it's too soon for you to be over me." She rested the palms of her hands on my chest. "I hurt you," she proclaimed, "but I still have feelings for you."

"You got some nerve saying that. With the taste of another man's dick fresh on your breath?" The laugh finally came out. "I might be into singers, but I never know I was living with a TV star."

I expected a slap, but she kept her hands on me. I felt her fingers tense. Then she spoke. "A reality show. She called a damn reality TV show. He never should've brought that hag over from Yugoslavia. That Eurobitch loves drama." She shook her head. "And you saw it?"

"Yeah. I saw that shit. I'm embarrassed to admit it," I said as I moved her hands off me. I began looking for something in the room to carry my stuff out. Deryn let out an odd, evil laugh. Totally out of place. I looked to make sure she didn't have a knife.

"Did it turn you on?" she asked.

"Huh?" I asked, slammed by her question. I know I didn't hear her right.

"While you were with that girl. Did it turn you on? The paper says her name is Amelia. Did you think of me while you fucked Amelia? I'll bet you fucked her good with that big black dick. *Was I on your mind, Daddy?* Were you really fucking me?"

Now she was scaring me. "You made your choice. Now I made mine. I'm through with you."

"No, you're not. You want to do to me what Marshall's done. You want to be sure this ass is yours and not his. Don't you, Daddy?"

"I came just to get my shit and leave."

Deryn backed up against me. Her tight, round behind playfully bumped against me. "You came to get your shit and leave," she said as she teased, lowering her pajama bottoms, revealing the crack of her ass. "Well get this shit, Daddy. Then you can leave."

"Deryn. Stop."

I placed my hands on her waist to push her winding ass away. At my touch, she straightened up, moving her body even closer to mine. We came in contact. My face, my lips were near her ear . . . her neck. She took my hands, wrapping them firmly around her waist. I didn't let go. I hated her, but didn't let go. Her body smelled of perfume and oils. Like how she used to surprise me in college. "Mmm. I missed this," she purred. "And I'm going to make everything all better."

"This ain't going down," I said as my dick rose in defiance.

"Yes. It is," she serenaded, having already worked herself up to near climax from the grind. I had slid her pajama bottoms down a little more and began raising her top. "We can talk about how you feel later."

"You want this dick that bad?" I asked, my voice wavering as her moist, sticky scent filled the room. My nostrils flared as I inhaled her unholy essence. Her top was on the floor. How I hated those pajamas. I felt her breasts, tense and swollen to the touch. I pinched her blistered nipples.

"Uh-huh," she grunted. "Yes. Marshall couldn't fill this up like you do, baby. I'm a dirty little girl and I want you to fuck me. Fuck me in my ass, Daddy."

Deryn knocked all of my stuff off the bed and bent across it, spreading her ass cheeks.

I debated, holding my belt buckle.

Before obliging her like a fool.

I quickly undid my pants, dropping them and my drawers before entering her just like she liked it.

Deryn let out a primal scream as my swollen dick bored into her. I drove her into the bed with the force of my thrusting pelvis. The mattress muffled the passion and profanity escaping her lips.

42

BODIE

I silently went about my job, unloading the loads of clothes from the dryer. To avoid another trip to solitary, I bottled up my rage. Some nigga had messed with Amelia's head and sent her in to do the same with me. The girl I knew wouldn't have said those things after all our history. Now more than ever, I needed to be free. If Aaron did what he was supposed to, I would have one less problem to deal with.

"Campbell!" the CO/talent scout yelled over the hissing of the pipes. He motioned me over. I wiped the sweat off my brow and rolled the basket out of the way.

"Got something from North?" I asked, hopeful of new developments with my case.

He chuckled although I couldn't hear him. "North got a note for you." He had been watching me with a newspaper folded under his arm. He continued overseeing the laundry as he slipped the paper into my hands.

Scribbled in pen were some comments in what I guessed to be North's handwriting.

> *Looks like your reputation is at stake. You've promised something, but maybe I should be talking to someone who can deliver. Someone getting closer to your little songbird? Take care of it, Mr. Campbell.*

I threw the "note" back at North's flunky. "North's late," I replied. "I got this taken care of. Whoever the fool is, he won't be a problem."

He put the paper back in my hand. "You sure?" he asked snidely. "I saw him on the last shift. He looked healthy to me."

"Shift? Who the fuck are you talkin' about?"

"Read the paper, man."

"I just did."

"Over," he motioned with his finger. I flipped the paper over to the side opposite North's note.

And saw Amelia's photo. I fixed on her image. Beautiful and full of life. That glow I hadn't seen during her visit.

"I didn't know that was yours. Nice piece of—"

"Winters . . ." I grimaced, finally looking at the face of the man beside Amelia, as if it would suddenly change. "Winters," I said as the air rushed out of me. I now realized how much I'd been played. "Fuckin' Winters."

I kicked a laundry bin over, then began hurling whatever I could get my hands on. The COs ordered me to stop, but I refused to listen. Eventually, they wrestled me to the ground and piled on top.

Imma kill him, I thought repeatedly, blanking out everything around me. Winters was dead.

43

AMELIA

I ran down the hall when I saw her. She looked like she had been crying. So unlike her. She gave me a hug.

"Thank you for coming so fast."

"What happened?" I asked.

"I don't know," Tookie replied. "They brought him here by ambulance. Montez' family is in there now. He hasn't been too coherent. He'd said your name, so I figured I'd call you."

"Me?"

"Yeah. He mumbled your name when he came to. Know anything about that?"

"No," I said, thinking back to Montez' visit at my apartment. "I don't know why he'd mention me." Tookie didn't need to be bothered with Montez' attempted indiscretion.

"Probably the painkillers," she said, relaxing the accusing stance she'd taken. "I don't know why somebody would do this to him."

"Will he be okay?"

Tookie shook her head. A nervous laugh came out. "They don't know. His leg is broken. His eye is messed up too. His scholarship is probably gone. That was his life."

"Do the police know how this happened?"

"Somebody beat his ass. What do you think?"

"Sorry. I didn't mean . . . Today's been terrible. Even before this."

"It's okay, girl. I'm just losin' my ever-lovin' mind. I shouldn't have called you. This ain't your problem."

"I don't mind," I reassured her. "Did they catch the people who did this?"

"No," she sighed heavily. "And if I knew who did this, they wouldn't have to. I'd bust a cap in them myself. I didn't think Montez was fuckin' anybody else, but I guess I was wrong. I usually can tell."

"Why would you say that? I mean . . . y'all two don't have a 'normal' relationship, but he didn't strike me as the type to be out there. You had him wrapped around your finger."

"You mean other than what happened with the three of us," she teased. "Yeah. I'd agree if they hadn't done what they did."

"Maybe it was just an argument or something. Maybe somebody—"

Tookie cut me off. "Amelia, you didn't see him. They stomped on him, kicked him between his legs over and over. Once the swelling goes down, the doctor said they might have to remove one of his nuts. A man doesn't beat another man like that unless it's over some young thang's kitty kat."

I shuddered at the imagery, starry-eyed from Tookie's revelation. "I'm so sorry."

"Don't be. You didn't have anything to do with it. Go home. You don't want to see him like this," she muttered. "I'm going to check on him again. I probably won't be in to work tomorrow."

I was waiting on the elevator when I ran into my cousin Me-Me. She held her little boy, J. R., at her side. The big man, Neal, was with her. I used to believe the baby was his until Tookie filled me in. She'd had a baby for a man who wasn't there for whatever reasons.

Reasons.

We all had ours.

Sometimes it was hard to tell when a reason was nothing more than an excuse. My visit with Bodie was a proof positive.

"Hey, cuz."

"Hey, yourself," Me-Me said, putting J. R. down so he could walk. He rubbed his eyes as he looked up at me. I smiled at him. "How is my girl? She said her boyfriend was beaten."

"Yeah. I just talked with her. Horrible what they did to him. Animals." As I spoke those words, my mind was working on something. Something I didn't want to face.

"Amelia, you're about to leave?"

"Yes," I sighed. "What a day."

Me-Me sized me up.

Knowing her too well for just a friend, Neal stepped in. "I'll take J. R. by the cafeteria. Maybe find some ice cream." Ice cream for them and an uncomfortable air for me and my cousin.

"C'mon. I'll ride down with you," Me-Me said.

I counted the numbers as they lit, then went out.

"Did you know this guy Montez?"

"Yes."

"When she called me, Tookie said he spoke your name."

"She told me, but I don't know why he did."

"I guess she's looking for anything to help. That's all."

"Anything?"

"Yeah."

The elevator stopped. I waited for someone to board when the doors opened, but nobody got on. "He came by my place. Yesterday," I volunteered as the door closed again.

"Montez?"

"Yeah. Please don't tell Tookie," I said, turning to grab her shoulders.

"Why? Something happen?"

"No . . . yes. I mean. He . . . he came by looking for something."

"*That?*" she quizzed with a motion of her finger poking through the circle created by her other hand.

"Yeah. I got him to leave though. Nothing happened, but I can't tell her. I feel like I did something when I didn't."

"Because of what happened to him?"

"That doesn't help. And his saying my name makes me feel worse. It's like he accusing me."

"Are you sure you don't know who did this to him? I mean . . . Tookie is a sweetheart. And it sounds like this boy got much worse than he deserved."

The elevator door opened.

"I need to go," I blurted out in an effort to alleviate the tension and unspoken accusations. I rushed free into the lobby.

Me-Me stayed on, prepared to rejoin them on the fifth floor. "Cuz?"

"Yes," I said, looking back.

"You still holding out for that Bodie dude?"

"No. I've moved on."

"Good" was all she uttered.

I watched the elevator doors shut.

44

IKE

We lay there atop the comforter. On what used to be our bed. Deryn's breathing was still labored as her nude body sought to regain its rhythm. Hair wild atop her head, basking in the fading glow of our encounter, she seemed content. It was a painful reminder that I'd fucked up. A leftover from the throes of misplaced passion and perhaps a touch of pity.

She wanted to cuddle under the covers like "very old times." Perhaps more. I declined. To have gotten under the sheets would've indicated comfort and acceptance. I was no longer comfortable with her and would never accept what she'd done to me. This sex hadn't been about that. It was a fight for dominance. It was about frustration and rage. Our bodies were the weapons in a war where words and reason made no sense.

Hate sex.

Most times, sex like that will curl your toes, have you dancing like an employed James Evans from *Good Times*.

I just felt "off."

"You okay?" I asked to fill the void.

"Yeah, Daddy. That was the bomb," she pushed out in a fading breath. "How about you? How do you feel, Isaac?"

I sighed. "Can't you just call me Ike for once? You've always made everything between us seem like a transaction."

Deryn rolled over, breasts on display like fresh melons at an out-door market. "I'm sorry, Ike," she said, sending hell into a deep freeze. "And I'm sorry I put you through all of this." Hell would never thaw.

"Why couldn't you have done little things like that before?"

"I feel way too good to fight. I know things have been shitty lately, but we had good times before. Maybe this is another chance."

"There won't be another chance," I shot off. "And if Marshall's wife hadn't 'busted' you—*pun intended*—you'd probably be the same old Deryn right now."

"You know this girl is only a poor replacement for me," Deryn proclaimed with a chuckle. "Sure I messed up with this whole Mar-shall thing, but me and you have too much history. She can't compete with that. Everything you find yourself doing now is because of me. What is she, a millionaire? If I hadn't pushed you over the years, made you strive for more, you wouldn't have dared reach out to someone like her."

"Like her? You don't even know her."

"True. But I know you," she voiced. "You didn't have it in you."

I sat up in the bed, noticing the stuff I'd come to pick up. "You're right," I softly muttered.

"Mmm-hmm," Deryn mumbled. "Now let me take *that girl* off your mind."

"Thank you."

"No thanks necessary, Ike," she said triumphantly. She pulled me to her, another act to seal her delusion of victory. I resisted, moving off the bed to retrieve my clothes.

"No. You don't understand," I said, gazing intently into the eyes of the woman I once loved. "Thank you for preparing me for the right woman once she came along. Amelia ain't no millionaire, but it doesn't matter to her that I'm not either. She makes me want to do more without trying. No put-downs. The way things were between me and you really showed me how much better things can be. And that I was stupid for coming here."

Deryn rose to her knees, stunned. "You're not serious, Isaac."

"Yes," I uttered. "Isaac is serious."

I finished putting my uniform back on, gathered the last of my stuff and left.

45

BODIE

The knee ground into my back, making me wince in pain.

"Get the fuck off me!" I yelled as the three COs stationed in the laundry worked me over. I got to one knee before being forced back down from a crack to my head. The one who'd set me off took that time to hide the newspaper message he'd delivered.

"Yo, this motherfucker's crazy," one of them voiced to his buddies. He was enjoying beating my ass the most. The other inmates stayed away, looking out for their best interests.

"Wait," North's scout pled, finally getting involved. "I just gave him some bad news about his mother. He'll be okay." Unsure if we'd been seen, he figured to cover his bought-and-paid-for ass.

The eager one wasn't sure if he bought it. "That true, Bodie? You gonna be okay?" he asked, applying more pressure on my back.

From my busted lip, I started to say something. Instead, I glared at the messenger. His eyes pled with me to keep my mouth shut. I spit blood onto the floor at his feet. "Yeah."

"I can't hear you."

"I said I'm fine. My head was messed up. I'm okay now." I looked beyond the pain, relaxing my muscles. A little while longer and they decided to let me up. They wore the uniforms, but my hate had to be saved for another. Winters was going to receive it all.

I was escorted back to my cell, trying to hide my new limp.

"You made the right move by keeping your mouth shut."

"I ain't no snitch. I'm good for that," I said, its deeper meaning escaping him. "I need something from you though."

"What? A conjugal visit?"

"Nah. If North does his shit, I won't need that. Wouldn't do her in here no way."

"Winters would," he laughed before clearing his throat. Escorting me back to my cell, he didn't have the other three to watch his back as close. "Uh . . . what you want?"

"The picture . . . from the paper."

"I can't do that. North said—"

"I don't want North's note. Just the picture. You can throw the rest away for all I care."

He hesitated, probably weighing all his options. Figuring it could do him no harm, he tore off the photo and handed it over. I didn't thank him.

"Just my opinion, but Winters crossed the line," he said.

"So you're saying you wouldn't fuck her?"

"No. I didn't say all that," he said, all flustered. "It's just that—"

"I gotcha. I gotcha. Know how long Winters been seeing my woman?"

"I don't know shit other than this picture. From their look, I'd say a while."

In my cell, I sat and stared intently at the picture, analyzing every detail. The closeness of their bodies. How Winters' hand caressed Amelia. The acceptance in her eyes, of wanting him near her. I agreed with North's CO. Winters was fucking her. Had been for a long time. Now I knew why Amelia had made herself unavailable to me. My CO . . . my fucking guard was filling that void. I imagined how he must've been dying of laughter inside whenever I would speak of her and what she meant to me. Acting uninterested, all the while stroking those thighs, touching those lips.

To go so far as to act halfway decent with me. That was the worst part.

It was all a fuckin' joke.

"Did Amelia know?" I asked myself.

She couldn't.

She wouldn't.

I ripped the rest of the picture away from those two. *Fuck Natalia's schemin' ass,* I thought as her image was torn away. She was as unimportant as these bars. Just another fake barrier between me and Amelia. Either one I could reach past.

"You tearin' out coupons, motherfucker?" Rewind chuckled from his top bunk. His high ass had just woken up. He was looking to fuck with me. "What they got on sale?"

I ignored the ignorance and tore the final strip.

"Nigga, I know you can hear me."

"Not now, man."

I made the final tear. The most symbolic.

"Bodie got coupons. Nigga hiding coupons like an old lady," he teased incoherently, mind clouded from whatever he was using to get by today. Rewind had been hitting that shit more and more.

I continued ignoring him, his taunts becoming unbearable. Intolerable.

He grumbled, hanging farther over his bunk for a better view over my shoulder. "Heeeey, a new picture! That's that same bitch you always crying over? Let me see."

He stretched, his hand flailing in my direction.

I reached up, grasping his wrist, and yanked him to the floor. Rewind hit hard, his body making a strange clapping sound on the concrete. I stood up, calmly walking over. He was barely conscious when I punched him once in the face.

He quit moving and went silent.

Rewind once more asleep, I returned to my bunk, lay down and resumed my thoughts of love and war.

46

AMELIA

"Whoa." Across the square table from me, Ike swallowed a piece of his waffle, preparing to dig into the seasoned fried wings. "Somebody had it in for him."

"That's what Tookie thinks," I added. The buzz of the late-morning crowd at the Breakfast Klub shielded our conversation. The freedom of kept secrets. I'd called Ike to meet me midtown before I went to work. Just across the Eastex Freeway, it wasn't far from his place. Although my catfish and grits were excellent, I wasn't as interested in that as in being near him.

Bodie had an ability to turn me upside down so easily. In such a short time, Ike had become my center, my balance. I needed his presence to reassure me in light of my lapses in judgment.

"You know he liked you." Ike picked up a piece of chicken, almost as if it offered him refuge from something. Definitely a little "off" today. I couldn't talk.

"Montez? No, I didn't know," I pretended.

"SkyBar. He was tryin' to push up on you. Fellas pick up on that stuff."

"Oh. That," I mumbled, forgetting he had caught part of Montez' display that night. "He was just a little drunk."

"Uh-huh. And horny."

"Like you?" I teased.

"Sometimes." Not the reaction I wanted. Instead, he flashed a troubled look.

"How's work? How was your double shift?"

"Shitty." That plate of food was his escape again. As he cut another piece of waffle with his fork, it was the most important thing on Earth. It held his focus instead of me. "And yours?"

"Rough," I acknowledged, keeping to myself what I'd really done that day.

He sensed the difficulty in my voice. Finally, he pulled himself back to me. "Anything you want to talk about?"

"I'm not sure." Debating over bringing up Bodie, I ran instead. A man hates a woman with issues. I was assembling a volume. "I think I just want to move on."

"Your ex?" he asked, bold enough to broach the subject. I was his plate of food now.

"Yes."

"Something happen?"

I saw him in prison. Behind your back. I kissed him. Now Montez is beaten and I hope Bodie has nothing to do with it. And if I brought up Montez, did I admit the threesome I was in?

"No," I answered. "And nothing ever will."

"That's good to know. I don't want to lose you. Ever."

"Damn, boy. You're not holding back, are you?"

"Just getting that off my chest," he commented, conviction expressed across his face.

"Any surprises with you or your ex? My car's cheap, but I don't want it keyed. I'm not one for drama . . . or at least not other people's drama."

"No." He wiped his mouth. "I've moved on. I had some feelings, but that's all behind me. No doubt."

"That makes me happy. Because I don't want to lose you either." I cast a wink his way. Toyed with his arm over the table. "Nothing to come between us?"

"Nothing," he dedicated across my heart, hope to live. His fingers intertwined with mine.

"Prove it." I cast a devilish gleam at him, squeezed his hand for emphasis.

"Now?"

"Yes." I licked my lips.

"Don't you have to be to work?"

"Mmm-hmm. Guess you better hurry."

Ike fished out the money for a tip.

We'd found a Chevron gas station with an empty lady's room just down Alabama Street. I entered first and he quickly followed. Now his jeans rested around his ankles and my panty hose dangled off one foot. My work skirt was scrunched between our grinding bodies, Ike's bare ass working overtime to take me *there*—that magical land where the right person and right lovin' come together.

"What took you so long?" I sang. My head sailed against the mirror as he hit my spot. My hips hopped closer to the edge, greedily swallowing more of him.

"I bought a lottery ticket." My bra hung open as he slid my shirt off my shoulders. As he took my wanting breast in his mouth, all speech ceased.

I panted in his ear, almost in tears as Ike slid inside. Atop the bathroom sink, I steadied myself with my thighs as his swollen dick entered, exited and reentered. My pussy flowed as his head sought refuge. He repeated this again and again, making me beg for him not to stop. He pressed his hand against the small of my back as he went deeper with each probe. Outside, somebody tugged in vain on the locked door.

He ran his fingers wildly through my hair, sending chills from my scalp down my spine.

"Oh shit, oh shit, oh shit." We were in a steady rhythm, the clapping of our bodies echoing in the small space. Someone tugged on the door again.

"That's it, Ike. Make me cum," I urged, turned on even more.

I pulled his head closer, our mouths finally joining. I filled his with my tongue. He sucked it.

The sink began to give, pulling partially out the wall from our weight. I fell toward Ike. He caught me, cradling his arms under my legs and lifting me into the air. Surprised, I let out a shriek, gripping his powerful shoulders for support.

"Don't worry. I gotcha."

And I knew he meant it.

Every which way.

At ease, I took all of him in me, slapping my ass against his thighs. He held me steady in the middle of the floor, finding the strength to come stronger. Deeper. I couldn't take it anymore. He looked me in my eyes.

"I love you, Amelia."

"I . . . I love you too."

I spread my hips, savoring every last inch until we climaxed together.

47

IKE

Tensions were high on the cell block. One death and several beatings overnight had put everything on lockdown. Things like this came in spurts. We could've been victims of averages or maybe Arnold's shit was just crashing down. On her watch, some COs had transferred to other facilities. Others had left in search of different opportunities. After months of smooth sailing, things were now unraveling.

And I was walking into it.

"Close four!" I yelled over the rampant yelling and catcalls throughout the block.

I wasn't the lead as we went cell by cell, but had to be ready. I adjusted my riot gear and took a deep breath. Whatever awaited me in the next cell, I had to man up.

"You aight, Winters?"

"Yeah. Let's do this."

The lead CO looked at me again. "If your head ain't here, let a brother know."

"Open five!" I yelled in response.

The bars clanked as the opening widened before us. The sole figure inside the tiny cell didn't move. Just lay deathly still in his bunk. A stark contrast to the rest.

"Rise and shine, Antoine," the lead officer prodded. I watched

Bodie slowly rise, conflicted about whether I wanted to break his neck or apologize for an honest mistake. But it wasn't honest anymore.

I wasn't honest.

And it was no mistake that I loved Amelia.

"Step to the side, Antoine. You know the drill."

It seemed hard for Bodie to focus, like either he was high or hadn't slept at all. He stepped away from his bunk.

"Back the fuck up," the lead instructed. "I ain't Rewind. You ain't breakin' my arm." The other CO laughed. Bodie didn't. The two of us moved in, anticipating a blowup.

"Rewind fell. He already told you that shit."

"Think that's what Rewind said?" he asked, goading Bodie. My hands tightened on the baton I held.

"Man, fuck you. I know that's what Rewind said. Otherwise, you'd have me in solitary. Rewind ain't a bitch."

Bodie turned and glared dead at me. He knew. The fresh fire that burned in his eyes killed all doubt. He continued.

"A bitch is a nigga that would smile in your face while fuckin' your girl. A bitch is a motherfucker that lies to a nigga, then stabs them in the back." He spit in my direction. There was no truce. I was the oppressor, his enemy.

I rushed the cell, claiming Bodie's tiny space as my own. The lead CO sidestepped to avoid being knocked over. We were looking eye to eye for the first time. "Got something on your mind? Something you wanna get off your chest, Antoine?"

"I should be askin' you, bitch." He didn't back down.

Neither did I.

Rather than using the baton, I rammed Bodie. He was forced backward, slamming into the cold concrete of the cell wall. He grimaced in pain. "I'm the last motherfucker you should be fuckin' with right now, Bodie," I said in his ear as he doubled over.

My team quickly broke things up, separating the two of us. Their amusement was apparent from the laughs they held in check, the smirks on their faces. They knew too. My life was a spectacle. Things didn't stay a secret long in here.

As I was forced to cool off, Bodie spoke. "What else can you do to me, boss?"

"You don't wanna know," I shouted over the lead CO, now trying to calm me. The other one wrapped up the search, rummaging through the rest of Bodie's things as quickly as possible. A piece of paper sailed harmlessly onto the floor. My eyes followed it as I ignored everything else being said. It was me and Amelia's photo again. Except my head was missing.

"It's clean. Let's go." He picked up the baton I'd dropped and threw it to me.

As we all cleared the cell, Bodie picked his photo from the floor. Cradling it, he smiled at me. More like an ice pick than something of warmth.

She's mine, his lips formed.

"Close five!"

Things had changed.

48

BODIE

"What it do, Bodie?"

"Aight, man." No contact allowed, we took our seats.

Aaron surprised me with his visit. He was heavier than I remembered, but still the same crazy motherfucker. As nervous as he was of prisons, he looked downright cheerful.

"I done good. Done right by ya."

"That's not what I hear," I mumbled, controlling my anger at his ass. Either he was a liar or stupid. Or both.

"I ain't been able to get in touch with ya. Nobody takin' my calls around here. What's up with that?"

"COs scared. Stuff been serious up in here this week."

"That's why I'm up here now."

"Good news?"

"Fuck yeah! I've been takin' care of that Lac fer ya. Remember that dude wantin' to buy it? He gone now. Don't think he liked the price, pawdnuh," Aaron boasted in his usual drawl. He flashed a mouthful of teeth, proud of his work.

"Why you gotta lie, man?"

"Huh? I ain't lyin', man. I took care of that. Best believe."

"Well, your stupid ass didn't do a good job."

"Nah, man. I know what I saw."

"And I know what I saw."

Aaron was going to say something else, but he was distracted. Rewind walked by, on his way to another table. The fresh blue cast on his arm stood out against the white of his shirt. The two of them stared each other down. Aaron usually would've got up in his face, but he remembered his surroundings. Rather than scowl or say something smart, Rewind just smiled. He kept cheesin' until he sat with his visitor.

"Why that motherfucker smilin' at me?" Aaron asked, still wary of Rewind. "He gay?"

"Nah, man. That's my celly. Quit worrying about him and start worrying about me."

"Bruh, I'm tellin' you what I did."

"Well, you did it to the wrong nigga."

He laughed. His hands nervously moved back and forth across the table. "Can't be. That's the nigga I saw with Amelia. I ain't crazy. Fucked him up myself. Left him in tears." He'd carelessly dropped all code, rambling loud enough for others to hear. I motioned for him to shut up.

"You fucked up. Straight up."

"No way. I got the right dude. Maybe Amelia's seeing two mother—"

"Amelia ain't like that, so just watch your mouth. I knew Ro shoulda been in on this."

"Ro don't need to be involved. I know what I'm doing. I'll—"

"Forget about it. I'll handle it myself."

Aaron seemed to shrink in his chair. The table, the whole room was swallowing him. My words were casting doubt on his actions. "Tell me who it is. And I'll do it. Right."

I just watched him before I spoke. "If I need something, I'll holler."

I pulled away from the table and left Aaron.

No North.

No Aaron.

I had to do it myself.

On the way back to my cell, I stopped to pick up something.

49

AMELIA

"Natalia! Natalia!" the place roared over and over again.

I screamed in unison with the rest of Reliant Stadium. Amid the throng of devoted fans, I was stunned at what I had witnessed. On the last number of the night, they'd gone all out. As the center stage rotated for all to see, Natalia raised her fist high above the throng of dancers. Perspiration covered them all. They had to be exhausted. As she breathed through her mouth, a piece of hair stuck across her sweaty face. The smoke from the pyrotechnics hung in the air, bathing them in a purplish haze.

Ike yelled something to me, but I couldn't hear. It was as if a thunderstorm had erupted inside. He was more amazed than me.

Owen had given us great seats for Natalia's concert, well within her view. Early in the evening, he'd disappeared to field his endless phone calls. As me and Ike stood and applauded, Natalia pointed at us. She was smiling.

Then the stadium went dark.

After the long stretch in traffic from Reliant Park, the limo delivered us to Club I-Life on Fondren for the VIP after party. The party was being hosted in Natalia's honor by Easy Al. A local basketball star in high school and college, Al was an acquaintance from back in South

Park. He played professional ball overseas, but was now famous in H-town for hosting the local Fox Sports show.

My cousin Me-Me had warned me not to trust Al, but it wasn't my party. Besides, Al hadn't done me anything and I didn't want to let my best friend down. I had my very own bodyguard with me anyway. And as our encounters had proven, Ike did a damn fine job of guarding this body.

"Wish they'd quit all this picture taking," Ike groaned, annoyed at the photographers lining the entrance to the club. Natalia had wanted some privacy and security was doing a great job of keeping them outside.

"They're just wondering who this handsome man is on my arm. Can't say I blame them. When I first saw you, I wanted to get to know you too." I snaked my arm around his and nestled closer. His manly scent was comforting. Ike fidgeted with his sport coat, probably wondering if his jeans and woven striped shirt were suitable. "And stop messing with your jacket. You look fine."

We left the photographers behind, entering the fantasy world created for one night. Black was the color of choice, the walls and furniture providing the feeling we'd just stepped into a cave. Accent lights of crimson showed the way throughout. Beside the crowd of celebrities and insiders were local well-wishers and contest winners. I overheard a few of them recognizing me from my night at Lullaby's. I cast an appreciative smile in their direction as we moved by.

"You might be more popular in here than your friend."

"I doubt it. I'm just a 'nobody' compared to her."

Ike snatched me, almost taking me out my shoes. "Nobody that's been around you thinks that and I certainly don't. Don't ever say that again."

I was unsure whether to be afraid or surprised. "Okay."

His face relaxed; the warmth returned. He kissed me in front of the onlookers. "Good."

Worming through the crowd, we stayed close to the walls. Playing on the flat screens mounted every few feet was Natalia's video for the "Call Me Caliente" remix with Fat Joe. The video trail lit the way as we moved into the next room. Guests were treated to scratching from the guest DJ from New York. As he went off on the turntables, the people on the dance floor cheered, bordered by the scantily clad women dancing in the cages perched atop each corner.

"Whose party did you say this was?"

"Him," I answered as the host of the evening approached.

"There's Miss Amelia! How ya been, baby?" the tall man said. The guy he'd been speaking to disapeared into the crowd. Easy Al wore a red suit that made him look somewhat like a devil. Probably a compliment in his book.

"Hey, Al." I gave him a kiss on his cheek. "This is my boyfriend, Ike."

"Pleased to meet you, Ike." They shook hands. "Amelia calls herself having a boyfriend now, but I remember when she and her cousin Me-Me were a bunch o' rugrats. She definitely all growed up now. Yessir." I could've sworn Al was undressing me with his eyes.

I gave Al a playful shove before things became any more creepy. "Stop it."

"So what do you think of the transformation? We worked overnight to get this place ready."

"It's wild, man," Ike chuckled.

"Wild? Sheeeeeeet. You should've seen the parties I used to throw at my crib in Sugarland. Unfortunately, those got too wild," he said, pointing to the faint scar on the cheek I'd just kissed. "Nah. Natalia's handlers told me to keep this reasonably tame. I tried."

"I just thought of something," Ike said over the loud music.

"What's that, man?"

"I don't know you, but I was wondering if you or some of your friends ever speak to kids. I have some boys at my old gym who could use a talking to."

"Sure, Ike. I know some people that would be glad to do that."

"Is Natalia here yet?" Call it intuition. I didn't feel right about Ike getting comfortable with Al.

Al shifted his attention back my way. "Yeah. I think she's doing interviews in one of the rooms. Don't worry. You'll run into her. When you feel the electricity in the air, just look around. That girl threw down tonight."

"Yes, she did."

"I hear you might join her on tour."

"Who told you that?"

"Never mind," he said coyly. "Look. Imma give your boy the grand tour. Introduce him to some Sixers and Rockets players I know. For the kids. You gonna be okay? Can y'all lovebirds handle being apart?"

"Are you okay?" Ike asked. "I can meet them another time."

I smiled. "Boy, go ahead. I'll be here."

"All right then." Al beamed. "Amelia, whatever you need, ask 'em. They know who you are in here."

After Ike and Al disappeared from my sight, I barely had time to be alone before a man said, "Long Island iced tea for the lady?"

"Yes, thank you," I said, reaching for the drink I assumed Ike or Natalia had ordered for me. When I realized the man wasn't a waiter, I dropped my hand. "Wait. Who are you? And how do you know what I drink?"

Mocha dimples, even brown eyes and an incredibly defined arm held the tall glass still. "Then it seems like a good time to introduce myself." The apparent athlete chuckled, brimming with confidence. "Ron Channing."

"From the Cowboys?"

"The one and only. The Fire starter knows a brother."

"Yes. You beat my Texans single-handedly in that game. And *why did you call me that*?"

"Because I heard it at Lullaby's."

"You were there? In the audience?"

"Ya know," he chimed, his voice smooth and melodic. "Would've talked to you, but you were occupied." He cut his eyes, obviously referring to Ike. "You had me wanting to rush the stage that night. Such a beautiful, soulful voice. You are truly gifted, sister."

I resisted a blush. "Thank you." Another track from the DJ interrupted us. "Are you enjoying yourself?"

"I am now. Would be better if you took this drink. I ordered it just for you."

"I can't. Like I said . . . I don't know you. And I don't think my boyfriend would like it."

"Oh." The single syllable rang distasteful on his tongue. "Can I let you in on a little secret?"

"I suppose."

"I'm not here for Natalia. I came tonight figuring you'd be here."

"That's weak."

"Well, I guess the truth is weak, because that's what it is. I even asked Al if he would get me some time with you . . . away from your shadow."

"Al set this up?" I remembered the two of them talking now. Me-Me was right about the snake.

"Relax. It ain't nothin' special. I just wanted to meet you." He set the unwanted Long Island on a tray as the waiter passed by. "Can I at least have your number?"

"Look . . . I'm flattered, but it just ain't gonna happen."

Ron licked his lips like he was LL Cool J or something. He came closer, as if to kiss me. Instead, he whispered, "How about if I drop a Bentley on you? Would it happen then?"

"Let me think about it." I moved closer to whisper back. My lip grazed his earlobe. He shuddered from the sensation. Probably a premature ejaculator. "Uuhhhh . . . no."

With no FOR RENT sign on my pussy, Mr. Touchdown tried to play it off. He shook my hand and moved on to easier prey.

I went in search of Ike, finding Al by himself instead. Well, not exactly by himself. Two attractive, petite Asian girls had parked themselves next to him as he held court. One of them wore her hair in cornrows.

"Where's Ike?" I huffed.

"He's with Natalia and that fag of hers, Owen. Out there," he said, gesturing toward the patio.

"That fag would probably kick your ass too." I said it as bitter as possible. The women smirked. "And that bullshit back there with your boy wasn't cool."

"Who? Channing?" He feigned innocence. "Hey. I'm just trying to keep everyone happy."

"You can keep me happy by keepin' my name out your mouth from now on. I'm not one for games. Me-Me was right about your shiesty ass."

"Well your trick ass cousin ain't shit! And neither are you!" he yelled to make himself look good. "Fuck you, bitches."

I had already walked off, leaving him to make a fool of himself.

I hastily worked my way toward the patio before something stopped me dead in my tracks. This whole party was beginning to feel like one big setup. Just inside the patio doors, Jason North rolled with one bodyguard. He fixed on me, enjoying my obvious discomfort. I had to walk by him to get to Ike and Natalia. I could've stood my ground and waited, but I was too heated for that. I charged ahead.

"Changed your mind yet, Amelia? Ready for the big time?" he sang as I came upon him.

"Just leave me alone, Jason. I'm not interested in On-Phire. Period."

"Of course you are, dear girl. Haven't you heard the buzz?" He put his hand to his ear, playing to his own warped genius. His bodyguard was the only one amused by the display. "We're ready to make millions."

"You're going to make it off someone else, 'cause you'll never have me." I kept moving, rather than engage him any further. I split him and his muscled protection, knowing he wouldn't attempt anything in front of witnesses.

"Does your new boyfriend out there know about poor Bodie? As much as he's trying to do for you? A shame to treat your felon so bad. You really should heed his advice."

I cast a final glance before pressing on. "Stay out of my life or you're going to make me a felon in here."

"If that will help with the Soundscan numbers, then so be it," he laughed. "To the future, Ms. Bonds."

This man was not rooted in reality.

Swinging the patio door open, the warm night air rushed over me.

I interrupted Natalia midsentence as she conversed with Ike at one of the stone tables. Owen stood at Nat's side. He wasn't on his phone for a change. Ike was placing a business card in his wallet.

I gave my girl a hug, congratulating her on the performance. "That's twice I've caught the two of you all secretive. Should I be concerned?"

Ike offered me his chair. As he stood up, he kissed me on my cheek. "Naw. Your girl was just offering some friendly advice."

Natalia looked at him. She lowered the dark sunglasses from her eyes. "Remember what I said, Ike."

He shook his head in agreement. A mystery for another time. This party had done nothing but fray my nerves and fuel my need for clarity.

"How are you enjoying your party?"

"Girl, please. That's why I'm out here. I would've preferred hangin' at Club Max's on Richmond, but you know how that goes. Gotta go with the flow." The many bangles on her arms clanked together as she motioned with her hands.

Ike excused himself, picking up on our body language. "Think I need another drink. Anybody else?"

"I'm good," I said.

Nat had one of her mojitos. Owen declined. I wanted him to leave too. Instead he moved away a few feet to check Nat's itinerary on his Blackberry.

"So what do you think of my party?"

"Honestly? I hate it."

She laughed. "Preach."

"I've been hit on, called out and bothered. And we just got here." Owen, pretending he wasn't listening, snickered. "Now . . . your concert? Girl, that was the bomb!"

"Thank you."

"I have a confession though. You're my girl and I need to get it off my chest. "

"That you're jealous of me?"

"Maybe just a little, but that's not it." I playfully flicked the table napkin at her. Sure to be somebody's photo: *Singer attacks Natalia in jealous rage*. "I just bought your CD yesterday."

"So when you said you bought it on the first day."

"I lied." I nervously avoided her gaze, hoping I wasn't diminished in her eyes. "But since I bought it, I can't stop listening to it. It's incredible. All of it."

"Do you mean it? Or are you lying again?"

"No. I mean it. I feel that much smaller for avoiding it. I guess deep down you make me confront things I wasn't ready for."

Nat cursed. "Damn, that Bodie."

"I don't want to talk about him ever again. I'm with Ike now. And I hope you haven't mentioned him to Ike."

She didn't answer. "Fine by me. So what do you want to talk about? Something's on your mind."

"Is Jason North paying you?"

Natalia almost knocked her drink over. "Why the fuck would North pay me? I ain't with his label."

"I just ran into his creepy ass, so it's fresh on my mind. Why are you trying to get me to sign with him?"

"I'm not." She sipped some more of her mojito.

"I heard you on the radio. Why else would you say that stuff when it wasn't true? I admitted my lie. Your turn."

Natalia chuckled. "That? That's just creative marketing 'n' stuff."

"If it was just that, you wouldn't have picked On-Phire. It's me, Nat. If North isn't in my face, Bodie is acting like North's my fuckin' salvation. I'm tired of the bullshit. Don't do this. Be straight with me. Please. Why are you helping North?"

She looked at Owen, an unspoken exchange between them. Her eyes went down onto the table. Words ran from her lips, but they were faint. Almost taken by the wind.

"Because he's blackmailing me."

"What?"

Nat looked up, a different person. Where energy had radiated with her voice, she was suddenly defeated, emotionally destitute. "You heard me. North is blackmailing me."

"Oh my God. Nat . . . I . . . I . . . how?"

"Because I was naive and stupid. That's how. I was at a club in Vegas. North and his people were there too. I had too many drinks and things happened back in my suite. He has a video of me in a compromising position with someone."

"That son of a bitch." I wanted to kill North myself. Natalia begged me not to make a scene. "But wait. You're a consenting adult. What you do is your business. Why don't you dare him to go public or sue him?"

"Because the *U.S. Icon* people would drop me."

"*And that's a bad thing?*" Owen cut loose. "Those people have done nothing but hinder your career."

"Yeah," I offered, trying to help in some way with her situation. "Look at Paris Hilton. You could turn this in your favor. You could—"

"I was with a woman."

"Huh? Oh. Okay. You were drunk—"

"Amelia. I'm a lesbian."

50

IKE

As soon as I made the request of Al, I regretted it.

She looked beyond compare in her olive dress. For all the makeup, hairdos, weaves, expensive clothes and breast implants around her, Amelia stood out. A simple beauty who was anything but simple.

I didn't want to leave her side. I couldn't leave her. Maybe the Bodie situation had me feeling possessive. Maybe something else had me obsessing.

It wasn't long ago. Another woman. A similar place. A similar party. A similar feeling of not quite fitting in.

Except Amelia was different. The ending wouldn't be similar. I was leaving with her, not a load of pain and hurt.

"Are you okay?" I asked. "I can meet them another time."

She smiled. I looked forward to it after every kiss. To make her happy. "Boy, go ahead. I'll be here."

Yeah. She was different.

"Bruh, how long you've known Amelia?" Al was probing, questioning my claim. Something men do when they feel something is worth their time . . . or interest.

"For a minute." Long enough to know I loved her, but that was none of his business. In his world, that would've labeled me a sucker. Instead, I'd left him frustrated.

"So where you from?"

"Third Ward."

"You in entertainment?"

"No. I'm a corrections officer."

"All right, all right." Al flashed a smile as if I'd finally given him something to size me up by. He knew I wasn't no punk so not to try me. "That's good of you to think about the kids."

"Somebody has to. We were once in their place."

"Right, right. Well, I'm sure some of my boys will be happy to stop by your gym." He took a few more steps singing, "For the kids," as if an afterthought. "Let me ask you something, man."

"Whazzat?"

"How did you and Amelia meet?"

"Right place, right time, I guess."

"Yeah," he chuckled. "Right for you."

My jaw tightened at the slight, but I let it slide. He wasn't going to push my buttons.

We circled the far end of the club twice, searching for these friends of his before he stopped. The longer I hung in his company, the more I wondered how he could have friends. We were in front of the DJ's booth. I could barely hear him.

"Wait here, bruh. I've got something to check on right quick."

"Don't worry about it, man," I shouted back. "You've got a party to run. Amelia's probably wondering where the hell I'm at anyway."

"Nah. It's no problem. I insist. Just stay right here. I'll have them come to you."

No one ever came. Instead, I stood as bodies danced around me. Some wanted me to join them. I passed. By the third verse of Chris Brown's "Is Your Man on the Floor? If He Ain't, Let Me Know," I decided to "run it, run it" back to Amelia.

Ron Channing.

Superbowl MVP.

Deryn bought me his jersey during one of her nicer periods. Too much bleach in the wash ruined it. Deryn was never cut out to be a homemaker.

He could've been one of the friends Al was looking for.

Except he found Amelia.

It didn't take a second to read his body language. The kids at the gym weren't on this guy's mind. I was an amateur in this world, just a broke, down-on-his-luck jailer. Al had played me. I'd reached my boiling point.

Perfect timing. Al made his appearance. Two Asian girls were engaging him. Amelia looked to be holding her own and would keep for another moment.

I closed the distance, clamping my hand on Al's shoulder. I spun him around, startling him out of his talk.

"H-hey, man!" He faked relief, having forgotten my name already. "I was just looking for you."

"Man, fuck you."

"Fuck me? I let you into my party and you wanna mouth off? To me? Bruh, you're way outta your league." He was going nuts, trying to impress the two women, no doubt. "Why don't you go out, get a decent job and buy you some nice clothes?" He opened his suit jacket and turned around 360 degrees, prancing like a clown. "Then come back and see me and we'll see what's on your mind."

He was much taller than me, but I knew I could take him. For all his flash and talk, Al was soft like drugstore cotton. I was getting ready to shred him when somebody wrapped me up from behind, lifting me up and away from Al.

As I was spun around, I struggled to free myself. People kept their distance, clearing out so as not to spill their drinks. I thought it was a bouncer until they let me go and shoved me toward the patio.

"You're Amelia's boy," Natalia's assistant, Owen, said between gasps, "right? *Whew.* You're a handful."

"Why'd you interfere, bro? That wasn't any of your business! I can take him!"

"Oh, I don't doubt that. But it's Natalia's party, so I can't have that mess up in here. If I didn't know you, I would've just let security throw you out. Word is bond."

*

"You don't understand. That motherfucker disrespected me! He's got one of his boys tryin' to push up on Amelia."

"And Amelia can handle herself." We'd both assumed a less confrontational stature. I was still locked on Al as he scurried away in his little red suit with his beauties. Owen snapped his fingers, bringing my eyes back on him. "Hey. She probably doesn't want you playing caveman up in here. She's beautiful and in the spotlight, man. You can't be going off whenever some dude finds her attractive."

His cell was blowing up, but he ignored it. I actively listened, wondering how the fuck he could be an expert on my relationship.

Then I calmed down. And listened.

"You're right," I agreed. "I'm not in my right mind. Haven't been for a minute."

"Her ex? The jailbird?"

In some strange way, I took offense. Almost took up for Bodie. "Yeah," I answered, moving on. "Her ex, my ex. *Is Natalia around?*"

"Yeah. I came in to order her another mojito. That waiter is about to be fired. Come outside and cool off."

Owen led me to the patio, following as to ensure I didn't run after Al. Natalia was sitting in a chair alone, recharging from her performance. Dark shades covered her eyes even though it was nightfall. Her hair was straight, different from how she wore it during her performance. Where most in attendance were dressed to impress, she made a statement simply in who she was: Natalia. A white sleeveless top and torn jeans didn't tarnish her star. When she saw me, she quit fishing for her drink among the ice and stood up.

"Hey, Ike!" The multicolored bangles clanked as she hugged me. Like we were old friends. No diva air about her. I considered whether it might be on account of Amelia.

"What did you think of the concert? Seats were fine?"

"Everything was great. Thank you."

"Anything for y'all two." She paused, a worried grimace formed. "You look riled up, boy. Still trippin' over Bodie?"

I sat down, able to confess to the one person who knew the deal.

"He knows. He knows I'm with her and he ain't happy. Can't say I blame him. I'm going to tell Amelia. Let her decide before this blows up."

"Don't. Bodie is no good. You've seen that already. Amelia doesn't need an excuse to be burdened with him again. I thought we talked about that."

"Yeah, but—"

"Bodie is dangerous. He has people that can and *will* hurt you and Amelia. If something happened to you, I don't know what she would do." I took her words to heart, remembering how distraught she was over that guy Montez . . . and he was nothing more than an acquaintance. "And I know you don't want to see that."

"True. But I don't have many options. I love your girl. No doubts. But it's either going to be him or me in there. I can tell."

The club manager delivered two mojitos, apologizing profusely on behalf of the club for the delay. Natalia took one, sampling it before sending him away. The diva air was there when she needed it.

"You see them?" Natalia gestured. Only then did I notice the two stoic men in black on the patio edges. That's how we were alone. Owen took a business card from his pocket, knowing this moment was coming. He gave it to Natalia; then she placed it in my hand.

"You need to get out of that job. Now. Call them before something bad happens."

51

BODIE

Something bad was about to happen.

And Winters brought it on himself.

The outdoor courtyard was the only place I trusted to say what I had to say. The guard in the tower above chose to look in the other direction while I talked on the cell.

Fuckin' answering machine.

"Yeah, I know about Winters, bitch! And about your fuckin' him! He ain't gettin' away with it! You hear me? He ain't gettin' away with it!" I went to slam the phone down out of frustration, but wasn't done. "How could you do this shit to me? Of all the niggas . . . *my fuckin' CO*? I gotta see this motherfucker in here and know he's goin' home to you? My woman? If you wanted to hurt me, then you did. You can't do no more, Amelia. But I ain't gonna be the only one hurtin'.

"Here," I said, chucking the phone back up to the tower. Quick hands, used to firing a high-powered rifle, snatched it from the air. The guard on watch was sure to dispose of it. The other CO stood ready to let me back in.

"Thanks, celly."

He nodded once. "If they catch you, I ain't seen shit."

I took the item, stowing it under my shirt. "You know I ain't talkin'. And that shit that went down before . . ."

"Man, I don't wanna hear no apologies." Rewind smiled. "My arm's already gettin' better. You just take care o' yo business."

"Fo sho. I got this."

The cell door opened on time. I walked out, heeding the call to lunch. My sources had informed me Winters was on duty. My hunger would be fed.

"Ay, celly."

"What?"

"That white boy you was seein' the other day. He got sumthin' ta do with all this?"

I paused, pondering Rewind's interest in Aaron. "No. He just my boy. And he ain't white."

In the chow hall, I wished I was white.

The COs acted like they were expecting something. They covered the whole lunch area, but there were more around us negroes. Winters was with them, glaring at me as I carried my tray of the day's shit. Some vegetables and more pork. I'd quit eating the shit. I wanted to hurl the tray at him, but it would've been an insult to the food. I had something better for Winters anyway. That thought made me particularly happy as I ambled to my seat.

Niggas was talkin' all that yap-yap, but I was deaf. Dumb for too long, but not so blind. Only my vision guided me. And only opportunity could I see. Winters relaxed enough to take his eyes off me. His cocky ass stood by the serving line. Against the wall, jokin' with his boys. I wondered if he knew most of them were on the take. If he weren't a CO, one of them would "do the do" for a few child-support payments. I ate my potatoes, biding my time and counting the minutes. Fifteen minutes to eat. I only needed one of those.

Tensions were high among the different groups. I'd just finished my tray when it jumped off. Not as planned, but better. The argument that was supposed to break out didn't happen. Motherfuckers scared of getting their wigs split. I just knew somebody had snitched to the COs. They were too prepared.

But not for the inked inmate on the other end of the chow hall.

As another dude walked by his table, he popped up, stickin' ole boy in the back, then walked away. As ole boy staggered, it got raw in a hurry. He reached for the table, pulling lunch trays down with him. Other inmates swarmed him, ensuring he was dead before he hit the floor. His group noticed and came calling in a hurry. We had a riot, everybody stepping up to settle scores amid the chaos.

A riot team had entered through a side door, rushing toward most of the commotion. Winters tried to take control of his little area, most of his backup having spread out. Two hundred fifty inmates wildin' out. Soon they would be hitting us with the gas.

I threw my plate to the side and stood up.

Rewind gave the go-ahead to some of his boys and I set off. I moved in Winters' direction steadily. He was occupied, separating two inmates and having a hard time of it. I moved closer.

Faster.

Only a few yards separated us. The distance was laced with hate; each step was like a drug. I could read the words on his shirt emblem.

Closer.

I pulled the shank from beneath my shirt. I admired it for a second. Rewind did his best work in the metal shop.

Over my shoulder, someone trailed me. One of Rewind's boys. He had something concealed in his hand. Someone else wanting to get at Winters, I guessed. Maybe he was fucking their girl on the outside too. But this was going to be mine and mine alone. No more time, I began running.

Winters was being rammed into the wall by the two, who suddenly decided to work together on him. His stomach was exposed. I was going to look into his eyes, get everything off my mind, as I plunged the shank into his gut. His eyes were going to bulge before shrinking and fading away.

I was in full stride, ready to drive it up in him. He hadn't seen me. Dammit, look up!

I was fixated on Winters; otherwise I would've seen it. The unexpected blow didn't knock me off my feet. Rather it knocked me off balance and sideways. My hand popped open. The shank I'd palmed sailed free. I stumbled for a second, but regained my footing. As flailing bodies rolled all around me, I looked around in desperation.

Then I found it.

My shank had rolled forward, stopping halfway between Winters and me.

The riot squad was prying inmates off him. Wiping his busted lip, he finally looked up.

And saw me.

And the shank.

In that moment of understanding, we both dove for it.

52

AMELIA

"I'm a lesbian," she'd said.

I was speechless, waiting for the punch line.

"I'm serious. Ever wonder why my family doesn't come around when I'm in town?"

"Yes . . . but I thought they just didn't approve of your career."

"Oh, they approve of that. And the money it brings in, but they're having trouble dealing with my sexuality." She killed the last mojito, bitter thoughts now rampant. Wounds opened. "How about you, Amelia? Are you still my friend?"

I shook my head. "Yes. Of course. I'm just surprised. But you and the different rappers—"

"Me and Penny Antnee cover for each other, just in case my tape leaks out. Owen says I should tell North to fuck off and release it."

Owen boasted. "Didn't hurt that Miss America's career. Or those two female rappers. Straight men eat that up."

"Can you keep it secret, girl, until I'm ready?"

"You have to ask?"

"No. But I have to ask you to forgive me for playing North's game."

"I understand now. You didn't have a choice."

"Yes, I did. And I chose my secret over my friend." Owen smacked his lips at the melodrama. "Sorry, Owen. I can at least get back at North by taking away what he wants. You."

"How?"

I'd been frozen at that moment at Club I-Life, the man's voice a surreal buzzing over the phone until now. I shook off the daze, sticking one finger in my ear. The lunchtime buzz had begun at Mirage. Deafening when trying to hold a conversation. In between orders, the cell phone Natalia had provided me rang.

"Miss Bonds, I have Mr. Lansky on the line," his assistant said, switching off the speaker phone with a click. I imagined some large office with lots of wood. Cigar smoke covering everything.

"Ms. Bonds, I am so pleased Natalia thought of me first. You are— dare I say it—a diamond in the rough?"

"Thank you, sir. But you've never heard me sing—"

"But others have. You see . . . I know when to listen. When Natalia says you're better than her, then . . ." I imagined the older man shrugging his shoulders. I'd read about him in *Vibe*. Marion Lansky made an entertainment empire from taking big risks with big reward. A biracial New Yorker, a black Jew raised in Harlem, he understood the art of the deal from both ends. His label had fallen off, but since his triple-bypass, he'd found that fire again. All the better to have a Fire Starter at his side on his way back to the top. "Well . . . I listen. You know how big Natalia's ego is, so I said I have to see this."

We laughed. Me concerned, him confident.

"I do have a serious question before I let you go."

"Yes?"

"Are you sure you're not signed somewhere with another label?"

"Absolutely not. I quit singing after *U.S. Icon*."

"Well, Miss Bonds, we're glad to have you back. And soon the whole world will be too."

"Thank you! Thank you so much!"

"Don't thank me yet. I'll see you when I get there for the audition. I want my whole team with me for this . . . including my nurse. If you're as hot as you sound over the phone, I'll need her to revive me. I'm out."

"Goodbye, Mr. Lansky."

I flipped the phone shut, trying to steady my hands for the lunch crowd.

I had an audition.

I picked the salad plates off the kitchen table and placed them on my arms. I was getting my orders right today.

I had an audition.

Ike was going to die when he heard this.

53

IKE

"Now I ain't losin' my job over this shit! So y'all need to get y'all's heads out y'all's asses!" Back listening to one of Arnold's rampages. A familiar scene.

"We had another 'accident' overnight. Another body. This little turf war has gone too far. And if you swingin' dicks can't get it done, I'll find somebody that can."

As annoying as she was, Arnold was right. Before all the drama in my life, I cared about this place. Still did. Just didn't know how things fit because of my new circumstances.

"Somebody's cutting in on someone's action, so we're gonna dry up the whole business. I want you to comb every inch of this block. I don't want no drugs. I don't want no shanks. No contraband. *Nada.* Do your damn job." She stood up from her table, feeling the need to parade her breasts in our faces. She always did this when we were seated in meetings. Tomas, the other sergeant who was sitting in on roll call, smirked. He knew the routine too.

"Most of this has been limited to fighting between the Mexicans and El Salvadorans. Now the brothers wanna act up. We understand something's planned for today. Don't know what, but the info is credible." She stopped in front of me. I tried to look around her, but couldn't. I heard the snickers and tried to contain mine.

"Glad you were able to leave your paparazzi and join us today, Winters. Brought any Cristal for us regular folk?"

It was their turn to laugh at me.

"Something on your mind, Winters?"

"No."

"What?"

"No, ma'am," I answered obediently. My eyes spoke otherwise.

"Don't I know it." She moved back to her table. "Maybe if you did have more on your mind, we wouldn't be having this meltdown. You've got chow hall today."

"What?"

"You heard me."

When Arnold assigned me here, I never expected a riot, struggling against two angry inmates. I'd been hit in the mouth with a lunch tray, then turned on by two who were trying to kill each other minutes ago. Two of our backups in riot gear bailed me out, quickly asserting control. The gas was coming and this would soon be over.

I wiped my lip, spitting my own blood. A second to catch my breath and I was going snag a gas mask. Looking down, I saw a shank. It was too far away to be from the two I'd been scuffling with. Besides, they would've just used it on me.

I looked out, seeking the shank's owner.

He had been searching for it too. Desperate as other fights spilled around him. Desperate for what he lost when his gaze met mine.

Bodie.

So this is what it comes to, I thought.

We both went after the shank.

54

BODIE

I got to it first and was bringing it up to stab him. He dove, his momentum carrying him into me. The tip grazed him, but he hit me solid, bowling me over. In as long a second, I was separated from the shank again. I rolled to the side and tried to crawl to it. Winters was dying today, but recovered. He climbed over me, almost grasping the handle. I pulled him back, the two of us rolling away from his sure death.

I dug my hands into his lying face, wanting to undo anything Amelia might like. He grabbed my wrist and punched me in the ribs with his free hand. The man's fist hurt, like he was a pro or something. I winced, cursing him through the pain. I grabbed his throat and began choking him. No one had noticed us as we struggled. I squeezed as hard as I could, knowing I didn't have much time. He struggled to breathe but was still fighting. He wasn't going to quit. I had to finish him.

He strained and we rolled back toward the shank. I could still get to it. Winters would be out of our life. I let go with one hand and reached. My tips almost touched it.

"Fuck you," Winters grunted, his shirt red with blood from the near miss. He flipped me onto my back. He now was on top and trying to gain control. He grabbed my head, banging it off the floor again and again. I knocked his hands away before I lost consciousness.

Over his shoulder, I saw Rewind's boy. He'd stepped back, lying in the cut to make his move. His shank was visible now, ready to be used on a motherfucker. Nigga was about to stick him and Winters' dumb ass wouldn't see it coming. Reeling from the head thumps, I still let out a weak laugh.

I didn't laugh long.

Rather than rush Winters and ventilate his punk ass, ole boy paced around like he was waiting for the perfect time or something.

Winters now saw him. In that instant, he froze. I strained as hard as I could and rolled Winters off me. I didn't have the strength to do that again. I punched him once to slow him from holding me. Crawling over him, I made another lunge across the floor. Winters grabbed my leg and tried to close the gap between us. I kicked his hand away and crawled for it. Between the two of us, Winters was in a bad way. One of us was going to get him.

I saw a shadow behind me. As it grew, I scrambled out of the way. I almost had the shank, but just missed the two bodies that came crashing down. One of them was moving.

Where I just had been now lay Rewind's friend. Facedown on the floor, his arms beneath his body and his head turned toward me at a bizarre angle. Although he looked dead at me, there was no recognition, no movement.

Then he blinked. He tried to speak, but all that came forth was a wheezing sound.

And atop his back was Winters.

Winters had tackled him as he ran toward me. His shank getting caught beneath him, it was now lodged in his chest. But why hadn't he stabbed Winters?

Breathless, Winters released his grip on the large body he'd brought down. He slid down, too weary to fight.

Our eyes met, telling me something I refused to accept.

The shank I'd had was still there. Just on the other side of them. I should've gotten up and finished him. He wouldn't be a problem anymore. But my mind was frozen. Trying to accept to the unacceptable.

Then the gas came. Pumped in through holes in the two doors leading to the chow hall. I coughed and wheezed as shadows came and dragged me away.

55

AMELIA

I was nervous about my upcoming audition. As it was in those dark days, my sleep was strained, labored.

Labored.

Labor.

Hard labor.

One the beginning of life; the other . . . a journey to the end.

Yes. Dark days.

"No," I moaned as I dropped the plastic device. I'd just left from Bodie's hearing. The judge had denied his bail. With every soul in Houston calling him a cold-blooded murderer, I was still down for him. Silly rabbit.

Except the rabbit died on the bathroom floor, its "positive" sign teasing me. From the toilet, I reached down and picked it up.

The cheap pregnancy test I'd bought on a whim played the cruelest joke. Crueler than my having to let Natalia go to Hollywood by herself, breaking the promise we'd made to each other. I don't think she's ever truly forgiven me for that.

I stayed for Bodie. And besides, I was too sick. I thought it was nerves over failure, maybe an ulcer.

Turned out to be nerves of the nine-month kind.

I couldn't have this now.

"Miss Bonds?" the soothing voice coaxed. I guess it was over.

I remember the white lights overhead when I came to.

I still see them when I sleep.

They're so bright they wake me up.

I sat up in the bed.

Sweating.

Alone.

Ike was at work so I wouldn't bother him.

I rubbed the back of my neck, reflecting for a moment the name etched back there. A drink from my bottle of Dasani; then I went back to sleep.

I try to imagine how she would've looked.

56

I K E

I saved him.

He wanted to kill me, but I saved him.

I was burned out. No energy left to fight and my backup had their hands full. I knew my life was at its end, but instead he overlooked me. In stride, he stepped over me and kept going.

He wasn't after me.

Bodie was crawling for his shank, oblivious to the one about to go into his back. All my problems would be solved. Natalia had warned me how dangerous this man was to me and Amelia. It would be easy.

Except I couldn't let that happen. I had a job to do.

I jumped to my feet and threw myself at the big man. My tackle caught him off balance as he bent over to stab Bodie. We went down, my weight atop him.

His shank wound up puncturing his lung.

Another black mark on CO Arnold and on our ability to do our job. We had two deaths in the dining hall. Everybody else was either in solitary or on lockdown, pending the investigation. I didn't tell them about me and Bodie's confrontation, but because of my condition, I was sent to the infirmary. Over my objections, they bandaged me up, ordering me home for the rest of the day.

I picked up my forwarded mail from my momma's house. She

wasn't home, so she was spared my prepared excuses for how I looked. I left her a brief note, then retreated to nurse my wounds.

"Hey. It's me." Amelia didn't know I was home, but I left a message for her just in case. "I'm calling to see if you'll take a raincheck for tonight. I'm feeling a little sick and need some sleep." The scrape across my chest stung beneath the bandage. In spite of Natalia's advice, I needed to tell her. Deception, as I'd learned the hard way, wasn't right, no matter how noble the intentions. "We need to talk about some things anyway. I'll call you tomorrow to come by. Love you."

The doctor at the prison infirmary warned me not to take medication with alcohol. I listened and left the pills on the coffee table.

One beer later, I limped off to sleep.

It was dark when I woke up. It wasn't my choice. The constant banging on the door disturbed me. Whoever it was, it must've been important. Maybe Amelia didn't get my message. Worse, maybe she knew about me and Bodie without hearing my side. That thought alone hastened my sprint from the bed.

I should've looked out the window first.

"Hello, Isaac."

The voice in my head screamed for me to slam the door.

"How'd you get here?" I had a hard head.

"Isn't it obvious? I drove."

"You know what I meant. How'd you find me?"

"Your mother."

"Bullshit. She wouldn't have done that."

"Well, she did."

I sighed. "What do you want?"

"I . . ." She spied my bandage. I should've put on a shirt. *"What happened to you?"* I almost believed her concern.

"Occupational hazard. You came all the way for this?"

"No. I needed to see you, Isaac. They burned my house. Our house."

I noticed Deryn's attire for the first time. Her top was silk . . . pajama. A pair of jeans and tennis shoes completed it. She never went anywhere uncoordinated. She always said she'd rather die. She was alive . . . kinda. No makeup either.

"Can I come in? I'm very tired."

"Deryn . . ."

"Please. It's late and I don't have anywhere to go. Don't you care?"

I was too tired for snappy comebacks. I motioned her in.

I fixed her some instant coffee and waited for her to compose herself.

"Did you see it on the news?"

"No. I've been asleep. You said 'they' burned the house." I'd picked up her "our" reference before. Trying to attach some importance for me. It worked. I had some fond memories of that house before I was kicked out. "Who?"

"Marshall's wife, I guess. I almost died. That's probably what she wants." She tried to be proud, defiant. You could see she was scared though. I refused to comfort her.

"She's that bitter?"

"Yes. I've been receiving threatening calls. Go look at my car. Somebody egged it."

"I'll take your word for it." I smiled, thinking she at least deserved that. "But what do you want me to do?"

"I didn't have anywhere else to go," she mumbled. "I . . . I thought maybe I could talk to you. Stay here."

I let out a laugh. "Sorry. Why don't you get a hotel or something? Maybe stay with your mother or one of your sisters."

Her eyes filled with venom. "You know I don't see them."

"Then maybe you should. They are your family. I mean, I never understood—"

"Isaac," she said, her voice proud yet wavering, "I didn't come here to be confrontational or to bring up those people. I just need to see a friendly face. And not be alone. This is too much for me to take."

"What did Marshall have to say? Does he know his wife is doing this? He's the HNIC of Houston. He can't keep her in check?"

"Marshall and I don't speak anymore. He's changed all his numbers."

"Okay, but how about at work?"

"He fired me. When you came by for your things that day, I was out of work."

"Oh."

"So . . . can I just stay the night? I'll be out of your hair in the morning."

"Okay." Call me a sucker.

I had to heal and needed my rest, so I fished a blanket from the box of unpacked things.

"Here," I said, dropping it in her lap. "I don't have a pillow to spare. Make yourself comfortable. I'm going back to bed."

As I slept, the bandage across my chest irritated me. It was sore, uncomfortable. Should've changed the dressing before going to sleep. Or least taken the pain pills.

I rubbed my hand across it, trying not to think about Bodie wielding a shank. Amelia was with me, not him. But when I came clean, would she still be there?

A light touch to my chest answered that. I felt her slender hand as it moved mine aside. It gently patted the area of my pain. A little bit slower and it would have pierced my heart. I let out a deep breath to assure myself it hadn't.

I rested my hand atop hers, comforted.

Her bare legs responded, rubbing against mine beneath the sheets. They were cool to the touch at first, but the friction was warming things up. I felt the mattress shift as she pressed up against me.

Just like she used to.

Used to.

That phrase clung on the edge of my consciousness, summoning me back.

I bolted awake.

"Does it hurt, Daddy?" Deryn purred.

I couldn't hear her seductive words over the calling of her naked, yearning silhouette. It threatened to drown out reason as blood rushed to my dick.

57

BODIE

*H*e *saved me.*

Nah. Can't be right. It couldn't be. Why would he want to? Especially when I wanted him dead. And why hadn't he turned me in?

Probably his twisted way of telling me I couldn't touch him, that I was beneath his concern.

I was going to prove him wrong.

Dead wrong.

My visitors were unaware that shit with Winters had me shook. Better that they didn't know anyway. Aaron's silly ass was still arguing. I tuned back in.

"I told you I could do it."

"I know what you said . . . and what you did. That's why my Lac is out there gettin' dogged. That's why your brother is here. You fuck up things when I tell you to do it. Something's wrong with your head, Aaron." I thumped my index finger repeatedly against my forehead.

"I wasn't wrong, Bodie. Shit, man . . ."

Ro shut down his brother with a gaze. Even though he was older, fatter . . . softer now, he still commanded situations with little drama. That's why I needed him. Fuck the bullshit, just get it done. "I came because you asked me."

"And that was mighty fuckin' nice of you, Ro." I didn't appreciate

Ro tryin' to sound all Jedi 'n' shit. Like he could talk down to me now just because he wore a cross around his neck. "Glad you decided to pay me a visit. Hope I wasn't keepin' you from somethin'. How's your family? Better yet, how's your fuckin' life out there?"

"C'mon, Bodie. You don't gotta talk all crazy. Ro did come. Let's get this straight so we can leave and do what we gotta do." Aaron didn't want to be here. As few visits as he made, this place spooked him. He was hard, but the fellas would take makin' his fair-skinned ass their bitch as a challenge. Foreplay for a motherfucker. If he ever wound up on my side of the fence, we both knew he would lose in the end.

"Aaron says you've changed, man. That true? You think everything's even between us all of a sudden? Too good to come around now?"

"Bodie, Ro the same. He just—"

"No, you're right, Bodie. I've changed. Seen things different. Kicked all that crazy shit to the curb. But as the Lord Jesus Christ is my savior, I owe you."

"Damn straight you owe me. 'Cause it's simple. My Lac ain't been runnin' right. It's time for a new mechanic. The old one thinks he's doin' a good job, but I need y'all to talk to him. Think your *savior* will mind?"

Ro contemplated things. "I can do that. Talk."

"*Talk?*" The word annoyed Aaron. "Who this motherfucker, Bodie? Where he at? Since I don't know what I'm doin' all of a sudden, tell me."

Without speaking, I nudged my head in the direction of one of the jailers. The Fontenot brothers looked in unison, each one grasping it differently. Ro smiled even though he was far from happy in what he was feeling. Aaron simply wigged out, leaning across the table.

"*A CO? He's one of them?*" he tried to whisper poorly. "Man, fuck that. That's almost as bad as a po-po."

"He works here?" Ro asked for confirmation. I nodded.

"Damn," said Aaron. "Why can't you just—"

"Not around here." I'd squandered the one good shot I'd had.

"If not around here, then how do we find him?"

"Under the hood of my Lac. That's where he'll probably be when he ain't here. He thinks he knows what he's doin', but he's in over his head with my car. He needs to be schooled. I'll get you a picture. Make sure you got the right one. When you tell him he's being replaced, do it somewhere else."

"Anything else?"

Did he save me? Save me from what? For what? I still wanted revenge, but some answers had to come first.

"Yeah. I changed my mind. Just check on him . . . for now. I'll let you know when to fire him."

Aaron and Ro looked at each other. "Suit yourself," they answered almost in sync.

58

AMELIA

My shift was almost over at Mirage. Ready for an evening with Ike. I was going to share more than my body with him tonight. It was time to share my diluted dreams and aspirations, which had been rekindled. I know. All backward. But sometimes, the flesh is easier to part than the heart.

"Where y'all two going tonight?" Tookie asked. She saw I was acting funny.

"I'll know in a sec." I had a break to play the voice mail. I entered my code and listened for Ike's voice.

"Hey. It's me," he opened. He sounded distracted, unsure. My brow crinkled. *"I'm calling to see if you'll take a raincheck for tonight. I'm feeling a little sick and need some sleep."*

It was going to be a big night. No parties, no drama. Just the two of us being close, intimate. I was to surprise him with news of my audition.

"Where's sexy Ike wining and dining you?" Tookie pressed.

Snapping my phone shut, I offered a smile. "It's a secret."

In my car, I imagined how beautiful a night it could be. How it might set the tone for many more nights.

But he was feeling under the weather.

All the better to go over there and give him some TLC. From the sound of his voice, he didn't seem up for that.

I decided not to push.

I got out my car and fished around my trunk. An old notebook lay beneath a stained apron. Maybe I could still set the tone for many more nights. I closed my trunk and tapped a pencil against my chin.

I made my way to the Franklin Street Coffee House by U of H–Downtown, where some cups of warm tea with lemon and honey nursed my creative spirit and emerging voice. Downstairs, a foreign film played for the patrons. Upstairs, I was alone and free to hum and harmonize undisturbed. I wasn't a songwriter, but tried to just scribble what the past years had brought me in terms of pain and an altered outlook on life. I hadn't realized it, but the film's score was providing an inspirational spark to my words. When the film ended, to the applause of the small audience below, I regretted it.

My caffeine buzz wearing off, I took leave with my new pages of pride. I took the scenic route home, driving through the Third Ward, which took me in front of a packed Lullaby's. I slowed long enough to lower my window. Over the cheers and driving bass, Me-Me's vocals were unmistakable. If not for her . . .

Yeah. If not for her.

"Thank you, cuz," I uttered to the night air before raising my window and continuing. I was so close to Ike. I wanted to share what I had accomplished tonight. As hard as it was, I honored his wishes, saving it for another day. Satisfied in one sense and unfulfilled in another, I made the lonely drive back to Stafford.

I hummed as I came into my apartment. Throwing my purse down, I set my notebook aside for the night. My stomach growled a little bit. I wished I'd taken something from Mirage, but Tookie would've known I wasn't going out. I had a message waiting for me. It could've been old, but maybe Ike was feeling better. I eagerly pushed PLAY . . . and regretted it.

"Yeah, I know about Winters, bitch! And about your fuckin' him! He ain't gettin' away with it! You hear me? He ain't gettin' away with it!"

I shuddered, listened to all I could before stopping the message and deleting it.

The only thing heard in my apartment was the thumping of my heart, the constant huffing of my breath. I felt trapped.

I ran back to my door, making sure I'd locked it.

No more doubts about Bodie. Only fears.

Dammit, how could he? What was wrong with him?

He didn't say it, but he had. He'd done it. Bodie had had Montez brutally beaten. I was certain. How long had he been watching me? He'd put in the hospital a young man who would probably never be the same again.

And now he was threatening Ike.

I looked at the time. Ike was sick, not to be disturbed. I had to warn him though.

I had to tell him about Bodie.

Even if he decided not to have anything to do with me.

I threw on something and ran out the door.

Into the night for Ike.

Like the title of a bad book. As if my life would fit within the pages.

On the way, I'd called, but there was no answer. That only made me drive faster.

The black car parked behind his truck should've been my warning. He was driving it the night we met. Instead, my concern for him escalated. Maybe they were there because something happened to him. He did say he was sick.

When I knocked on the door, it was my turn to be sick.

She opened it quickly, recklessly. As if no regard for her safety this time of night.

"Oh." Disappointment clung onto her response. The tone I was familiar with. "May I help you?" She was beautiful. Even in just the pajama top and panties she tried to shield behind the door.

"Where's Ike?" I demanded.

"Isaac's not here." She let me see her fully now. No longer caring what I saw . . . or thought.

I looked at Ike's truck tucked away in the shadows. It hadn't been moved. Bodie's message was replaced by Ike's in my head.

"Where is he?"

"I really don't know." She braced her arm across the doorway, piercing eyes glistening like emerald crystals. "Is there anything else you need?"

I wanted to knock her on her ass, storm inside and find him. I didn't want to believe it, but couldn't shake that he'd claimed sickness to get with her. His ex. I knew how strong those bonds could be.

"Are you sure Ike's not here?"

"Positive. Want to see for yourself?" She dropped her arm from barring my entry. Almost daring me to rush in and see evidence of what they'd been doing. Damn. Why'd she have to be beautiful? She seemed so polished, so refined. Something else was there although I couldn't put my finger on it.

"You'd probably like that," I replied, giving in to my true feelings for her. "I'll pass."

"Suit yourself," she said, cracking a smile. Beautiful and evil.

I began to leave.

"Want me to tell Isaac anything?"

"No," I responded. "If I have anything to say, I'll tell him myself."

I hadn't gotten two yards.

"Hmm. That's interesting."

I stopped. "Excuse me?" I didn't like her. On some level, I wanted an excuse to beat her.

"You're prettier in person than your pictures, Amelia. That's all."

"You know my name?"

"Of course I do. Me and Isaac were talking about you . . . earlier when we . . . before he left."

"Okay. I asked. Well, fuck you and fuck him."

I came by out of concern. Because I cared about what we had. Ike had just made it easier to let us go.

59

IKE

I stopped on the 288 overpass on my way home, watching the faint traffic forming. My hands gripped the chain link fence, supporting me. Sweat soaked my clothes in the dark predawn air. My breathing was steadying. Two miles to Hermann Park. Two miles back. But back to what?

Until just recently, Deryn was my all. I knew no other woman, didn't want any other.

"One more time," she breathed more than spoke as I became fully awake. It was as if her body had its own seductive language. And I wished I weren't fluent in it.

She turned her attention to my erection, which was rising to the occasion. She draped her body across me before I could react. "I just need you tonight. Okay?" she reasoned, her hand toying with my dick through my boxers. She gripped it, gathering the fabric around it like some sort of Halloween ghost. She kissed the head affectionately. Moistness from my tip created a stain. She lapped at it with the tip of her tongue. I felt myself swelling.

My chest still ached as I tried to sit up. The pain brought me back to Amelia. I felt reason returning to my clouded mind.

"Deryn. Stop."

"Just one more time." That same seductive refrain. She released my dick and climbed atop me. She took my wrists and pinned my arms down. Still weakened, I fell back onto my pillow. "You're hurt. I'm hurt. I'll take away your pain . . . and you can take away mine." She slid down, her warm stickiness tracing across my dick. "Okay?"

I felt her clit, pulsing and throbbing, as she worked herself on me. I twitched at her beck and call. She placed my hands on her breasts and held them there. She ground harder as she coaxed my fingers to squeeze them.

"C'mon. Stop. I didn't let you stay for this. I mean it."

"Put it in, Daddy." She panted as she rose for me to enter her. She began sliding my boxers down. I let go of her breasts and placed my hands around her waist.

And moved her off me.

Before she could respond, I sprang out the bed. Quickly grabbing some clothes.

"What are you doing?"

"Leaving."

"Now?" Deryn, ready to be fucked to no end, was at a loss for words. I avoided looking at her, lest I give in to weakness. "Where are you going?"

"Out."

I'd done enough soul-searching on the jog. A chance to put everything in perspective. Not close to the miles I used to put in when I was boxing, but good enough. I took a final look at the traffic below me and headed back to Truxillo Street.

The sun was about to break when I got back. Almost time to report back to work. Nevertheless, I walked the final block.

Deryn was still there. I was lucky Amelia hadn't dropped by. Now I just needed to do what I had to.

My door was open. I found her in the kitchen playing homemaker. She'd grabbed a few eggs from the fridge and was turning the stove on. Deryn had put on some clothes, which was a comfort. Still she could've put on some pants.

"Hey."

"Are you going to tell me where you went? Or why you left like that?"

"I went running. Needed some time to think." I hung my keys on the hook by the telephone.

"Oh. Want me to fix you some breakfast?"

She surprised me, but didn't derail me. "Um. No." I took position by the sink, looking in her eyes. "I need you to go. If Amelia comes by, I don't want her thinking—"

"That we?"

I nodded. "Yeah. She's my girlfriend now, Deryn." I liked the sound of my proclamation. "And even though I should care less about what you're going through, I do . . ."

"But."

"Yeah. 'But.' " I chuckled. "I was stupid to let you stay the night. You have to go. Now."

She dropped the skillet in the sink. I watched her eyes shift as if a big revelation was coming. "Your decision."

"Yeah." I thought back to my jog. "It is my decision."

60

BODIE

"Shit's fucked up, man."

"Yeah." Rewind put his nose to the straw, inhaling his cares away. One of his envelopes was filled with the white stuff: cocaine. The personal letters from home. That's where most of the letter dust was hidden. As hard as the isolation was, I'd avoided the stuff. "All that shit that went down and you ain't got nothin' to show for it. You don't get chances like that around here."

He took another long sniff atop his bunk. Rather than sleeping, I sat on the cell floor. Looking up at him. It was dark, but I wanted to at least imagine I could see his face.

"What was your boy doin'?"

Rewind wiped his nose, licking the residue off his fingertips. "Who?"

"You know who. Big motherfucker. I seen you with him before. He was tryin' to run up on Winters too." I assumed.

"Jackson? I dunno nuthin' about that, man." He giggled, soaring beyond the walls of the prison on his latest journey. "I could find out, but he's in the infirmary. And under guard. 'Course, I'd have to give a flyin' fuck." The last remark amused him to no end.

A roach scurried by my hand. I could've squished it, but I didn't. He didn't want to be here either. Just trapped like me. I focused on Rewind again. "If I didn't know better, I'd swear he was tryin' to stick me. Not Winters."

"Nigga, you just paranoid because you fucked up. Shit. Everything was right there for you and you blew it."

It was. I had him. Winters was run down. Too tired to stop me. All I had to do was get up, grab the shank and take care of the motherfucker. But I hesitated. Punked out and it cost me.

"Interesting conversation, ladies? Antoine, how come you're not in your bunk?"

CO Arnold's voice was unmistakable. She stood outside the cell door with two backups. Rewind's head had disappeared as he stowed his envelope.

"What do you want?" I asked as the flashlight from one of them beamed in my face.

"For you to stand up and step back."

I listened, rising to my feet and not knowing what to expect. The cell door clanked open. Arnold entered solo. Her visit to me in solitary came to mind as I guarded my nuts. She looked up at Rewind's bunk.

"Movin' time, Rewind," she sang.

"Why me?" he asked, his head reappearing.

"Just get your shit. I ain't got all night."

I stood by while Arnold quickly, quietly had Rewind's belongings removed. He gave me a pound on the way out.

"It's been real, celly."

"Ya know."

As peculiar as it was, I didn't dwell on it. People have their reasons for doing stuff. I'd made it this far by keeping my nose out of people's business.

Still, as volatile as things could get, I was going to miss Rewind. He was good for a laugh from time to time. Tomorrow, I could have someone better or worse for my celly. I just had to move on.

I went to rest on my bunk and saw something trapped between the mattress and the wall. I reached for it, pulling the envelope free. Rewind must've let it fall when Arnold and them came in. I opened it and peered inside.

Still full of letter dust and the straw. The rest of his mail was gone with him. I set it to the side, considering flushing it later.

My eyes were getting heavy.

They shut.

I quickly opened them. I went for the envelope again. This time I took the straw in my hand.

If I fell asleep, I'd have a visit from Abdel at the pawn shop. He came for me on these nights. When I was feeling weak, uncertain. I wasn't up for it tonight.

Rewind said everything was right there for me and I blew it. Both times. With Amelia. And with Winters.

Well, I didn't blow this time. Ironically, I inhaled. Inhaled deeply. Then did it again.

The cell grew larger. My bars disappeared. I felt power. More power over my life than I'd felt in a long time.

My pulse quickened; then everything was better because it didn't matter.

61

IKE

"On five!"

I was beginning to hate that number. The prebreakfast shake-down, a regular routine since the chow hall incident, guaranteed I'd see him again. Didn't plan on it being this soon, but I was given instructions by Arnold. And like a good little boy, I followed orders. As the door slid open, images of our struggle had me tense. Another attempt and I was taking him down.

Hard.

For good.

But when I saw him, I knew something was off.

Rewind was gone. Bodie . . .

Bodie was in a stupor. He hung partially off his bunk, mouth open catching flies. He didn't even hear the rumble of the cell door as it opened. There would be no struggle today. At least nothing I couldn't handle.

I poked at him. He barely moved, a mixture of a groan and a laugh escaping his lips. He was a joke. It would be so easy to end it now. No more problems for me and Amelia. Except I wasn't a murderer. I wasn't Bodie.

"Get up." I poked him with my baton.

Whatever dream he was experiencing had him carrying a smile until he saw me. His eyes were swollen.

"I shoulda killed you," he uttered through a sore throat.

"Get your high ass up, Bodie."

He wiped his nose, staggering to his feet. He fell once, but I didn't help him.

"Come to fuck with me some more, boss? Well, you can't touch me. Like that AK song, I'm bulletproof, my man."

"Uh-huh. I got that album too. And ain't AK dead now?"

On the floor by his bunk, I found what I suspected. Letter dust. The envelope still had traces of cocaine in it. Bodie made a mistake normally reserved for the new boots. He left it out, too strung out to care. Maybe he wanted to get caught.

"You gonna take that away from me too, bitch?" he cackled. I glared at him.

"Everything all right, Winters?" my backup asked.

Bodie had tried to kill me. I clenched the envelope, shielded from my backup's view. Bodie was drifting asleep as he stood. I closed my eyes, deliberating.

"Yeah. Everything's okay."

I placed the envelope back with his other personal effects. I glanced around the cell a final time, then left it.

I was about to order it closed when I was stopped.

"What?" I asked of the other CO who'd joined us.

"Gotta check it."

"What the fuck? I just did it."

He shrugged his shoulders. "I know. Arnold's orders."

He ordered Bodie to stand up and back away again. When Bodie groggily complied, he noticed his state. He looked back at me. I didn't flinch. I just watched him as he tore through the cell, until he got to Bodie's personal mail.

Then he found it.

Bodie spit on me as the other CO and my backup hauled him past. Something else to wrongly blame on me. Another trip to solitary for him.

And Arnold wanted to see me.

* * *

"I've had it with you, Winters! Is fuckin' with an inmate's girlfriend fuckin' with your ability to perform a simple shakedown?"

"If you didn't think I could perform my duty, then why send me?"

"I thought about that myself. Figured I'd give you a chance . . . baby you. With all you've been through. All your little booboos you picked up in chow hall. I'm sure it's been hard on your party schedule."

"Serena, you need—"

"Serena?" Arnold stormed from behind her desk. Filings from the last week were scattered across it. I wondered how many trustees had done her there. "Oh. So now the rank don't mean shit. It all goes together. The lack of discipline. The lack of respect. That's your problem."

"Give me something to respect and I will."

"Keep it up, Winters. You're this close to being written up!"

"Then you need to write up to stay out of my personal life while you're at it."

"That's just it, dumb ass! Your life ain't personal. Hell, this bitch you're fuckin' is comin' by the prison to see Campbell when you're off."

"What?"

"Uh-huh," she taunted. "Secrets, secrets, secrets. Didn't know that, huh, genius? Just the other day, I worked visitation. Bodie had his tongue all down her throat until I broke them up."

She'd silenced me. My mind tried to wrap around it, but was having trouble.

"Tell me . . . how does Bodie taste?"

I resisted the white-hot rage, channeled it. "I don't know. But you might be able to tell. Half the inmates on this block have been in your mouth. And who knows how many COs? I don't know how you keep your job." In the end, I was more destructive than if I'd hit her.

"Get out! Get out of my face before I do something you'll regret."

I fixed my gaze on her. I smiled. A calmness came over me. "I won't regret a damn thing. I quit."

"Get off the premises! Now!"

I slammed her door as I left. Something she threw smacked against the wall.

Everyone in the locker room had heard us. Some were afraid to approach me. Fear of retaliation. Others came running for the 411. I declined their requests. Just waved them off before gathering my belongings and taking my last walk. I felt something close to sadness, having put so much of my life into this. I'd like to think I made a difference for some of them. Chance had ensured Bodie wasn't included in that number.

I threw my bag in the back of my pickup when Tomas, the other shift sergeant, came up. He was winded. Probably from running to catch up with me.

"You want to talk about things, Winters? Maybe cool off? I've never been in charge of you, but know what I've seen. You're a good CO."

"Thanks. But I think this was meant to happen. This is my fork in the road."

"Very well, amigo." He grinned, understanding that a man has to do what a man has to do. "But do you want me to squash things with Arnold? Maybe talk things over with the warden? You and I both know how vindictive she can be. Maybe you should leave on better terms."

"Nah. Any other terms would be worse. I'm really beginning to think Arnold's crazy. Besides, she can't do shit to me now."

Enough of the bullshit. I drove for Amelia's.

62

BODIE

Naked in solitary.

My punishment for fighting back. I had to laugh even if no one was there to hear it. Winters had me thrown in here, but he just didn't know.

I soared.

I had Amelia.

In ways he never could.

Half here, half in another time . . . another place, she was mine. I had her heart on lock.

The last time we made love. A week before our last breakup. Two weeks before I caught that ride to the pawn shop with Aaron and Ro.

"Bodie . . . I . . . I . . . oh shit. Ooooh *shit*." Her legs tightened around my neck. I felt her toes curl. I smiled, knowing I was tearing it up. What had begun as an argument, again, ended with us pulling into a Motel 6 off Northwest Freeway. We had that intensity . . . that burn. When Amelia loved you, it was like being trapped in a fire. Heat and flames everywhere with no escape.

"You love me?"

"I . . . I," she panted.

"Huh?" I doubled my efforts, felt another gush as she came. My sweat dripped onto her firm, sexy body.

"Yes! Yes! Yes! I love you!"

People two rooms over knew it.

Keys in the door disturbed me. But it wasn't the door to the hotel room. It was my dark cell. I tried to focus, still holding my hardened dick in my hand.

"Busy, Antoine?"

I went to say something, but giggled instead. My "I don't give a fuck" trip was still in effect. "What you want? You're messin' up my dream."

I wagged my dick at Arnold, laughing. She didn't laugh back. She was alone. She pushed the door shut behind her.

"Wasting all that dick in your hand? 'Cause I really need to unwind."

"You can unwind on this." I held it erect for her to see.

"What happened to playing hard to get? I know. This place finally got to you."

"Whatever." I blew out. "Can't you and your boy Winters leave me alone for a few fuckin' minutes?"

"Winters." She laughed after stating his name. Bitch might've been high herself.

"What's so funny?"

"Nothing." She undid her uniform belt. "You really don't like him, huh?"

I didn't answer. Before Winters made a fool of me, she was at the top of my list. I watched her take off her striped pants. A laced thong decorated her thick round ass until she slipped that off too. My dick, still in my hand, began hardening again.

"Can I still unwind on it?"

I hated her as much as I wanted to fuck her. But a nigga has his limits. As I watched her play with her clit, sliding her fingers in and out of her pussy, I wanted to know hers.

She climbed atop me on the cell floor. I squeezed that ass as she guided my dick up inside her. I hadn't had pussy in so long, I almost nutted from the sensation.

Arnold wound that ass round and round, spiraling down my pole like a pro. She rode me hard, making her ass cheeks clap with every bounce of her pussy on my dick. I grabbed her shirt, yanking her down harder each time. She unbuttoned it so I could see her big old titties almost coming out her bra. I pulled her bra down, letting them bounce freely.

"Oh yeah. That's it, nigga. That's it." I felt her pussy quiver uncontrollably as she came hard.

I wasn't done with that ass.

Before she knew it, I had her bent over on her knees. I took all my frustrations out in that moment. She begged, pleaded and cursed as I wore that ass out doggy style, trying to drive my dick into her lungs. "Tear it up," she taunted as she smacked her ass defiantly against me. As her legs gave out, she fell over. I rode her down to the floor, pounding that pussy every step of the way. I pressed atop her hot, sticky body as I worked the dick in and out of her.

"That's it, baby. Cum like I'm that bitch Amelia."

And I did.

Only moans escaped her lips as I bust my nut. The coke was deserting me as I rolled off her. Emotionally and physically spent, I drifted off while Arnold gathered her clothes.

"Get up."

The baton poked me in my side. I tried to roll away, continue my sleep. When it hit me upside my head, I came to.

"That was some good shit, Antoine. Thank you." Arnold had put most of her uniform back on. Her shirt still hung out of her pants.

She tapped on the cell door and others walked in. I sat up, quickly moving back into the corner. My head was ringing, but I tried to focus.

"What's wrong, Antoine? This pussy too much for you?" She laughed and the others joined in. About four of them. Men. I still couldn't make out their faces.

"What you want now? And why they here?" I squinted in their direction. Arnold walked over, stooping beside me.

"I forgot to tell you earlier. Winters is gone."

Her voice made my head hurt worse. "What the fuck you talkin' 'bout?" I groaned.

She got closer so I would hear perfectly. "Winters left. But he has a parting gift just for you for trying to kill him."

The other four came closer. I could see them clearly now.

"What the fuck . . . ?"

"What's up, celly?" Rewind grinned like he'd won something. His boys looked more anxious. I knew what was up.

Arnold pushed my head with her hand before she stood up. Rewind put his arm around her waist. They tongued while he reached under her shirt and squeezed one of her breasts. She looked back at me, singing, "Just remember, whatever you did to me . . . they're gonna do to you." Then she instructed, "Don't do anything permanent. I got too much paperwork as it is." Arnold tucked in her shirt, whistling as she left the cell.

I tried to get on my feet, but couldn't. When they saw me move, Rewind and his boys teed off on me. While they punched, kicked and swung, Rewind ran his mouth.

"Think you can break my arm and get away with it, nigga? Thought you was a tough motherfucker? That's what you thought? Well, you ain't shit!"

When the beating was over, they lifted me up. I couldn't see Rewind anymore. Don't really know if I'd lost consciousness. Everything was numb. I felt wobbly like spaghetti. They pinned my arms and legs, bending me over.

"What's your white boy's name, Bodie?" Rewind was behind me.

The question didn't make sense. I tried to get free, but they beat me some more. I had broken ribs. They held me in place again.

"See, I remember him. I don't forget faces. Especially his. By the Chinese restaurant on Antoine. 'Bout five years ago. Your boy put my cousin in a coma. Y'know . . . I always wondered where I knew that picture of your Caddy you had on the wall. You were sittin' in it that night while he did it. Nigga, this is gonna be so much fun."

They all laughed.

All of my past dealings and the turf wars we'd fought came slapping me in the face in that instant. I could've tried reasoning with
them, but that shit don't work. Rewind dropped his pants.

Winters had gotten me good. I didn't know he had it in him.

Rewind forced his dick in my ass. I felt myself tear as I resisted
screaming by biting into my lip. Pain like I'd never known before had
me wishing they'd just kill me. But they didn't. Just took turns over
and over. I don't know when they stopped. I just prayed for it to end.

But my prayers stopped being answered long ago.

63

AMELIA

I left Memorial City Mall with my prize. With my audition coming up, I'd found the perfect outfit at Camille la Vie. On my arm was an exquisite black dress with a gold sequined halter strap. One left, on sale and just my size. As if meant to be.

I could've dwelled on Ike, but he'd played me. What could have been if he weren't a grown ass man still playing kid games.

He was good.

Had me fooled.

Still, I worried for his safety. Maybe it was for the best. If I wasn't with him, then maybe Bodie would leave him alone. That's it . . . reasoning my hurt and disappointment away. A few more days of telling myself that and I might believe it.

I hung my purchase in the back of my car, preparing to leave. I backed up until a truck almost hit me. Traffic was always bad here, but this was ridiculous. I honked for it to move, but that didn't work. Still spooked by Bodie, I locked my door and rolled the window up.

I saw someone in uniform, probably mall security, in my mirror as they walked up. He knocked on my window.

"Ma'am, would you put your window down?"

I obeyed.

"Gotcha," he said as I recognized the voice. I almost wanted to smile. He wanted to kiss me. I didn't let him. Played distant . . . cold.

"Your uniform?" I asked.

"Yeah," he said, giving me a nervous smile. The colors, the stripe on the pant leg. It looked a lot like . . .

"Just got off work?"

"You might say that. I quit."

Like that was supposed to make me concerned. I looked back like I was in a hurry. "What are you doing here?"

"I was looking for you, boo. Went by your job. Tookie said you'd be here. Took forever to find your car."

"Yeah. And you almost missed me."

"You're not answering your phone."

"Kind of like you when you were sick."

He looked at me strangely. "Something you want to say?"

"I'll leave that to you, player. What do you want?"

"We need to talk. Now."

I reached out my window and slapped him.

"What was that for?" Yeah. He was good.

"I met her."

He opened his mouth to form that word. I banged him with the car door, knocking him back. "What the fuck is wrong with you!"

"Don't say 'who' because you know who I'm talking about."

"Deryn?"

"At least you know when to drop the act." I was out of my car. Pointing my finger at him as I stormed about. Fuck it. There was gonna be a scene. I swung a fist, but he sidestepped it. "I went by there, Ike! I went by there last night when you called yourself being sick. I saw your ex in all her glory. Or maybe she's not your ex. Probably never was. To think I went by there to warn you. Because I was worried . . ."

"About what? Bodie?"

He stopped me in my tracks. My turn to look dumbfounded.

A Honda wanted to pass to leave the mall. Ike's truck blocked them and they began honking.

"Go the fuck around!" he barked. They sped around his truck and got away. His attention came back to me. "Yeah. I know about Bodie. I know you've been by the prison to see him. Probably one of those days you were supposed to be working."

"You've been following me?"

"No. You already know the answer." I read the patch on his uniform, put my eyes on what I'd been avoiding. Texas Department of Corrections. Our eyes met. Truth revealed. I didn't want him to speak it. "I'm a guard. A corrections officer. Fuck." He pinched his brow between his eyes. He lowered his voice, looking like he wanted to cry. *"Was* a corrections officer. I was Bodie's CO, Amelia."

"Lord. No." I brought my trembling hands to my mouth.

He cautiously approached. Cradled my hands in his. "Please. Like I said. We need to talk."

64

IKE

Once she was able to drive, I followed Amelia here. She led me downtown near the aquarium on the bayou, where she fetched a notebook from her trunk. We walked through the back entrance of the Questcom Theater as if they were expecting her.

"What are you doing here?" My eyes adjusted to the darkened corridor as we snaked toward the center of the facility. Amelia, still fuming, was moving so quickly that she almost left me.

"Rehearsing." She stopped at the end of the corridor. I could see the theater stage behind her and rows of empty seats. "They're letting me rehearse. Natalia got me an audition with Marion Lansky." She let her enthusiasm show . . . shared it with me, if just for a second. It was difficult being cut off. "I wanted to surprise you with the news last night. When you claimed you were sick. But you surprised me instead."

"When I called, I wasn't well. Seriously. Things had happened at work."

"Did fucking that bitch heal you? No . . . wait. I shouldn't call her that. I don't know her like that. And I don't know you either."

"Can I tell you my side?"

"Maybe. I have to rehearse first. Take a seat."

I did as ordered, letting her work through her anger in her own way. From my front-row seat, I watched her deliver a powerful rendition of "I'm Going Down." It reminded me of when I first heard her sing, that night when she cried her soul out. She asked if Deryn had healed me last night when she stayed over. No. Deryn couldn't. Deryn just made wounds worse, more raw. But just closing my eyes . . . listening to Amelia and imagining, made me think she could.

When she finished, the sound people and I applauded. She curtsied and waved. The Amelia I'd come to know smiled at me. She walked to the edge of the stage and sat down. Her legs dangled before me.

"Now. Talk."

I looked around, curious if anybody was paying attention to me. They weren't. "I didn't know it was you. You look different. I've only known Bodie since his transfer. He'd talked about his girl, but I honestly didn't know it was you . . . that you were his."

She shook her head, things weighing heavier than I could imagine. "You make it sound like I'm his property. Is that how he described me? Is that what you think?"

"Baby, I don't know what to think." I sighed. "This is so surreal, y'know? I never meant . . . I never would have . . . I mean if I hadn't gone to Lullaby's . . ."

"Do you regret that you did, Ike?"

I felt my chest. The bandage was irritating. "No," I replied. "No, I don't."

Her eyes watered. She stood up, moving gracefully across the stage. Like Natalia, but different. This is where she belonged. Part of her wanted to move on. She came back to me.

"How long have you known?"

"Not long." I put my head down. "Too long. I should've come forward when I first found out. Part of me was afraid. Afraid the best thing to happen to me would walk away. That maybe I needed you more than you needed me."

She hummed a little tune to herself, not looking at me. Looking back somewhere else. "I've known him since I was eighteen. I was young. Liked the attention he showed me. He was dangerous, different. And he loved me. No matter what we went through, he never scared me. But when he said he was going to hurt you . . ." She revealed her eyes to me. "I loved him. Damn."

"Exactly. Damn."

"What's wrong with your chest?"

"Huh? Oh. Just a scratch." She looked at me strange. "Okay. The truth. More than a scratch. Me and Bodie had a run-in. We're both okay if you're wondering. It's the reason I didn't see you last night. And one of the reasons I quit. I know if I'd stayed things would only get 'permanent' for one of us. I'm not a murderer."

" 'Not like him' is what you're saying."

"You're putting words in my mouth. And I'm not trying to kick a brother while he's already down."

"You really cared about Bodie."

"Don't go there. I'm not his biggest fan at the moment."

"But I've become one of yours, Ike."

"Thank you. That means more than you know. But I gotta tell you, nothing happened with me and Deryn last night. She needed somewhere to crash and I called myself doing the right thing. Honest. She didn't tell me you'd been by."

Amelia sat down again. Her feet swayed from side to side. "Speaking of honesty, I lied to you once. When I said I had to work, I did go see him. Only once since I've known you. I went to end things for good."

"For real?"

"Yes. I did lie to you another time."

"Oh."

She patted her neck. "My tattoo."

I got up from my seat. Walked up to the stage. I touched her ankles. Grazed the backs of my hands against them. "I already figured that out. It was Bodie's name before you changed it . . . Antoine to Antoinette."

"No. It wasn't."

65

BODIE

"**Y**ou need to tell us what happened, Campbell." She used "Antoine" to get to me. Now she didn't need to. She'd found more severe ways. "There's nothing to be ashamed of."

Alvarez, the other sergeant, sensing she was going somewhere she shouldn't, gave it a shot. "Son, this happened on my watch and I won't stand for it. I know you have your code and all that bullshit, but you need to talk so I can handle this."

I just glared at Arnold from my hospital bed. The fake concern she was showing was the ultimate torture. When they got me out of solitary, they had to stitch me up and administer an AIDS test. I was bandaged for my ribs and my other lumps were tended to. Rewind and them beat me good. After fuckin' with that powder, I didn't want shit else, but they forced the pain meds on me. Meds for pain, but not for rage.

"I don't know shit." My throat was dry, cracking.

They exchanged looks. "Told you," Arnold huffed at Alvarez.

Alvarez shook his head. "Son, if you change your mind, you know where to find me. If this is COs' doing, I'll have 'em on the street and brought up on charges."

They left me, but not before Arnold got a parting shot in. She patted me on my thigh, pretending she was concerned in front of her boy. When she was sure he couldn't hear her, she hissed, "The gown looks good on you, Antoine. Or should I call you 'Antoinette' now?"

I didn't respond, but my heart monitor shot up. Too weak to choke the ho.

I summoned the CO on guard over when they left. "I need to speak to my lawyer. Now."

"Arnold said no calls for you. Since you are technically still in solitary when you get outta here."

"Do you want to be the one denying my lawyer access? Have your ass working at the Waffle House, motherfucker. I said I need to meet with my lawyer today."

The CO sent it up through the channels and got in touch with him. I refused to let him see me looking defeated. Against their orders, I put on my prison uni and met him in visitation.

"You look terrible, Mr. Campbell," Jason North said as I walked slowly toward him. It took all my effort not to drag my leg. I worried my ass was bleeding again.

"Don't get up," I said as he tried to rise. "This won't take long."

"I hear times are hard, Mr. Campbell."

"They won't be for long. I got the contract for Amelia. It's binding. You can have it. Just get me the fuck out of here. Now."

"Do tell. Dear boy, you made my day." If a snake could smile, it would look like him.

"Good. Now make mine."

"Anything else I can do? Assist with relations on your side of the wall?"

I began limping away. Pain meds had me spacin'. I turned to acknowledge him a final time. "No. I got this. But if you try to fuck over me and Amelia, I'll kill you."

"I don't doubt it for a second, dear boy."

66

AMELIA

"**N**o. It wasn't."

"If the tat on your neck's not Bodie's name, then what did you lie about?"

The lights dimmed in the theater. I'd have to return another day if I wanted to rehearse. I picked up my notebook and rose to my feet. I flipped through the pages of verses I'd written at the coffeehouse. The finale to *U.S. Icon* was held in a similar type theater. Looking up from my writing, I imagined the empty seats filled with fans holding signs with my name. It must've been close to what Natalia felt.

Ike climbed onto the stage, looking out beside me. I took his hand in mine and caressed it.

"I'd say, 'penny for your thoughts,' if I had one."

"I was in this position before. When I quit singing. It was supposed to be the biggest day of my life."

"What happened?"

"Bodie got arrested . . . for murder. I choked. He went to jail. Natalia went on." I wiped the tear with my finger before it ran down my cheek. "Then I found out I was pregnant."

I turned to him, the man who had seen the father of my child more times than I had in recent years. No more secrets.

"That's my other lie. My middle name is Loretta, my grandmother's name. Not Antoinette. Antoinette is the name of my daughter."

"Daughter?" It wasn't intentional, just instinctive. Ike's hand pulled away. Releasing his grip, he took a step back. He folded his arms as if attempting to restrain his emotions. "You have a daughter . . . with Bodie?"

Silence.

How do you broach the subject of abortion?

"No," I answered. "She's not here."

He wrestled with my answer, finding its meaning without further questions.

He surprised me.

Ike unfolded his arms. He wrapped them around me and held. Not because he had to.

Just because.

"I'm sorry, boo. I'm sorry."

"Don't be. I don't want anybody feeling sorry for me. I hate pity even though I've engaged in a lot of it lately."

"Does he know about it?"

"What do you think?" I chuckled from a case of nerves. I remembered how alone I felt when I took a cab to the clinic. Natalia, my best friend, was away in California as her drama unfolded before the nation. At the time, I felt that God had deserted me too. "He never saw the tat when I visited him. It's just my way of honoring her. If he did, he'd just think I got mad at him and changed the name."

"I can see why. I sure did."

"Sometimes men have trouble seeing the obvious."

He smiled, knowing it applied to him in so many ways. "Wanna know what I see?"

"Shoot."

"I see me and you growing old together. Maybe three kids."

"Three?"

"Well . . . yeah. After you blow Lansky away at your audition and go quadruple platinum, we'll have plenty time to fit that in."

"Still interested in me?"

"Do you see me runnin'?"

"You're crazy, Ike."

"Crazy over you. Yesterday is over, so don't sweat it. Just go out and make tomorrow the best it can be."

"Where'd you get that from? Your mother?"

"No, my boxing coach. Speaking of my momma, I need to introduce y'all."

"I'd like that, Isaac."

"What did you call me?"

I winked. "Get over it."

"Coming from your mouth, it sounds beautiful."

We left the theater . . . together. I'd be back for my big shot and Ike would be with me. Not a superstar and her bodyguard. Just a waitress and a former prison guard trying to make tomorrow the best it can be . . . together.

67

IKE

Amelia didn't want to go home and didn't want me there. Bodie's threats still had her frightened. It bothered me, made me briefly rethink how I'd handled him, that someone who claimed to love her so much would cause her so much pain. Love was something you knew, but was also something you learned.

To make her feel safe, I went by the ATM, then checked us into a motel for the night. We chose one in Baytown, east of town. Someplace far enough from both our places, she figured. She'd offered to pay the bill, but I refused. I was out of a job, but not out of pride.

Due to the hurricanes, the only room available was a suite.

Maybe I shouldn't have been so eager to refuse her offer.

"You could've let me go home and get some clothes." I fumbled with the card key, frustrated with the red light every time I inserted it.

"You can do it in the morning. Unless you have somewhere you'd rather be." She clung to me despite what my uniform represented.

"Naw, I'm where I belong."

"Good," she said as the door finally flashed green, granting us entry.

The room was better than we expected. Roach free, from the ones that crawl and the leftover ones from the cleaning lady with glaucoma. Even the carpet you could walk on barefooted.

Amelia ran for the bed, springing through the air before bouncing on its surface. I laughed at the sudden burst of energy she showed.

"My feet were killing me," she said as she kicked her work shoes off. I was a little more reserved, checking the room. The bathroom surprised me with a large garden tub with whirlpool jets. Now that's what I'm talkin' 'bout. I hummed to myself, imagining soaking my sore body in a mass of bubbles.

"What did you find?"

"Heaven," I accurately replied.

I ran the water, finding some shower gel to add to it. As the tub filled, I began taking my uniform off. Amelia was on the bed flipping through channels to catch up on the day.

"Look, *Busted* is on. Want to watch it?"

"Please, not tonight," I chimed. I got to my uniform shirt and began unbuttoning it. Concerned about her seeing too much, I pushed the door partially closed. I took a final look at the patch I'd worn since college, then balled it up and tossed it in the garbage. The door bumped me in my back.

"Can I come in?" From behind the door, Amelia revealed herself. Her eyes tired yet brimming with the infectious enthusiasm I loved about her. She was anxious to shed her work clothes too. She joined me in the bathroom, her bare form bathed in the light of the mirrored bulbs. I still wore my undershirt.

Hiding.

She came closer. I froze, admiring the gentle curves of her hips, the slope of her breasts. She raised my tee over my head. My bandage was exposed. She paused.

"He tried to kill you."

"But he didn't."

"Maybe I should talk to him. Try to get him to stop this."

"Let's not talk about him. Not here. Not tonight. Remember . . . we're here to get away."

We kissed, free of lies and all the bullshit, revealed fully to each other. Grasping her hips, I carried Amelia to the tub. We descended into the bubbles, where I descended into her depths again and again.

"I love you, Ike," she gasped as I loved her harder. Water splashed, overflowing onto the bathroom floor.

"What do you think?" Amelia donned her dress from the car, giving me a preview of what she would wear at her audition.

We'd ordered Domino's. I lay across the bedspread, replenishing my energy with a slice of pepperoni. "You look beautiful. Perfect for your evening."

She turned, allowing me to admire her fully. I dropped my pizza in the box. "Y'know, I thought about something less formal. Maybe some nice jeans. Go with the understated look."

"Don't. You look fit to be crowned. That's going to be your night. Let Lansky see you ready to take the throne."

She scowled, irritated with my choice of words. "I'm not there to compete with Natalia. If it weren't for her, I wouldn't even have the audition."

"I know, I know. But in the industry's eyes, you are her competition. Are you prepared?"

"Yes."

"Good, 'cause I got your back."

She brought her fingertips across her lips, as if to prevent foolish, hasty words from escaping. When she was ready, she removed them. "I believe you," she said.

We could've made love again that night. Probably wanted to. We turned off the TV and cuddled instead. No sounds save the beating of our hearts. Content with each other and more important . . . ourselves.

When I knew she was asleep, I slid my arm out from under her. I quietly walked over to my pants pocket, where I pulled my wallet free. I looked at her, enjoying the peaceful expression on her face.

Will it last? I wondered.

I couldn't expect her just to wait while I found myself.

I went to the bathroom, where I read the numbers on the business card. I dialed them on my phone.

"Sorry to call so late," I replied upon their answering.

68

BODIE

"You know you shouldn't be saying this to me." He dropped his cigarette, extinguishing what was left with his foot. His mirrored sunglasses hid his eyes. Inmates called him Ashtray, but not to his face.

I wasn't cleared, but was weightlifting anyway. I needed the outlet. To make myself feel everything was normal with me. To admit I was patched together and feeling less than a man . . . that was death. "Why not?" I asked. "From what I hear, most of y'all feel the same way."

"I can help you with your former cellmate, but I'm stayin' outta that other mess." He leaned against the wall, already fishing another cigarette from his pocket. I thought they'd outlawed that in here.

"I'm offering a shitload of money. And you can't do this?"

"How 'bout Winters?" he offered. "He ain't workin' here anymore. I can do that."

"I ain't askin' you about Winters. I'm asking you to take care of Arnold."

"Sorry, Bodie."

"You sure as hell are." I sat up from the weight bench, glaring at Ashtray. I imagine he scowled back behind his knockoff Ray-Bans. "Did you bring the phone?"

Instead of nodding, he moved his glasses up and down. Joe Cool, that one. He debated on lighting his cigarette first, but reached in his pocket for the burner.

"Give it to me. I'll let you know when I'm done."

I quickly dialed the number. With what had gone down, my stroke around here was gone. I had to be careful. Pick and choose my spots.

"What it do?"

"Put Ro on, motherfucker."

"You ain't gotta be so bitter."

"Did you get the picture?"

"Yeah. We got it. You sure that mug a CO? That motherfucker was in the paper with her?"

"You'd know that if you read. Now put Ro on."

Aaron had a few words as he handed the phone over. He was getting cocky. I wouldn't be able to trust him much longer.

"Hello."

"You watchin' him?"

"Yeah. But he didn't come home last night. He ain't at Amelia's either." I could hear Aaron in the background, bitchin' about being parked all night outside Winters' place.

"Find him. I want him gone before I get out."

"Out? You bein' released, bruh?"

"Yeah. I got something in the works. Got a problem with that?"

"After takin' the hit for me and my brother, man? Hell no."

"So you got it, right?"

He paused, telling Aaron to shut up. Ro regained his calm. "Are you sure you want to do this, Bodie? You're talking about taking a life. The Scripture says—"

"Don't you owe me?"

"Yes."

"Well, do what I fuckin' say. I've been through more shit for y'all asses than you'll ever know and it's time y'all motherfuckers paid up."

"That's it?"

"No. I got another favor."

"What's that?"

A plane flew overhead. Free. Taking off from the airport named for the daddy of the former governor. A man who liked frying niggas. I'd be free like that plane soon.

"Tell Winters it's from me before he dies," I said, never taking my eyes off the plane.

"Your will be done then. And may God have mercy on all our souls."

69

AMELIA

"**A**re you gonna do some Jennifer Holliday? You gotta do some Jennifer Holliday. It always sets them off at the Apollo."

"We're not in Harlem, Tookie," Me-Me reminded her.

"So. The judges still *gonna looooove it*," she sang, imitating her favorite singer.

"There aren't any judges."

"What? Well, don't tell Amelia."

I held my little cousin J. R., bouncing him on my leg. Watching the two friends carry on reminded me of why I missed Natalia. She wanted to be here for my audition, but had an independent film she was trying out for. Onward and upward for her.

Marion Lansky and his people were in the theater, taking their seats. I was backstage, seeing relatives I hadn't seen in years. Mainly, I was with the people I trusted. And wondering what was keeping Ike.

"Amelia, did you hear me?"

"Huh?" I said, bringing my attention to the soft-spoken teddy bear, Neal.

He wore a nice blue tailored suit, looking like he belonged out there with Lansky's people. "Do you need me to do anything?"

I sipped some of my tea. J. R. swatted at my nose, spurring Me-Me to yank him from my lap. "No, I'm okay, Neal. Thanks."

He'd done enough, having bunches and bunches of flowers awaiting me when I arrived. He and Me-Me had also had a limo pick me
up from the hairstylist's. Natalia had had a designer number flown
in overnight, but remembering Ike's reaction, I stuck with my choice.

"Ms. Bonds?"

Me-Me and myself looked.

"Amelia?" the assistant said, pointing explicitly at me. My cousin
laughed. "We're almost finished with setup. We'll be ready for sound
check in fifteen minutes."

Everybody paused while I took a deep breath. Me-Me suggested
they clear out to give me some quiet time. Before she left, the two of
us did a quick vocal exercise, climbing the scales in harmony.

"Remember, you got this," she sang as she walked out the door.

"Tookie . . . wait," I called out.

She came back in. "I know you ain't worried about Ike. He's
gonna be here."

"I'm not worried. Could you close the door?"

Tookie, looking beautiful with a ton of ringlet curls in her hair,
pushed it shut. She paused.

"I've been needing to tell you something."

"What's that, boo?"

I looked at her reflection in my dressing room mirror. "I know
what happened to Montez."

"And what's that?"

"My ex did it. I mean . . . he had something to do with it. Montez
didn't do anything. He was just in the wrong place. I wanted to let
you know. And apologize."

Tookie was quiet for the longest. It made me a little nervous. Then
she spoke. "I knew it. It didn't make sense when he was mumbling,
but I figured it had something to do with you."

"I'm sorry."

She came closer, putting her hands on my shoulders. She gave me
a kiss on the cheek. "I ain't mad atcha. Well . . . maybe a little for not
telling me sooner. The real motherfucker I'm mad at is your jailbird

ex. If he was out, I'd bust a cap in his ass. But get all that stuff outta your mind, boo. Think positive thoughts because that's what I'm going to be doing for you."

I reached up, placing my hand atop hers. "Thank you, Tookie. For everything."

She left me. I finished the last bit of tea and hummed a little more, tuning up.

As I remembered one of the songs I'd written, I wondered what surprises awaited me on that stage.

And what surprises awaited me and Ike beyond today.

70

IKE

"Yeah!" I shouted over the radio blaring in my truck. I sped along, ignoring the potholes and construction work. Soon this piece of shit would be retired anyway.

"Impressive credentials, Mr. Winters," he'd said. The man in black looked over the few sheets I'd put together in the folder. I figured I'd dress the part, wearing an expensive black suit as well. I had the tag and the store bag outside in the truck. I had one other use for the suit though—one more important than this interview. Amelia's coming-out party. "And you used to do some boxing? We like our associates to have some hand-to-hand expertise. I think you would do nicely."

"Thank you."

"Natalia mentioned you to us already. I was wondering what took you so long to call."

I smiled. "Timing, sir. Leaving you waiting builds the anticipation."

We shared a laugh and a handshake.

And I was offered a six-figure job as a supervisor with their security firm.

I slammed on my brakes to keep from running a red light. Looking at my watch, I saw I was late. Amelia would be pissed. But I think I could make that smile return with what I had to say.

I stopped at my place, ignoring the busted kitchen window. A rock rested on the kitchen floor. Probably done by Deryn. She was still pissed and trying to vandalize her way into my heart.

In my bedroom, I secured the jewelry case from its hiding spot. The jewelry store was nice enough to grant me a line of credit and I was foolish enough to take it. What was two months' salary when I didn't have one? With my good news, it no longer mattered. I opened it, making sure the ring was resting comfortably.

Another glance at my watch and I was on my way, bolting out the house and back into my truck.

To avoid traffic, I took the back streets. Highway travel at this time of day could be murder. *Clackety-clack* went my engine every time I gunned the motor. I decided to leave Third Ward for downtown by crossing 288 at Wheeler Street.

Behind me was an old Monte Carlo. Its paint job was all I could see as it rode my bumper. The sun was dipping behind the clouds, but its color created its own light. Wouldn't have minded having one like that myself back in the day. I rolled down my window and motioned for it to go around. No need keeping them from their destination.

Still it stayed behind me, so I continued on.

I got to the overpass. The same spot I'd jogged across the week before. The same place I'd stopped at to sort through my baggage. I smiled, knowing that it was carrying me over into another chapter in my life.

Then the car passed me.

As it sped by, I noticed the white boy glaring at me. He cut a wink. I nodded my head, wondering now if he was truly white. Boy looked pretty ghetto if you asked me. I almost didn't notice the muzzle of the rifle as it inched out the window.

I saw the flash.

My leg burned before I heard the gunfire erupt. Whistling sounds filled the cab of the truck. Then my forearm squirted blood.

My first thoughts were to the suit I'd just ruined. And that Amelia was going to be pissed.

Then that I might die.

I sped up, trying to pass the car. They accelerated too, still spraying my truck with automatic gunfire. I ducked as the windows shattered.

When the Monte Carlo got even with me, I slammed on my weak brakes. It was enough to slow me and make the car overtake me.

When it did, I rammed it.

The car slid sideways, its driver jarred from behind the wheel. It came to rest against the rail, smashed and smoking.

Everything was happening so fast. My truck killed on me after bouncing off the wall, taking a portion of the fencing down. I tasted the blood coming up my throat. I was hurt bad. I tried one last time to get it to start. Nothing.

I tumbled onto the street after opening the door. One of my arms was numb. Tingling. Behind me, a car door creaked. I rose to my feet again and tried to run. Someone walked up on me, kicking me in my back. I tumbled, falling against the railing. The ring box spilled out my pocket. I tried to grab it, but it rolled off my fingertips.

Dude, different than the driver, pulled out a 9 mil and pointed it at my head. I'd never seen him before in my life. My leg quivered, weak from the shots that had already found their mark. My black pants felt cold, soaked. The driver of the car had come to and was trying to walk. I heard a lady scream from the far end of the overpass. I looked back at the crucifix around dude's neck. Amelia's ring was right between his legs. So close.

He cocked the hammer back as I looked on. For a second, I thought I heard him whisper a prayer.

"I have nothing personal against you," he spoke. "And wish nothing but peace and a better world to come for you, my brother."

I tried to speak, but found it hard to talk. I still had some feeling in my arm. He placed the muzzle to my forehead.

"I have a message for you. Bodie said to tell you this is from him."

The mention of his name made my adrenaline surge. I brought my arm up, crushing dude's nose with a punch. The hit knocked him silly, his eyes rolling up. He spun, trying to find his balance, but it didn't work. I watched him tumble against the railing before flipping over the side. Cars honked as he plummeted onto 288 below. I heard the dull thud. His crucifix hung up. It dangled from the piece of open fence where he'd just been.

I'd never been a murderer.

But I'd killed someone before.

Same punch. Back when I was boxing. My opponent fell to the mat and died in the hospital later. It was unintentional, but it led me to hang up the gloves.

"You killed my brother, motherfucker!" the driver snarled. Bloodied, he screamed like a mad dog as he ran at me. Tears clouded his eyes as he brought the AK-47 up. I stayed on my knees, blood loss overwhelming me. I was done.

I stretched out my hand, trying to will Amelia's ring into it. I began crying because it was all I could do.

He kicked the ring box away. Wiping the snot from his nose, he muttered, "Fuck you."

He unloaded the clip into me.

And I died.

71

BODIE

"I'm doing this only because Arnold has gone too far."

We were talking outside the metal shop door. The grinding inside shielded our voices.

"Bullshit. You're doing this because you want the money. You'll be able set your family up with some nice things." He didn't deny it.

"Sure you want to give up all your stash? On this? That kind of money buys you a lot in here."

"It'll be worth it for what that bitch did. And I'll be gone soon. I'll make the money up on the outside."

Winters was being taken care of and North had the contract. He'd had his lawyers check it. It was binding. Amelia wouldn't be able to sign with anyone else.

And I would continue as her manager.

I'd protect her. Make sure she was safe from North and anyone else.

"I'll do it," Alvarez, the other sergeant, agreed. An unlikely choice to go to, but I was desperate. "I'll take care of Arnold. But I'll do it my way."

"I knew you would." I grinned as I went to open the metal shop door. He barred the way with his arm. "Something else you want to say?"

"You don't have to do this, Campbell. You have the ability to stop. Like you said, you'll be gone."

"I'm like Santa, boss. I'm making a list and checking it twice. Now are you gonna let me go?"

Alvarez dropped his arm, moving aside. He had no stomach for the path he was on by making this deal with me.

Everyone else in the metal shop got word to clear out.

I entered and the door locked behind me.

Rewind wore goggles as he performed his work. When he noticed me out the corner of his eye, he flinched. He dropped the piece of metal at his feet. "What's up, celly?"

Only one of us was smiling.

72

AMELIA

"Miss, are you ready?" I looked again and saw the *U.S. Icon* judge, not Marion Lansky, sitting politely in the front row.

My palms were sweaty. Had a cold, damp feel to them as the air-conditioning in the theater kicked in. I cleared my throat and closed my eyes.

Ike hadn't shown. Same as the other time when I depended on someone to have my back. But he would be here. I'd heard his message on my phone before I came onstage. He was running a little late, but he would be here.

And he loved me.

"Miss, are you ready?" I opened my eyes again. I was back in the Questcom Theater. No three judges to tell me I was going to Hollywood. Everything else was yesterday. This was my Hollywood.

Ike still hadn't shown. I looked among the faces, searching for his smile. The smile wasn't there, but somehow I heard his words.

Just go out and make tomorrow the best it can be.

"For tomorrow," I whispered before signaling the sound crew I was ready.

The lights dimmed to where a solitary cone of light encased me. I adjusted the microphone stand out of habit. Lansky stared intently, his gaze analyzing every subtle nuance of my performance and translating it into dollars.

I wasn't the same scared girl.

Time to break the bank.

Time to start a fire.

Lights exploded behind me, jarring my audience. I snatched the microphone, kicking the stand aside as I went into my own version of Mary J. Blige's "Be Happy." Very appropriate for the recent lessons I'd learned.

To quit condemning myself for my mistakes while vowing to truly learn from them. How could I love Ike if I couldn't love myself enough to know it was time to let Bodie go?

I was letting go. Every verse, an exorcism; every note, a prayer.

I bounded down the stairs, uplifting the very same listeners who were lifting me. Just like that night at Lullaby's, I won them over and made them my own. Some of Lansky's inner circle stood and danced as I walked by. I stuck out my hand, high-fiving all of them, twirling past as I worked the notes. Lansky remained seated, playing his cards like a gambler. My eyes pleaded for a response, but he wasn't giving one. I moved on, dancing back onto the stage.

Lansky only gave me two numbers to wow him. A habit of his from what Natalia had told me. He claimed all he needed to know could be determined from an audition's song choice and vocals. He had to be back in New York by morning, so I knew the next number would be my last shot.

I'd switched the song selection. Somewhere between leaving the dressing room and getting to the stage, I'd made the decision. As everyone settled back into their seats, I cued the keyboard player. I'd gone over the song with him, humming what I wanted for accompaniment. He was good. Figured out what I wanted even when I wasn't sure.

I was going with my own song. One of the ones I wrote at the coffeehouse. A big gamble. But not that big for someone with nothing to lose.

Then I saw him.

In the top section, where it was closed off to everyone. He stood, hunched over the railing as he looked down at me.

Ike.

He was dressed all in black, the diamond stud in his ear twinkling from way up there. We smiled at each other before he left, walking back up the stairs and out the exit to the rear.

"I'd like to do a number for you that I wrote. Something I needed to put out there to help me move on . . . and I hope you enjoy."

I poured my heart into my final act, a melancholy number about passion without love. Halfway through it, I was crying. I pushed on, digging deeper into my soul to finish. And when I was finished, they cried with me.

Tookie was the first. Standing up and applauding. Me-Me and Neal joined her. Then another. And another. The roar was deafening.

But Lansky was still speechless. He stayed glued to his seat. I didn't know what he felt about it.

Then I realized he was wiping his eyes. He was crying too.

Lansky left, but had his people take down all of my information. He was flying me up to New York next week to meet his image team and legal staff. He wanted them to check on the Fire Starter tag . . . see if it was trademarked. I was going to be signed.

"Cuz, you were amazing," Me-Me said as we hugged goodbye. She and Neal had to be to Lullaby's to open it up.

"And I owe all to you."

"Free concert tickets when you come to town is all I ask," she teased. "Didn't know you were a song writer too."

"Me neither," I admitted. "It just felt right."

"Sure you don't want to come to the club?"

"Maybe later. Have you seen Ike?"

Me-Me shook her head. "No."

"Maybe he had to move his truck or something."

"So you saw him?"

"Yes. In the upper tier."

"That was open?"

"No, but he got up there somehow."

Knowing I had him there, they left. I stayed inside the theater, waiting for him to return. Everyone had left by now, but I stayed put. I called his cell, but got his voice mail. I decided to go out the back door, where he might be waiting with a surprise or something.

I was starting to worry.

Then I heard it. I walked from behind the theater and looked down Bagby Street in the direction of the noise. It was dark, but I knew Ike's truck when I saw it. It putted and sputtered as it approached, smoke escaping from under its hood.

He must've had car trouble.

That's what took him so long.

I wasn't the prissy one, so I ran down Bagby to meet him, my dress trailing behind me. The truck rolled to a stop at the curb on the corner of Prairie Street.

"Did you see it? Did you see it?" I yelled, unable to control my excitement. I quit running when I saw all the bullet holes and broken glass. The door to Ike's truck opened.

"*Aaron?*"

The last words I said.

I screamed as bullets rang out from his gun, slamming into me. I flew off my feet, tumbling to the concrete.

"Th-this shit all your fault," he rambled. I hadn't seen Aaron or his brother since Bodie went to jail. Blood streaked his shirt, but it wasn't his. Ike was dead. I knew it like I'd never known anything in my life. I tried to scream, but couldn't. Only a horrible gurgling sound escaping.

He came up on me and kicked me once. I winced in pain.

"You don't know how much mess you caused, do ya? All this shit is because o' you. Because of you." I could make out several police sirens, coming closer. They wouldn't be here in time. I'm not quite sure I wanted to live anymore anyway. He aimed at my head.

Two shots rang out.

Blood splattered on Aaron's shirt again.

Except this time it was his.

I trembled, losing consciousness as I began convulsing. I tried to scream again with the same result as before.

Aaron looked at his chest, then fell face-first to the sidewalk. Behind him stood Tookie, her purse dangling open on her arm. She clenched the gun she'd just fired, afraid to let go.

Then I made my exit.

No more songs to sing.

73

BODIE

North worked fast. They came to get me from my cell, telling me I was to meet with one of his attorneys at the courthouse. Rather than cuffed and transported in my whites, I was given a brand-new suit to put on.

I was really gonna be free. Not no dream or nothin'. My dreams had been cruel. This tasted sweet—as sweet as Amelia's lips. The thought made me dress quicker. When she saw me, she wouldn't know what to do.

Before I left the cell, I gathered my pen and paper and finished a letter I'd been working on. It was a reply to a letter of mine that had been found. I had fumbled with what to say in it, but today's news was what I needed. I wrapped up my reply to my moms, telling her how Amelia and me were going to be so happy together and get it right this time. I handed it to the CO to be delivered as he escorted me out of my block.

Down the row, I slapped the hands extended through the bars, tellin' them to keep their head up. Waiting for me by the prison transport to sign my papers was Sergeant Alvarez. Arnold should've been there. A light went off in my head.

North wasn't the only one who worked fast.

"I got this," he said to the assigned driver. "I need to make some stops on the way back."

I adjusted my lapels and stepped into the back.

We took I-45 into town. It was a rainy, nasty day. Like the sun had decided to sleep in. The only thing close to warmth was the glow of the transport's flashing yellow light on the traffic we passed.

"What's going on with Arnold?" I asked to break the silence. Alvarez didn't even put on the radio for a nigga. He was as glum as the weather. Not me. I felt alive.

"She was arrested last night," he said calmly as he looked into the rearview mirror. "A half kilo of coke was found in her trunk."

"Damn. I guess crime doesn't pay," I responded slyly. Didn't know if the van was wired. If Alvarez had a change of heart and was tryin' to set me up.

"It gets worse. She's also been implicated in the murder of Rewind."

I blinked on that one. He impressed me. I guess all my money was well spent. "C'mon now."

"Looks like she'd been supplying him on the inside. Maybe he threatened to talk or something. None of your concern though. You won't be around."

"You seem pretty certain, Alvarez."

"I am. A friend of yours, Roland Fontenot, signed a confession yesterday. You won't be staying with us any longer."

I moved up, grabbing the security grill behind his head. "Don't fuck with me like that."

"I'm not. Got the order this morning. That and those high-powered attorneys of yours got you a hearing today."

"I'll be damned."

"You might be. Winters is dead." He switched lanes on the dime, rocking the van and knocking me into the door. "You remember Winters, right?" His tone was gruff, accusatory. He liked Winters.

I controlled my satisfaction. Alvarez only knew so much. "Yeah. So."

"You know anything about that?"

"Winters had enemies. That's all I know."

"If you were innocent to begin with, you didn't have to go this route. You killed a good man."

"I don't know what you're talkin' 'bout, boss."

"My name's not 'boss.' It's Tomas." We never spoke again. Business transacted. Business finished.

I was delivered at the courthouse. One of North's attorneys was there, two guards with him. A smallish white man in expensive eyeglasses, he wore a black trench coat as he spoke on his cell. Used to see cats like him all the time by the Galleria, all important in their own heads. He motioned his hand at me like I was a servant or something, too busy to speak to me like a man. I followed him inside like a good little boy . . . for now.

Inside the courthouse, people were scrambling around. A lot of chatter. I wasn't used to all the noise. Sounded like mice or something. Maybe it was normal. But it didn't seem right.

"What's going on, man?"

"Crazy day in Houston. A lot of violence overnight. C'mon, let's get this over."

We went through a set of metal detectors. I liked that they didn't treat me like a criminal. Must've been the suit. On the second floor, we entered the clerk's office for a judge. He turned to me.

"With the new developments, Mr. North was able to get this expedited. Don't say a thing. Just smile and nod. Can you do that?"

I put this big fake-ass smile on my face and moved my head up and down like a dog.

"I guess that will do." I took a seat at the back of the courtroom while he spoke with the ladies in the office. A small black-and-white TV on their desk had them talking. My attorney shook his head at whatever was being said. After fishing paperwork out of his briefcase, he handed it to them and returned. He sat on the side of me, looking straight ahead. He only broke his concentration to look at his watch.

"Where are they holding Ro?"

"Who?" he answered, looking at his watch again instead of me.

"Roland Fontenot. My boy. The one who confessed."

He laughed. A first. "Probably in the Harris County Morgue right about now."

"Shit ain't funny, man."

"I wasn't joking. It was a deathbed confession. Your 'boy' is room temperature."

I felt sick, began sweating. While I came to terms, he got a phone call. His cell on vibrate. Made the pocket on his suit wiggle. He took it out, looked at the number.

"Yes, Mr. North. Uh-huh. Yes. He's here. Uh-huh, uh-huh . . . uh-huh."

He lowered the phone, covered it with his hand.

"Mr. North needs to speak with you."

I couldn't talk, but he knew when I was on the phone.

"We have a problem, dear boy. I offered to help, but you declined it. Now your idiots have cost both me and you."

"I—"

"Don't talk. Nothing you can say will suffice. You have cost me time and money, Mr. Campbell. That is something I do not like. You can have your contract back."

"I don't understand. Why?"

"Because it's no longer worth anything to me."

"I don't understand."

"Understand this. Let us not cross paths in the future. Now put your former attorney back on the phone."

I'd barely moved it from my ear when the lawyer snatched it away. He listened to his instructions, then stowed the phone away.

"I'm about to lose my mind up in here if somebody don't tell me somethin'. What the fuck is North talking about?"

"Your 'arrangement' is over. After this hearing, I no longer represent you."

"That's some bullshit. We had a deal."

"Well, I guess the deal broke over that." He gestured toward the TV the clerks were gathered around. Most shook their heads in pity.

Even though he objected, I got up from my seat and went over. About five people were gathered around the old wooden desk. I could see over their heads—different pictures from around town on the news. I tried to make out what was being said:

   ". . . bloody night on the streets of Houston."

". . . rather graphic images . . ."

      "Police are still investigating . . ."

  "The alleged shooter, Roland Fontenot . . ."

    ". . . where he fell from the 288 overpass."

  "Killed on the scene was Isaac Winters, a former corrections officer with the Texas Department of . . ."

     "Aaron Fontenot, brother of Roland . . ."

  ". . . went on a maddening rampage."

". . . if Amelia Bonds, a resident of Stafford, is a random victim or not . . ."

    ". . . is unknown if others are involved in this. . . ."

  "Sources tell us . . ."

"Amelia . . ."

When I repeated her name, the ladies all turned around and looked at me.

My world began swimming. I tugged at the stupid necktie, preventing it from strangling me.

"No . . . no . . . this is all wrong."

Images swirling. Aaron's and Ro's pictures flashed on the TV set. Everyone began moving away from me. One of the ladies ran out the office to get help.

My attorney came over, tried to calm me down. I swung on him, dropping him on the floor.

"Get the fuck off me, man!"

He crawled away and ran out the courtroom.

I broke down crying, clawing at my eyes to make it stop. But it didn't. I couldn't make it stop. Why couldn't . . . I . . . make . . . it . . . stop?

"No, no, no. Amelia, I'm sorry," I whimpered. "Baby, no."

Security had arrived, surrounding me. "Sir, put your hands up. Now!"

"Or what! What the fuck you gonna do to me, man? Look at them! Look . . . at . . . them! I killed them, man. All of them." I pointed at the TV, but they didn't flinch. They were going for their guns.

And I knew what I had to do.

I ran at them. Got to one, wrestling him for his gun. They pulled theirs. I got his away.

They aimed.

I aimed.

I pulled.

Darkness. Just like my dreams.

I was alone.

Not for long.

Somebody walked up, joining me in the emptiness.

"I've been waiting for you."

Abdel. I expected him.

"Now you look like me, my friend," he said, pointing to his blown-open skull. We probably did look alike.

"Man, that shit was funny." The laughter seemed familiar.

A pair of tennis shoes stepped out of the dark. It was Aaron, two large holes in his chest. "What it do, Bodie?"

"What it do, man? Ro, here?"

"Yeah, yeah. You always askin' 'bout him. He around here some-where. You know he like to be alone."

"Get up," Abdel offered his hand, helping me up. "Let's go find your partner."

The three of us went to search for Ro.

Aaron was still talkin' shit. He never shut up.

74

EPILOGUE

The hosts took the stage, a country music singer and a girl from that ABC sitcom everyone was raving about. They always matched odd couples. I was as nervous as could be listening to them announce the nominees. Tookie, Me-Me and Neal were seated on the side of me, waiting and wondering. During the pause between nominees, you could hear a pin drop. When they got to my song, the roaring applause gave me goose bumps.

The hosts joked some more. The audience laughed a little.

"Come the fuck on," Tookie muttered. Me-Me hushed her. Neal looked at me and smiled. This was the moment.

They opened the envelope.

Me-Me gripped my hand although I could barely feel it.

"And the winner for Song of the Year is . . ."

My eyes widened.

"Natalia!"

Natalia rose from her seat and waved at everybody. Everyone screamed in the place as she took the stage.

You would've thought we were there from the noise we made. Anyone outside my apartment probably wondered what was going on.

Natalia had taken home the Grammy.

And I had won.

Tookie jumped out of her chair and ran over to my wheelchair. She kissed me on my cheek and hugged me warmly.

"I'm so happy for you, boo. All you've been through and you're still doin' it."

"Thank you," I strained to say. I never let my smile leave me though.

I can't sing anymore. Barely have a voice after that bullet ripped through my throat.

But I was still writing. Ghostwriting for some. Singing the songs in my head. And in my heart.

Natalia had won Song of the Year.

One of the first songs I'd written. I sang it for my audition with Lansky. When I came out of surgery and the doctors gave me the news, I gave it to her.

Just like someone had once given something to me.

Their heart.

I love you, Ike.

. . . And no matter what you did, part of me still loves you, Bodie.

Life can be so cruel, but in the end . . . it is still life.

Photo by JWP Studio

Eric Pete is an award–winning author. His previous novels include *Real for Me, Someone's in the Kitchen, Gets No Love,* and *Don't Get It Twisted.* He has also contributed short stories to the erotica anthologies *After Hours: A Collection of Erotic Writing by Black Men* and *Twilight Moods: African American Erotica.* A graduate of McNeese State University, he currently resides in Texas, where he is working on his next novel. Visit his Web site at www.ericpete.com.

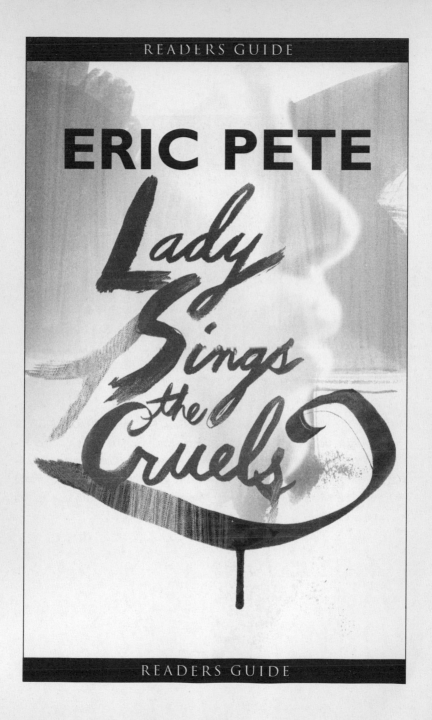

ERIC PETE

Lady Sings the Cruels

A CONVERSATION WITH ERIC PETE

Q. *How did you come up with the title* Lady Sings the Cruels?

A. It was between that and *Ain't No Sunshine*, but thankfully the latter had been recently used. I thought about the way fate and chance permeated the book, so *Lady Sings the Cruels* came to mind. The whole "fate as a cruel master" thing. The title also has that "old school" feel in that it's similar to *Lady Sings the Blues* and is a play on words.

Q. *How did you come up with the story?*

A. The story came from an innocent conversation I was having with a friend during a previous tour. She mentioned a friend leaving her picture behind after his incarceration ended and how she found out it was being "circulated." My mind went off on a tangent from that point on, weaving together the story you hold in your hands.

Q. *What do you think will be the reaction from some of your readers?*

A. A lot of mouth dropping.

Q. *How is the Eric Pete of today different from the last time we talked?*

A. I'm older, wiser, and have been tested. I'm in a different place and don't quite know if and how that will be reflected in my writings.

Q. *What do you hope to accomplish in your career?*

A. To keep people guessing what I'm going to do next. To be able to say I've tried it all and that maybe have mastered "some" of it.

Q. *Anything you want to tell the readers?*

A. I think I touched on most of it in my acknowledgments. I do thank them all for the feedback. If anyone is wondering how to reach me or about my other books, just go to the Web site: www.ericpete.com.

QUESTIONS
FOR DISCUSSION

1. How did the raw nature of the story line affect you, if at all?

2. Who do you feel Amelia should have chosen? Why?

3. Do you think Ike was wrong (or right) in pursuing Amelia once he learned of her connection to Bodie?

4. What fault, if any, do you feel Amelia bore in the conflict between Bodie and Ike?

5. Do you feel Amelia would have reacted differently if she'd known Bodie didn't kill the pawnshop owner?

6. Given Bodie's temperament, do you think things would've been different between Amelia and him had he been free?

7. How do you feel the title *Lady Sings the Cruels* fits with the overall story?

8. Did the characters seem realistic? Who would you consider the biggest villain of the story?

9. How would you have handled catching your significant other in a situation like that of Deryn and her boss?

10. Which one of the characters do you want to learn more about?

11. How did you feel seeing characters from previous novels (the various characters from *Someone's in the Kitchen* and Jason North from *Gets No Love*)? Is there someone you'd like to see with his or her own story? Why?

12. Do you feel Natalia had any jealousy toward Amelia or vice versa? Why or why not?

13. Do you feel Jason North would've double-crossed Bodie?